FUSE

Cerberus Personal Security Specialists
Book 4

ELLIE MASTERS
MASTER OF ROMANTIC SUSPENSE

JEM Publishing

This book is dedicated to my one and only—my amazing and wonderful husband.

Without your care and support, my writing would not have made it this far.

You pushed me when I needed to be pushed.

You supported me when I felt discouraged.

You believed in me when I didn't believe in myself.

If it weren't for you, this book never would have come to life.

Rescuing Lily

Rescuing Jinx

Rescuing Maria

Bravo Team

Rescuing Angie

Rescuing Isabelle

Rescuing Carmen

Rescuing Rosalie

Rescuing Kaye

Cara's Protector

Rescuing Barbi

Charlie Team

Rescuing Rebel

Rescuing Stitch

Rescuing Mia

Jenna's Protector

Rescuing Sophia

Rescuing Malia

Rescuing Ally (Part 1)

Rescuing Ally (Part 2)

Delta Team

Rescuing Ember

Rescuing Aria

STANDALONES IN THE GUARDIAN HOSTAGE RESCUE SERIES YOU CAN READ ANYTIME

Ellie Masters writing as L.A. Warren
Vendel Rising: a Science Fiction Serialized Novel

If you enjoyed this book by Ellie Masters, the LIGHTER SIDE of the Jet & Ellie writing duo, and aren't afraid of edgier writing, you might enjoy reading BDSM themed books written by Jet, the DARKER SIDE of the Masters' Writing Team.

The DARKER SIDE

Jet Masters is the darker side of the Jet & Ellie writing duo!

Romantic Suspense

Changing Roles Series:

THIS SERIES MUST BE READ IN ORDER.

Command Me

Control Me

Collar Me

Embracing FATE

Seizing FATE

Accepting FATE

HOT READS

A STANDALONE NOVEL.

Down the Rabbit Hole

Light BDSM Romance
The Ties that Bind

To My Readers

This book is a work of fiction. It does not exist in the real world and should not be construed as reality. As in most romantic fiction, I've taken liberties. I've compressed the romance into a sliver of time. I've allowed these characters to develop strong bonds of trust over a matter of days.

This does not happen in real life where you, my amazing readers, live. Take more time in your romance and learn who you're giving a piece of your heart to. I urge you to move with caution. Always protect yourself.

Grab the First Book in The
Guardian Hostage Rescue
Specialists Series for Free

https://elliemasters.com/RescuingMelissa

ONE

Talia

———

STATISTICAL PROBABILITY

Victor Lawson is twenty-three minutes late, and in my world, that means he's probably dead.

The café's ambient noise—clinking cups, muted conversations, the hiss of the espresso machine—should provide perfect acoustic cover. Instead, each sound sharpens into a threat variable. The ceramic strike of a saucer hitting a table mimics the click of a hammer locking back. A sudden burst of steam masks the scuff of approaching footsteps.

My fingers trace the edge of my phone, tapping a silent, nervous rhythm against the case. I'm ready to call the FBI contact who might be our only hope. If Victor's still alive. If they haven't found him. If my calculations about corporate assassination aren't about to become deadly accurate.

Last night's conversation replays on a loop, a corrupted file I can't close.

"They know, Talia. They're watching me." Victor's voice crackled through the phone in panicked bursts, the frequencies clipped by

poor reception. *"I was followed from the lab. They've been parked outside my apartment all night."*

My throat tightened—the familiar constriction that arrives when variables shift too fast.

"Are you certain? Coincidences happen, and in a city this size—"

"It's not a coincidence." The certainty in his voice makes the hair on my arms stand up, even in memory. *"Black sedan. Tinted windows. Same one from yesterday and the day before."*

"Where are you now?"

"I'm at my sister's place across town. She's out of the country, but I have a key."

"Here's what we're going to do." I kept my voice steady, professional, forcing the tremor in my hand to still. Probability calculations spiraled through my mind, assessing risk vectors. *"Meet me at the Westlake Coffee Shop on Third. I have a contact at the FBI—James Morrison. He can help with protection."*

"You think this is really that serious?"

The fear in his voice was a physical weight, transmitted through cellular towers into my apartment, where my very recent ex-boyfriend's boxes still lined the hallway like tombstones.

"Seventy-three deaths and a pharmaceutical company willing to cover them up? Yes, Victor. It's that serious. Bring the drive."

"Okay."

Eight months ago, Meridian began human trials for ML-273 —their "miracle" cancer drug. Initial results were promising, the kind that make stockholders salivate and executives order champagne.

According to Victor, kidney and liver damage appeared in the first trial phase, but management pressured the research team to exclude the data points. *Statistical outliers*, they called them. By the third phase, the outliers became the norm. Patients were dying. Organ failure. Massive internal bleeding. Hearts simply stopping.

Victor documented everything. Seventy-three fatalities that

Meridian buried in paperwork, falsified results, and pushed for FDA approval anyway.

"I've created a database tracking every death," Victor told me three weeks ago. *"Names, dates, autopsy results. The evidence is irrefutable."*

"The families—do they know?"

"Meridian paid them off. NDAs so thick you'd need a forklift. But the patterns ..." His voice cracked. *"You can't hide patterns from someone trained to see them."*

My hand tightens around my teacup until the ceramic bites into my palm. Mint steam curls into my face, sharp and grounding, but it can't mask the underlying scent of the café: burnt coffee. Bitter, acrid, institutional. Someone ordered a dark roast and left it too long on the warming plate. It smells like a mistake.

A mother at the next table wrestles twin toddlers while texting someone who isn't responding fast enough—the frustrated thumb jabs give it away. Her engagement ring catches the light, but a paler band of skin rings her finger beside it. Recent removal of the wedding band. The way she touches that spot creates a somatic loop of guilt. Affair, probably.

Or abandonment.

The businessman in the corner reeks of cologne—something expensive and recently applied. Too much for a regular workday. Job interview. His hand gestures are rehearsed, his pulse visible in his neck as he checks his watch. High anxiety.

The barista has dark circles under her eyes and keeps checking her phone between orders. The pattern—quick glance, forced smile for customers, back to phone—reads personal crisis, not professional negligence.

I process these details automatically, cataloging patterns and anomalies. It's not a choice. It's an operating system.

"You don't experience life, Talia. You dissect it."

Nathan's voice slithers through my thoughts. Three years of

his observations, his critiques, his careful dismantling of who I am. Last night's fight echoes in my skull.

"You're like a computer pretending to be human," he said, standing in our bathroom—my bathroom now—while I packed his toothbrush. *"Every response calculated for optimal outcome. Every emotion filtered through some probability matrix."*

"That's not—" My fingers fumbled with the toiletry bag, dropping the zipper pull.

"It is." He stepped closer. His cologne, usually pleasant, became sharp in the small space. Invading. Claiming territory one last time. *"Three years, Talia. Three years of living with someone who processes feelings like data points."*

I exhale slowly, shoving the memory into a mental subfolder. *Delete.*

Focus on Victor. He's never late. The man sets his watch to the atomic clock. Twenty-three minutes constitutes a massive deviation.

My gaze tracks across the café for the twentieth time. Three laptops glow at separate tables, their owners hunched over screens, islands of isolation. A man in a gray suit scrolls through his phone. The barista with a rose tattoo climbing her collarbone leans against the counter, attention flicking between customers and the clock above the door.

Outside, late-afternoon light casts long shadows across rain-slick pavement. A delivery truck idles at the curb, hazard lights creating rhythmic orange pulses. Across the street, a black SUV sits in a no-parking zone.

Tinted windows. Engine running. Exhaust pumping a gray cloud into the cool air. No driver visible. A parking ticket curls beneath the wiper, rain-spotted and ignored.

Anomaly.

Everything about that vehicle screams wrong.

A cyclist coasts past, head ducked against the wind. Two

teenagers laugh near the corner, sharing earbuds, oblivious to everything beyond their bubble of youth and music.

Movement snags my peripheral vision.

Victor. Finally.

He darts down the sidewalk across the street like prey that knows the predator is upwind. His usual professorial shuffle is gone, replaced by quick, jerky movements. Shoulders hunched against more than cold. The messenger bag he clutches against his ribs might as well be welded there.

Our eyes meet through the glass.

Relief softens his features for a heartbeat. He lifts a hand.

The cup burns against my palms. I set it down carefully, deliberately. No sudden movements. Nothing to draw attention. My heart hammers a frantic rhythm against my ribs, entirely at odds with my still hands.

Victor steps off the curb and into the crosswalk.

The SUV's engine roars.

No.

The word dies in my constricted throat—lost in the sudden scream of tires. The vehicle launches forward. Zero to forty in the span of a breath. No horn. No brake lights. Just mechanical violence given purpose.

Time fractures.

The meaty crack of steel striking bone echoes through the glass. A sound, wet and ruinous, physics winning against biology.

Victor pinwheels through the air. The messenger bag tears free. Papers explode like startled birds, white confetti raining down on a murder.

His body hits the asphalt with a wet slap that silences the street.

Behind me, sharp gasps. Ceramic shattering on tile. A child's piercing scream. The mother clutches her twins, pressing their faces into her chest to shield them from the data.

The SUV fishtails. Corrects. Vanishes around the corner. Tires squeal. The stench of burning rubber floods through the door as someone rushes out. Chemical and acrid. It tastes like violence.

I'm already moving. My legs obey before my brain finishes the calculation.

Blood spreads beneath Victor's skull in an expanding crimson lake. The metallic tang hits my nostrils—copper and iron, sharp enough to make my stomach heave. His left leg bends at an angle that defies anatomy. Bone pierces skin just above the knee. White stark against red. The raw meat smell of exposed marrow rises in waves.

I drop into the slush beside him. My fingers find his carotid, slipping on sweat and rain. A weak flutter against my fingertips.

Still alive.

Barely.

His eyes swim into focus, pupils blown wide with shock.

"The drive." Blood bubbles on his lips, pink foam. Punctured lung. "Inner pocket … Messenger bag … Hidden seam …"

My hands move. Checking vitals is useless—the damage is catastrophic—but I do it anyway because the alternative is screaming. Coffee-stained notebook splayed open. Pages fluttering in the wind. Laptop with a spiderweb crack across the screen. The messenger bag lies three feet away.

"Take it. Run." His fingers claw at my wrist with strength that defies his injuries, nails digging into my skin. "They'll come—for you next."

Pressure builds in my throat. Words trapped behind the constriction.

"Don't talk." My voice sounds thin, distant. Inside, calculations spiral: survival rate with these injuries is less than one percent. Response time for paramedics in this neighborhood is four to six minutes. Too long.

His grip tightens, bones grinding under skin. "Promise … Evidence—gets out."

I nod once. Tears sting my eyes, unbidden, blurring the data. My fingers slip inside the bag's outer pocket. Papers. Receipts. Nothing. Then the inner pocket—finding the small slit he mentioned, barely visible unless you know the pattern. The USB drive sits there. Small and warm, like it's been absorbing his body heat.

It disappears into my bra while my other hand stays on his wrist. To any observer, I'm checking his pulse. Good Samaritan doing what she can.

"Go." More blood now. Pooling faster. Darker. Arterial. "Before they come back."

He's dying. The realization hits not as a fact, but as a hollow ache in my chest.

"I'm not leaving you." My throat burns.

"Have to." His eyes drift shut, then snap open with desperate clarity.

Ice floods my veins. If they tracked Victor here. If they know about me …

"Go." The word is a gurgle. "Run …"

Sirens wail in the distance—bouncing off glass and steel. The crowd presses closer. Phones out. Recording tragedy for social media consumption. Someone's livestreaming. Digital vultures circling the carcass.

"Did anyone see what happened?" An older man kneels beside me, hands hovering uncertainly over Victor's broken body.

"Black SUV. No plates." I stand. My legs shake violently, adrenaline crashing against shock. "The driver aimed right for him."

Victor's breathing grows shallow. Stops. Starts again. Weaker. Then nothing.

The variable becomes a constant.

I back away as more people crowd in. Someone claiming to be a nurse pushes forward. Another calls 911 again. Voices overlapping in chaos.

I walk away. Each step measured. Normal. Don't run. Running attracts the eye. The drive presses against my chest—seventy-three deaths encoded in silicon and plastic.

Single point of failure.

The thought crystallizes with mathematical clarity. If they take me now, the evidence dies with me. Victor's death becomes meaningless.

Seventy-three victims stay buried.

High probability they're already mobilizing to sweep the scene. Near certainty this drive won't survive if I'm taken.

Need redundancy. Now.

An internet café three blocks north flashes in my memory—anonymous terminals, no account required, cash only. Risky, but less risky than carrying the only copy. Every second without backups increases the odds of total evidence loss.

I duck inside. Burnt coffee and desperation assault my nostrils again—stale air recycled through cheap filters, unwashed bodies, the chemical sweetness of energy drinks. The teenager behind the counter doesn't even glance up from his phone. Earbuds blocking out the world.

Perfect.

I slide into a terminal at the back, angled so I can monitor the door. My movements are automatic, disconnected from the shaking in my hands. Fingers flying across keys. Three minutes to copy the drive to a new USB from the basket of extras they sell. I slip both drives inside my bra for safe keeping. Another minute to upload encrypted backups to cloud servers I maintain under false identities.

Habits from my FBI days. Habits that might save my life.

My phone vibrates. Morrison's number.

"Singh. What's up?"

"Remember that whistleblower situation?" I keep my voice low, back pressed to the wall. "High-priority corporate malfeasance with significant casualties."

"Yes?" Keys click on his end.

"Victor Lawson was just hit. Professional job. I have what he was carrying."

Silence stretches. Two heartbeats. Then his breathing changes—controlled, operational.

"Where are you?"

"Internet café, Third and Madison."

"Stay public. I'll be there in twelve minutes."

"Will do."

The upload completes. I pocket both drives, leave a twenty on the counter, and step back onto the street. The rain has started again, a soft mist that makes everything look like a watercolor painting slowly dissolving.

Morrison's sedan slides to the curb exactly eleven minutes later. Government plates. Bulletproof glass. Subtle tells for those who know the pattern. The passenger window lowers.

"Get in."

I slip inside. The interior smells like coffee and gun oil—burnt grounds and CLP solvent. It smells like safety. Morrison looks exactly as he did when I left the Bureau. Crisp suit that never wrinkles. Sharp eyes that miss nothing. Worry lines that have deepened into permanent grooves.

He pulls into traffic, smooth but fast, eyes constantly scanning mirrors.

"Do they know about you?" His tone is conversational. His knuckles are white on the steering wheel.

"Unknown." The original drive burns against my skin. "Victor was paranoid. Thought he was being followed."

"Paranoid people—"

"Live longer. Usually." I pull the drive free. It's warm from my skin, slightly damp with sweat. "Clinical trials. Cover-ups. Payoffs. All documented."

He pockets it with the kind of ease that comes from years of handling dangerous evidence. "Backups?"

"Multiple."

"Good girl." A sharp right turn, then a left. Anti-surveillance driving. "This goes deeper than Meridian?"

"Four other pharmaceutical companies. Same patterns." The words come clipped. Factual. It's easier to speak in data than to think about the pink foam on Victor's lips. "Connected through parent company—Nexus Holdings. Statistical probability of coincidence—"

"Zero. I know how you think, Singh." Another turn. "Protected by?"

"People who commit murder in broad daylight."

That gets his attention. His eyes flick to mine in the mirror. "Come again?"

"Victor said he was being watched." My fingers find my collarbone, pressing into the scar tissue there. Grounding myself.

Morrison reaches into his jacket and produces a plain business card. No name, no logo. Just ten digits in black ink.

"If something happens to me, call this number." He presses it into my palm. "These people operate outside the system. They're ghosts."

"That's paranoid, even for you."

"After what you just witnessed?" His smile lacks humor. "Paranoia seems like basic math."

He pulls over six blocks from my building. "Go home, pack light, get somewhere safe. I'll dig into this quietly, build a case the right way. I'll contact you when I have protection in place."

"James—"

"No arguments. You know what these people are capable of."

I exit without another word. Morrison's taillights disappear into traffic, red dots swallowed by the city.

At my apartment door, I check for signs of tampering. Doorframe dust undisturbed. Lock scratches match my key pattern. The wood around the deadbolt shows no fresh marks. Inside, Nathan's boxes line the hallway—monuments to last night's relationship funeral.

I step around them, each one labeled in my precise handwriting: "Kitchen - Fragile," "Books - Study," "Bedroom - Misc." Three years condensed into cardboard and packing tape.

The laptop waits on my kitchen counter. The USB slides into the port with a soft click. Files cascade across the screen—spreadsheets, documents, video files. Deaths, cover-ups, payoffs, all meticulously documented. Victor's obsessive nature might be the only reason these victims get justice.

I create more copies. One hidden behind the bathroom mirror. One under the kitchen drawer. One in the freezer inside a vacuum-sealed bag labeled "Soup Stock 3/15."

Redundancies. Paranoid people live longer.

The espresso machine on the counter catches my eye—the Williams-Sonoma model I bought Nathan for Christmas. I calculated how much we'd save versus daily coffee shop visits. Practical. Analytical.

"Three years of this, Talia." His voice echoes from last night, when everything finally shattered. *"Three years of calculated responses, measured reactions. You don't feel things—you process them. You simulate emotions because real ones might mess up your data."*

"That's not fair—"

"Isn't it?" He stepped closer, his cologne sharp and pungent. *"When we make love, you're cataloging responses. When we fight, you're analyzing patterns."*

My throat tightened. *"I do love you."*

"No." His laugh was bitter. *"You've determined that saying those words produces optimal relationship outcomes."*

The memory hurts more than the bruises on my knees from the pavement.

The television drones in the background as I work, local news recycling the same stories. I'm only half-listening, hands moving automatically to hide more copies in the cloud, when the anchor's tone shifts—that particular cadence that signals breaking news.

"This just in. FBI Special Agent James Morrison was found dead in his office at the Federal Building, an apparent suicide according to preliminary reports. Morrison, a twenty-year veteran of the Bureau, was discovered by cleaning staff at approximately 6:45 PM ..."

The room tilts.

Morrison. Dead. "Suicide."

The screen fills with his official photo—dress blues, American flag behind him, slight smile that never reached his eyes. Then crime scene footage—yellow tape, dark suits guarding the entrance, rain making everything look like a fever dream.

"Preliminary reports indicate a self-inflicted gunshot wound," the anchor continues. "Morrison left no note."

No note. Morrison would never kill himself without explaining why. The man documented everything.

First Victor. Now Morrison. Two bodies.

That's not cleanup. It's a message.

If they got to Morrison, then they have to know about me.

My fingers find the business card. Ten digits in black ink that suddenly feel like the only lifeline in an ocean of threats.

I dial before fear can paralyze me.

"Cerberus." Male voice, calm and professional. No accent, no identifying characteristics.

"This is Talia Singh. James Morrison gave me this number."

My voice remains steady despite adrenaline flooding every cell. "He's dead."

Keys clicking in the background. "Status and location?"

"Chicago, North Side. Fifth-floor apartment." I move to the window, keeping to the shadows. "Morrison was murdered because of what I gave him. I have evidence they'll kill for."

"Understood. Is your current location secure?"

"One entrance, fire escape outside the bedroom window." My fingers trace the window lock. "Neighbors on both sides, family above, elderly couple below."

"Lock your doors. Stay away from windows. Our operative is four hours out."

"Four—" The word sticks in my throat.

"Minimum. Do you have a weapon?"

"Kitchen knives."

"Find one. Keep your phone charged and with you. We'll use it to track your position."

"Track me?"

"In case you have to run. For now, stay put. The operative will text a code phrase when they arrive: 'Statistical probability.' You'll respond with 'Acceptable margins.' Clear?"

"Clear."

"Four hours. Stay alive."

The line goes dead.

I pocket my phone. My fingers tremble despite my attempt at control. A kitchen knife—eight-inch chef's knife, sharp enough to matter—fits in my hand like it belongs there. The weight is wrong. The balance unfamiliar. But the edge catches the light and promises violence if necessary.

Every creak in the building becomes footsteps on stairs. Every gust of wind sounds like the fire escape groaning under its weight. The clock on my phone counts down.

Four hours to outlast whoever sent that SUV. Four hours to survive what Morrison couldn't.

My pulse hammers against my ribs, trying to escape the cage of my chest. The apartment feels too quiet, too exposed.

I move to the living room, putting my back against the wall where I can monitor both the front door and the hallway to the bedroom. The knife rests across my lap. Nathan's boxes provide cover if I need to duck behind them. The cardboard smells faintly of his cologne—chemical sweetness mixed with something sharper underneath.

Four hours.

The city sounds filter through the windows—sirens, car horns, a dog barking. Normal sounds of life continuing while mine hangs by probability calculations and a stranger's arrival time.

I grip the knife until my knuckles turn white. And I wait.

TWO

Jackson

PRECISION CONTROL

The C4 sits in my palm like a promise—1.4 ounces of controlled destruction, waiting for my command.

I place it against the concrete pillar, measuring exactly seven centimeters from the support beam's stress point. The training warehouse reeks of dust and metal, Seattle rain drumming against the roof in a rhythm that matches the steady beat of my heart. Four Cerberus operators watch from behind the blast barrier. Four Axion Construction contractors look nervous as hell.

They should be. One millimeter means the difference between a clean breach and bringing down the whole structure.

"Questions?" My query comes out clipped, minimal.

"Shouldn't we use more explosives for a beam this size?" Collins, Axion's lead engineer, steps forward. His cologne is too strong for close quarters, a chemical sweetness mixed with nervous sweat.

"More explosives equal less control." I connect the detonator wire, feeling the familiar snap of the coupling. "Less predictability. Larger collateral damage radius. Your company's paying Cerberus to teach you precision, not brute force."

Brass smirks from his position by the door. He's seen this scenario before—corporate types questioning my methods until they witness the results.

"Time?" I ask without looking up.

"Three minutes." Brass's voice cuts through the ambient noise without effort.

Calculations run automatically in my head. Load capacity. Explosive force. Blast radius. Numbers never lie. Never betray. Never demand more than precision.

"Perimeter?"

"Clear," Halo confirms from overwatch. "Fifteen seconds to optimal window."

The floor vibrates slightly—Whisper moving into position on the catwalk above. No need to check. Each Cerberus team member will be exactly where they're supposed to be. We operate on trust. The only trust that matters—trust earned through blood, verified through action.

Not the kind of trust that gets people killed.

"Everyone behind the barrier," I order, measuring the distance. Eighteen feet to minimum safe position.

I move back twenty-two feet. Always add a margin for error when civilian lives are involved.

The Axion team scrambles to comply, their movements sloppy compared to my team's fluid efficiency. Brass slides in beside me, shoulder bumping mine in silent camaraderie.

"You good?"

I give a minimal nod. My teammates have learned to read volumes in my silence. Brass has been with me long enough to know when to push and when to let it go. Today isn't a pushing day.

"Detonation in five, four, three …"

The sound comes first. Not the explosion itself, but the microsecond before—that distinctive compression of air molecules as the C4 ignites. Then the controlled boom, precisely calibrated to take out only the target support without compromising the surrounding structure.

Heat washes over the barrier. Dust billows. Concrete particles coat my tongue—gritty, alkaline, mixed with the metallic tang of explosive residue.

And suddenly I'm not in Seattle anymore.

I'm in Syria. Three years ago. Different dust, different heat, but the same taste of explosive residue coating my throat.

"Trust me, Jackson. Intel's solid. Building's clear."

Colonel Mitchell's voice crackles through my earpiece, confident and reassuring. My team moves on his word—Kowalski first through the door, then Vega, then Brennan. I'm fourth, the demolitions kit heavy on my back.

"Structural charge here," I mark the wall with chalk. *"Sixty seconds to breach the compound next door."*

"Confirmed hostile location?" Kowalski asks, always careful, always checking.

"Confirmed," Mitchell responds without hesitation. *"Three high-value targets. No civilians."*

The explosion rocks the building differently than my calculations predicted. The wall doesn't just breach—it collapses inward. Screams pierce through the dust. Not adult screams.

Children.

The dust clears like a curtain pulling back on hell. A classroom. Seventeen kids, maybe eight years old. Some still moving.

Most not. Blood spreading across scattered homework papers written in Arabic.

"What the fuck, Mitchell?" My voice breaks over the comm. *"You said it was clear!"*

"Collateral damage happens, Jackson. Targets were priority."

But there were no targets. Never were. Mitchell sold our position to the highest bidder and traded our coordinates to pad a Swiss account. The intel wasn't just bad; it was a weapon aimed at us.

The ambush hit us forty seconds later.

Kowalski takes the first bullet—a high-velocity round punches through his throat. He drops mid-word, hand reaching for the wound that's already pumping his life onto Syrian dirt. His eyes find mine, confused, betrayed. He mouths something I can't hear over the gunfire.

Vega goes next. Three rounds center mass, ceramic armor useless against armor-piercing rounds they shouldn't have. He falls forward, tries to crawl, leaves a red trail for six feet before going still. His wife was pregnant. Twin boys he'll never meet.

I'm dragging Brennan behind rubble when the grenade rolls in. The explosion tears him from my grip, shrapnel turning his left side into hamburger. He bleeds out in my arms, trying to say his daughter's name through bubbles of blood. *"Tell Sarah ..."* But he never finishes. Just goes slack, eyes fixed on nothing.

Hendricks screams for his mother in Spanish while his intestines spill through his fingers. Nguyen takes a headshot so clean it looks like special effects until you see the wall behind him. Patel burns alive when the white phosphorus hits, and there's nothing—nothing—I can do but listen.

Seven teammates dead in four minutes. Dead because I trusted the intel. Because I trusted Mitchell's voice in my ear saying "building's clear" while he counted his blood money.

The extraction team found me three hours later, still holding

Brennan's body, calculating over and over how different it could've been if I'd verified the intel myself. If I'd trusted my instincts instead of Mitchell's words.

"Fuse!" Brass's voice cuts through the memory. "Assessment."

I blink hard, forcing myself back to Seattle. To now. The training warehouse snaps into focus. No dead children. No dead teammates. Just a perfectly executed breach.

"Clean breach." My voice remains steady despite the acid burning my throat. "Seven-point-two-second window. Sufficient for extraction."

Brass's eyes narrow slightly. He noticed the hesitation. Of course he did. But he doesn't call it out. That's the code among us—cover each other's blind spots without advertising them.

Whisper drops from the catwalk, landing silently despite his size. The Axion contractors stare with barely concealed awe. Most civilians react that way to Cerberus operators.

We're just built differently. Forged in places that break normal people.

Collins approaches the breached pillar, running his hand along the precise cut. "That's—impressive. Not even a hairline fracture in the surrounding structure."

"Precision matters," I tell him. "In demolition, one degree of miscalculation compounds exponentially."

But miscalculation doesn't get people killed.

Misplaced trust does.

The contractors file out, still murmuring among themselves. Brass escorts them to the elevator, his bulk a casual reminder that Cerberus operates in a different league. Halo gives them a mock salute that somehow feels like a warning.

Ghost watches from the observation deck. Arms crossed. When the civilians are gone, he descends the metal stairs. Footsteps echoing.

"Good work. Debrief in twenty."

The team disperses to clean gear. I stay behind, staring at the breach point. Seven centimeters from the optimal stress point. Exactly as calculated. My calculations are never wrong.

Only people lie. Especially the ones with "intel."

Ghost finds me in the equipment room, setting detonators in their designated positions. Each one precisely aligned, because precision is all I can control.

"You good?" Ghost asks, but it's not really a question.

"Functional," I answer truthfully.

He studies me for a long moment. We've never discussed Syria in detail, but Ghost pulled my file when he recruited me. He knows about Mitchell. About the betrayal. About the seven teammates and seventeen kids who died because I trusted bad intel.

"Take the night," he says finally. "We'll talk tomorrow."

"Copy that."

But we both know what he's not saying. That the memories are getting worse, not better. That *functional* might not be enough forever.

Later, the walls of my apartment close in. The flashback left familiar tension crawling under my skin—that itch that demands either violence or sex to scratch. The gym's closed. The heavy bag in my bedroom won't be enough tonight.

I need something more immediate. More consuming.

I pull on dark jeans and a black button-down. The fabric stretches across my shoulders, sleeves rolled to expose forearms mapped with scars. The mirror reflects someone polished enough to blend in, dangerous enough to make people think twice.

Three bars within walking distance serve my purpose. Anonymous. Dark. Loud enough that conversation becomes impossible.

I choose the furthest one, letting the Seattle rain soak through my shirt. The cold grounds me in the present, washing away phantom blood and Syrian dust.

Titanium Bar throbs with bass heavy enough to feel in my bones. The air reeks of perfume, sweat, and desperation. Perfect. I scan automatically—exits, sight lines, potential threats. Old habits.

The bartender slides a whiskey neat across the bar without being asked. I've been here enough that my preferences are known, even if my name isn't. The burn down my throat is familiar, necessary.

My gaze moves methodically through the crowd. Not hunting, exactly. More like target acquisition. Looking for someone who wants what I need—release without connection, control without consequences.

She's at the end of the bar. Alone. Designer dress, expensive shoes, nursing a martini, like it personally offended her. Recent breakup, probably. The way she keeps checking her phone confirms it.

I slide onto the stool beside her. Close enough that she has to acknowledge me. Her perfume hits—floral, expensive, trying too hard. Mixed with the faint salt of fresh tears she's covered well.

"Your date's not coming."

Her eyebrows lift. "How do you know I'm waiting for someone?"

"You're not." I hold her gaze steady. "But you're waiting for something."

"And what would that be?"

"Same thing I am." No smile. This isn't about charm. "Quick, simple, and very, very good."

She laughs, low and interested. "Pretty sure of yourself."

"Not sure. Certain." I lean closer, voice dropping. "I can read your body like a blueprint. Every breath, every tell, every response mapped and measured." My fingers graze her wrist, feeling her pulse spike. "Right now, you're pressing your thighs together under that dress. Your breathing just shifted. You're wondering if I'm full of shit or if I can deliver."

Her inhale catches. "That's—"

"Accurate. And I always deliver." I pull back slightly, maintaining eye contact. "I know exactly how to take you apart. Which pressure points make you gasp. The precise angle that makes you forget your own name. How long to hold you on the edge before you break."

"You're either very good or very delusional."

"First one." I stand, extending my hand. "I don't do names. I don't do numbers. I don't do breakfast. But I can make you come twice before we get to the main event. Your choice."

Her pupils dilate. Most women would walk away from such bluntness. The ones I'm looking for never do.

She takes my hand. Her skin is warm, her pulse racing against my palm.

The bathroom is cramped but private. The lock clicks, and I press her against the wall, giving her a moment to reconsider.

She doesn't. Her hands reach for my belt, but I catch her wrists.

"If you want this to be good," I keep my voice low, controlled, "you do exactly what I say, when I say it."

Her eyes widen slightly. "And if I don't?"

"Then we're done." Simple. Direct. "I don't waste time on negotiations."

She studies me for a heartbeat, then nods.

"Strip."

She hesitates just long enough to gauge my seriousness, then lets her dress pool at her feet. Lace and skin and vulnerability. She doesn't try to cover herself. That willingness tells me everything—she needs this as much as I do.

I pin her wrists above her head with one hand, using my body to cage her against the wall. "Don't move them."

The command makes her shiver. Good. She wants to surrender control. I want to take it.

Control is everything—in demolition, in combat, in this. Every touch is measured and deliberate. Every response is catalogued and utilized. I work methodically, learning her reactions like memorizing a schematic.

Her breath catches when I find the spot below her ear—that precise junction of nerve endings most people miss. She arches when my free hand traces her ribs, counting each one like reading braille. I catalog every shiver, every gasp, building a mental map of her responses.

This is what I do best. Two things in life respond to absolute precision: explosives and the female form. Both require total focus, perfect timing, and the confidence to commit fully. Half measures get people killed in combat and disappointed in bed.

I work her body like defusing a bomb in reverse—finding every wire, every connection, knowing exactly which sequence will detonate. The spot where her neck meets her shoulder is the one that makes her knees buckle. The pressure point on her hip sends electricity straight to her core. I find a rhythm that takes her from zero to desperate in forty-five seconds flat.

"There," she gasps. "Right there."

I maintain the exact angle, the exact pressure, the exact speed. No variation. No improvisation. Just ruthless consistency until her whole body goes rigid, then shatters.

The first orgasm tears through her with a strangled cry. I don't stop, working her through a second one until she's shaking, gasping.

"Twice," I murmur against her ear. "As promised."

She's liquid against the wall, held up mostly by my grip on her wrists. The power of it—of her complete surrender—satisfies something dark and necessary.

"On your knees."

She drops instantly, eyes glazed with endorphins and submission. This is what I need. Control absolute. No questions, no trust required. Just simple, mechanical dominance.

I unbuckle my belt. She watches with hungry eyes, already reaching, but I catch her chin.

"Exactly like I say. No improvisation."

She nods, eager and compliant. I thread my fingers through her hair, controlling pace and depth with the same precision I use setting charges. Shallow, then deep, then holding her still while her throat works around me. The wet heat makes my eyes close involuntarily, but I force them open. Control means awareness. Always.

I watch her surrender to the rhythm I set, measuring my own response, delaying gratification the same way I delay detonation—building pressure, holding, building more. Each stroke calculated to edge closer without tipping over. The tension coils tight in my spine, but I maintain the pace. Steady. Measured. No rushing.

When I finally let go, it's on my terms. The release hits like a controlled explosion—contained, directed, exactly as planned. My grip tightens in her hair as everything narrows to this singular moment of perfect control over both our bodies.

Just sensation and control.

When I finish, she's still on her knees, looking wrecked and satisfied. I help her stand, hand her the dress, and put distance between us while she dresses.

"That was incredible," she says, voice rough. "Maybe we could—"

"No." I'm already at the sink, washing my hands with the same thoroughness I use when cleaning explosive residue. Soap, hot water, twenty seconds minimum. "This was exactly what I promised. Nothing more."

"Come on." She steps closer, her dress only half-zipped. "That was incredible. You could at least—"

"I could. But I won't." I dry my hands on paper towels, each movement deliberate. "You got what I said you'd get. Twice, as promised. I got mine. Transaction complete."

"Transaction?" Her voice pitches higher. "That's what you're calling it?"

"That's what it was." I check my watch. Eleven minutes total. Efficient. "We both knew the terms going in."

"But the way you just … You knew exactly …" She reaches for my arm. "Nobody's ever made me—"

"Stop." I step back, creating a clear boundary. "You're looking for something I don't have. Can't give. Won't pretend to."

She stares at me, frustration and desire warring on her face. "You're seriously just going to walk away? After that?"

"Yes."

"Most guys would at least want to fuck me properly."

"I'm not most guys." I move toward the door. "Got what I needed from your mouth. Don't need anything else."

"That's it? Just going to use my throat and walk away?"

"Yes." I meet her gaze directly.

Fucking requires more than I have left. Eye contact. Vulnerability. The pretense of connection. A mouth is simple friction and heat—better than my hand, simpler than dealing with the rest. Clean. Controlled. No one has to pretend it means anything.

And I won't make Mitchell's mistake. I won't let intimacy become a weapon aimed at my back.

"She's perfect for you, Jackson. Local asset. Been feeding us intel for months." Mitchell's grin in that Damascus safe house. *"Why don't you get to know her better? Build some trust."*

Amara.

Dark eyes, dangerous curves.

Three nights of her wrapped around me, whispering intel

between orgasms. My body buried deep while she fed me lies Mitchell scripted. The warmth of her skin just another trap, another betrayal. She'd radioed our position while I was still inside her, my guard down, vulnerable in the most primitive way.

Seven teammates dead because I trusted the person I let close.

Never again. Transactional sex can't betray you the same way. It can't make you vulnerable while you're lost in it. Can't whisper lies that you want to believe. It's just friction. Nothing more.

I unlock the door. "Find someone else if you want more."

"You're an asshole."

"Accurate." I open the door. "But at least I'm an honest asshole."

She finishes zipping her dress, movements sharp with anger. "You know what? You're right. I did get what you promised. But you're going to die alone with that attitude."

Probably. But alone means no one else dies because I trusted the wrong person.

She leaves without another word. Smart woman.

The sex helped, but the hollow sensation remains. Always does. Some men drink to forget. Some find God. Some put bullets in their heads.

I considered it once. Six months after Syria, after my discharge papers came through stamped "medical" instead of "honorable" because I couldn't speak for three weeks after the extraction. Sitting in a VA hospital room that smelled like disinfectant and despair.

I had a loaded Glock heavy in my lap. The weight felt right. The solution felt clean. No more calculations. No more flashbacks. No more waking up with Brennan's blood on my hands that no amount of washing removes.

Ghost found me there. Don't know how. Don't know why.

"That's sloppy," he said, looking at the gun. "Permanent solution to a temporary problem."

"Doesn't feel temporary."

"Never does." He sat down beside me, close enough to grab the weapon if needed, far enough to show trust. "But you're too valuable to waste. I need operators who understand the real cost of war. Who've been betrayed and survived. Who know the price of trust."

That was three years ago. Now I calculate explosive yields and fuck strangers in bar bathrooms. Not healing, but functional.

And functional is all I need to be.

My phone buzzes. Cerberus priority alert.

Twenty minutes later, I'm in the briefing room. Ghost looks exhausted. Brass and the others filter in, alert despite the hour. The wall display shows a woman's face—angular features, dark hair pulled back, intelligent eyes that seem to see through the camera.

"Talia Singh," Ghost announces. "Former FBI analyst. Two of her contacts are dead in twenty-four hours. Morrison was one of ours—the suicide was staged."

"Phoenix?" Brass asks.

"Unknown, but probable. Morrison gave her our emergency contact before he died. She reached out seventeen minutes ago." Ghost's expression hardens. "Fuse, you're on protection and extraction."

He slides a tablet across the table. Her full file loads—FBI commendations, case histories, psychological profile. An analyst. Someone who provides intel. Someone who expects others to trust her assessments.

"A fucking analyst?" The words escape before I can stop them.

"Problem?" Ghost asks, but his tone says he already knows. He's testing me.

The rest of the team exchanges glances. They know my history. Ghost sure as hell knows—he pulled my file, read every detail about Syria, about Mitchell's betrayal. He knows exactly what putting me with an analyst means.

"No problem." My jaw clenches hard enough to crack teeth.

But we both know better. She's precisely the type of person I can't afford to trust—the type who gets people killed with bad information, whether through incompetence or betrayal.

Ghost dismisses the others with a look. When we're alone, he leans back in his chair, studying me.

"You're wondering why I'm assigning you." Not a question.

"The thought crossed my mind."

"Because you're the best at keeping people alive." He pauses. "And because maybe it's time you remember that not everyone who deals in intelligence is Mitchell."

"That's a dangerous assumption."

"So is thinking you can operate forever without trusting anyone outside this team." He slides another photo across—a crime scene in Morrison's office. "She's not the enemy, Jackson. She's a witness. A victim. And right now, she's breathing because Morrison trusted her enough to give her our number."

"Morrison's dead."

"Not because of her. Because of what she knows." Ghost's voice hardens. "I need you functional on this. Can you handle protection detail for someone whose job was intelligence analysis? Yes or no?"

The photo shows Morrison's body, a staged suicide that any professional would spot as murder. He was solid. Trustworthy. One of the few outside Cerberus I could almost respect. And he died for trusting this analyst.

Or died protecting her.

"I'll keep her alive," I say finally. "But I'm not trusting her intel."

"I'm not asking you to. I'm asking you to keep her breathing long enough to figure out who wants her dead." Ghost stands. "Maybe in the process, you'll remember that betrayal isn't the only possible outcome of trust."

"Doubtful."

"That's not an order, Jackson. Just an observation from someone who recruited you out of a VA hospital with a loaded gun in your lap." His eyes hold mine. "Sometimes the thing we resist most is exactly what we need."

I study her photo during the flight to Chicago. Talia Singh. Brilliant analyst who sees patterns others miss. Probably thinks her assessments are gospel. Probably expects immediate trust and compliance.

She's in for disappointment.

My job is to keep her alive, not to believe her. Trust is for people who haven't learned better.

I learned in Syria. Seven teammates paid for my education in blood because I listened to the intel instead of my gut.

I won't make that mistake again.

THREE

Talia

STATISTICAL PROBABILITY OF SURVIVAL

The kitchen knife rests across my thighs; eight inches of German steel that's supposed to make me feel safe.

For the first hour, I huddle behind Nathan's boxes, back pressed against the wall where I can monitor both the front door and the hallway. Every sound in the building makes my heart stutter. Mrs. Patterson's television murmurs through the walls—some crime drama with dramatic music and shouted dialogue. Mr. Delgado's heavy footsteps echo on the stairs as he leaves for his night shift at the hospital. Normal sounds that should be comforting. Instead, they feel like threats closing in.

My phone shows 11:47 PM. Almost three and a half hours since I called Cerberus. Their operative should arrive soon.

Should.

The knife handle grows slick with sweat. My legs cramp from staying in one position too long, muscles screaming for move-ment. One USB drive is tucked in my bra, warm against my skin, slightly damp. Victor's original is hidden in my sock. Unnecessary with several versions uploaded to servers, but the duplicate physical copy provides some form of relief. Seventy-three deaths compressed into silicon and plastic.

I can't stay frozen forever.

Moving carefully, silently, I unfold from my hiding spot. My laptop waits on the kitchen counter where I left it. The need to understand what Victor died for overwhelms the need to hide.

The files bloom across my screen—seventy-three deaths documented in meticulous detail. Medical records. Falsified trial data. Internal emails discussing "acceptable losses" as if they're talking about quarterly earnings rather than human lives. The pattern spreads across five pharmaceutical companies, all subsidiaries of Nexus Holdings.

Morrison died for this. Victor died for this.

The statistical probability that I'll survive the night is decreasing by the minute.

My fingers fly across keys, uploading encrypted backups to servers in three countries. The progress bar crawls—67%, 74%, 81%—

The doorknob turns.

No warning. No footsteps in the hall. Just the soft scrape of metal on metal as someone tests the lock.

The deadbolt disengages with a whisper.

Three men flow into my apartment like oil spreading across water—silent, inevitable, deadly. Black tactical gear absorbs the kitchen light. Suppressors already threaded onto their weapons. They move in as one, overlapping coverage, no blind spots.

My hand finds the knife.

I throw it.

The blade whistles past the lead man's ear, embedding into the wall with a solid thunk. He doesn't even flinch.

"Impressive reflexes, Ms. Singh." His voice is cultured,

amused. The kind of voice that belongs at charity galas, not home invasions. "Though your aim needs work."

My hand finds a second knife from the block. This one I keep, backing deeper into the kitchen. My breath comes too fast, too shallow.

"We're here for a simple exchange." He takes a measured step forward, his partners fanning out to cut off angles. "You have something that belongs to our employers."

Seventy-three dead people. Falsified data. Premeditated murder.

Words crowd my throat. Won't emerge. They never do when fear takes over. My throat constricts, a physical lock turning in my larynx.

"The drive, Ms. Singh. We know you have it."

I throw the second knife. This one catches the shoulder of the man on the left, tearing through fabric but not flesh. He adjusts his stance, unperturbed. Probably wearing body armor under that tactical gear.

"That's enough of that." The leader's tone hardens. "Three trained operatives versus one analyst. No exits. No backup. I can see you calculating, measuring distances. But the math doesn't work in your favor."

He's right. But Nathan's boxes tower between us—twenty boxes of our dead relationship, filled with his books and kitchen gadgets and the life we built that he dismantled with a paralegal named Rebecca.

I slam my shoulder into the stack.

Boxes cascade in an avalanche of bubble wrap and breaking glass. The espresso machine I bought Nathan for Christmas crashes across the tiles with a sharp crack that makes one of the men flinch. Books scatter like dead birds, pages fluttering. The smell of cardboard dust and stale cologne rises—Nathan's scent still clinging to his belongings like a ghost.

In the chaos, I bolt for the bedroom.

I slam the door shut behind me. My hands shake as I wedge the security bar under the knob—stupid, should've had it at the front door where it belongs. The door shudders immediately as someone tests it. Then silence that's worse than the assault.

"Break it down."

The window. Paint-sealed and humidity-swollen from Chicago summers. My mother's silver jewelry box is heavy in my hands—ornate and solid, the weight of family heirlooms and old money. I smash it against the glass.

Once. Spiderweb cracks appear.

Twice. The cracks spread like lightning.

The door frame groans behind me, wood splintering under sustained force.

Third strike. Glass explodes outward.

Chicago night floods in—diesel exhaust sharp in my nose, the promise of coming rain, garlic from the Thai place three blocks over. And below, five floors of empty space yawning like an open mouth.

The fire escape squats outside like a rusted skeleton, metal corroded by decades of weather.

Five floors.

My body locks, feet rooting to the floor.

Seven years old. Mom calling from below: *"Get down from there!"* The garage roof rough under my palms. Reaching for the yellow Frisbee. The shingle sliding. That moment when solid becomes air. The ground rushing up—

The door crashes inward.

No choice. No time.

I squeeze through the jagged glass, feeling it catch my shirt, slice through the fabric—hot line of pain across my thigh. The fire escape groans under my sudden weight, rust flakes raining down—metallic taste mixing with the copper tang of fear. The metal is cold under my palms, gritty with decades of Chicago winters. The texture bites into skin already cut from the glass.

Don't look down.

I look down.

The alley yawns like a throat ready to swallow me. Dumpsters look like toys five stories below. My vision tilts, vertigo hitting like a physical blow. Seven years old again. Falling. The snap of bone—

"She's going up!"

Up. The roof. The door to the internal stairs should be there. Has to be there.

My legs shake as I climb, each rung protesting under my weight. Bolts grind in crumbling brick. The structure sways—or maybe that's me. Blood from my cut palms makes the metal slippery. The wind picks up, whipping hair across my face, carrying the smell of rain and rot and city exhaust. Something sharp like ozone means a storm is coming.

The roof access appears. I haul myself over the edge, grit biting through my jeans. Chicago sprawls in every direction— millions of lights, each one a life that has no idea mine is ending.

The rooftop is a graveyard of dead technology. HVAC units squat like tombs, humming their mechanical prayers. A forest of TV antennas from the analog age juts toward the sky. Rusted lawn chairs circle a Weber grill that hasn't seen flame in years. Beer bottles scattered like offerings. Some broken. A child's tricycle in the corner, its red paint peeling, abandoned by someone who moved away or grew up and forgot it existed.

The door to the internal stairs is exactly where I calculated.

But there's no handle on the outside. Of course not. Fire code requires exterior access, but building owners ignore regulations until someone dies. Building code violations everywhere except the one that would save me.

Metal scrapes behind me. They're coming.

I sprint for cover, wedging myself between the water tower and an HVAC unit. The metal is warm from the day's heat, humming with mechanical life. Pigeon droppings and rust coat everything—the smell thick and organic, ammonia and decay mixing with hot metal and old grease. I pull out my phone; fingers slick with blood.

"Status?" The Cerberus operator's voice is clipped, professional.

"Roof." The word scrapes out of my constricted throat. "Three men. Armed—"

"Two minutes out. Stay alive."

One hundred twenty seconds. One hundred twenty reasons to keep breathing.

"Spread out." The leader's voice carries on the wind. "She's here."

Footsteps fan across the rooftop. Methodical. Patient. They know I'm trapped.

Ninety seconds.

A bottle clinks against concrete. A chair scrapes.

Seventy seconds.

A shadow falls across my hiding spot.

"Behind the water tower!"

Rough hands grab my arms, yanking me into the open. My phone flies from my grip, screen shattering against concrete like ice on stone. The stocky one wrenches my arms behind my back. His breath reeks of coffee and cigarettes. His grip is iron, fingers digging into my biceps hard enough to bruise. My shoulders scream, muscles stretching at angles they weren't designed for.

The leader approaches with measured steps, adjusting his suppressor with the same care someone might clean their glasses. Up close, he smells expensive—cologne, leather, and spice. But underneath, gunpowder and violence.

"The drive."

I stare at him. My mouth opens. Nothing comes out but a wheeze. My throat constricts—that familiar strangling sensation. Nathan's voice echoing in my head: *You dissect life instead of living it. You're like a computer pretending to be human.*

His fist drives into my stomach.

Pain explodes through my core, white-hot and nauseating. My knees hit the rooftop hard, skin tearing through denim. I retch, tasting bile and blood—coppery tang coating my teeth. The night air burns my throat as I fight for breath that won't come. Grit digs into my kneecaps, sharp edges cutting through fabric.

"Search her."

Hands pat me down—invasive, violating, checking every pocket, every seam. They find the decoy USB in my bra immediately, fingers rough against my ribs, against my breasts, taking liberties that make my skin crawl.

"The copies."

Blood pools in my mouth. I spit, watching red splatter across his Italian leather shoes.

His boot connects with my ribs.

The crack echoes across the rooftop. White fire spreads through my chest. The pain is so sharp it steals thought, reduces everything to sensation and survival.

"Pain is remarkably persuasive, Ms. Singh." He kneels, gripping my chin, forcing me to meet his gaze. His eyes are gray, empty as a winter sky. His breath is mint-fresh—grotesque contrast to the violence. "The copies. Where?"

The stocky one hauls me upright. The movement sends lightning through my bruised ribs. City lights blur through tears I refuse to acknowledge. Wind cuts through my torn clothes, raising goose bumps, making me shiver. Cold air stings the cuts on my palms, my thigh, every wound a separate chorus of pain.

The third man—younger, nervous—shifts near the roof's edge. "We should hurry. Cops could—"

"The cops aren't coming." The leader presses his suppressor against my forehead. The metal is cold, a perfect circle of pressure promising oblivion. "Last chance. The copies."

My throat muscles seize. My mouth works soundlessly. Terror has stolen my voice completely. No sound emerges, not even a wheeze. Just silent opening and closing like a dying fish gasping for water.

"Wrong answer."

The suppressor swings away from my head toward my knee. I close my eyes. As if that will change the outcome. As if not seeing will make it hurt less.

But then, something wet and warm spatters across my face.

The grip on my arms goes slack. I open my eyes. The third man by the roof's edge—the nervous one—has a neat hole in his forehead. Perfect circle, like someone drew it there with a marker. He topples backward without a sound, already dead before he hits.

"Contact—" The leader spins toward the shadows, weapon raised.

The stocky one shoves me aside, reaching for his sidearm. His head snaps back. The back of his skull explodes outward in a spray of blood, brain matter, and bone fragments. He drops, his weight clipping my shoulder as he falls. Hot blood soaks through my shirt, sticky and thick. The smell hits—copper and meat and something organic and wrong, nauseating in its intimacy.

The leader fires three times at the darkness. Desperate. Wild.

A shape emerges from shadow—tall, moving with controlled violence. The leader swings his weapon around, but the man is already there, one hand deflecting the gun while driving an elbow into the leader's throat.

The leader staggers back, gasping. They trade blows faster

than I can track. The shadow moves like water, each strike precise, economical. No wasted motion.

Defense becomes offense, then becomes defense again in a fluid dance of violence.

The leader pulls a knife. Steel catches city light, blade gleaming.

The man shifts, catches the leader's wrist, twists sharply. The wet snap of breaking bone fills the air—a sharp crack like a branch breaking. The knife clatters across the surface. In the same fluid motion, he drives his knee into the leader's solar plexus, then brings his elbow down on the back of his neck.

The leader crumples. Doesn't move.

Three men down.

Maybe fifteen seconds total.

The man turns to me. Light catches his face—angular features, dark stubble, eyes that catalog everything in one sweep. He's breathing normally, like he just finished a casual jog instead of killing three people.

"Talia Singh?" His voice is deep, controlled. Barely more than a whisper. "*Statistical Probability*." He says it with emphasis, and it takes me a while to figure out why he would say those words right now. Then it hits, what the man on the phone said. The code word. I'm supposed to respond, but my voice has fled.

I nod, mute. My voice is a dead thing in my throat.

"Jonah Jackson. Cerberus." He extends a hand. "We need to move. Now."

I stare at his hand. Blood-slicked, strong, steady. I take it. His grip is solid, warm, steady against my shaking. Calloused palms. Strong fingers that know exactly how much pressure to apply.

"Can you walk?"

I nod.

"Can you speak?"

I open my mouth. Close it. Shake my head. The mechanism is jammed.

His jaw tightens. A muscle jumps. "Injured throat?"

I touch my throat, shake my head again.

"Shock." Not a question. "Follow me. Stay close. Nod if you understand."

I nod.

He moves toward the roof's edge. My body locks, feet rooting to gravel like I've been bolted down.

"Fire escape. Only way down."

I shake my head violently, backing away.

He turns, impatience flickering across his features. "You climbed up—"

I point at the bodies. Then at myself. Make a throat-cutting gesture. Then point at the fire escape and shake my head harder, whole body trembling.

"Heights." Understanding crosses his features, softening them fractionally. "But you climbed anyway. To survive."

I nod, wrapping my arms around myself. My ribs protest—sharp pain lancing through my chest with each breath.

"Can you do it again?"

No. God, no.

Footsteps in the stairwell. Voices. More coming.

I force myself to nod.

He swings onto the fire escape—no hesitation, no fear, moving like the rusted metal is solid ground. I snatch both my phone and the USB from one of the dead men and follow on legs made of jelly, hands welding to the railings. The metal groans, shakes, threatens to tear free from the brick. The rust is rough under my palms, flaking away, leaving orange residue on bloodied skin.

"Eyes on me." An order, not a suggestion. "Don't look down."

I lock onto his face. Strong jaw, dark eyes that don't waver. An anchor in the spinning world.

"One level. Then the next."

We descend into a nightmare. Each step is calculated terror. My hands won't release the railings. He has to pry them loose at each platform, his fingers warm against my frozen ones. Patient. Methodical. Like he has all the time in the world, even though we're both going to die.

"Two more floors."

Glass explodes above us. Gunfire erupts, suppressors spitting their mechanical coughs.

Without warning, he grabs me, throws me over his shoulder in a fireman's carry. His shoulder drives into my stomach, reigniting the pain from earlier. One arm locks around my legs, holding me secure as he descends fast—taking steps three at a time.

There is no romance in it. Just efficiency. Mass and velocity and the quickest way to clear the kill zone.

The world inverts. Blood rushes to my head. His body is solid beneath me, muscles shifting with each movement. I smell gunpowder and sweat, leather and something clean like cedar. My hands clutch at his back, feeling a tactical vest, weapons, and controlled power.

We hit the alley hard. He sets me on my feet but keeps one arm around my waist when my knees buckle. His grip is firm, supporting without hurting my bruised ribs.

A motorcycle waits—black, anonymous.

"Get on."

I stare at it, then at him.

"Now." The word is an order, clipped and absolute.

I climb on behind him. My arms wrap around his waist on instinct. He's solid, real, radiating heat through his jacket. I can feel his abs through the leather—hard planes of muscle, body honed for violence.

"Hold tight."

The engine roars. We launch forward. Alley walls blur past. My ribs protest with each bump, each jarring impact. Wind tears at my torn clothes, stinging every cut. But his body shields most of it—a solid wall between me and everything trying to kill me.

We hit the street. He leans into a turn. I lean with him—instinct, survival, trust I didn't choose. My arms tighten around his waist, feeling each breath he takes, each shift of muscle as he controls the machine.

Sirens wail somewhere in the distance. He weaves through traffic, taking side streets, alleys, routes that make no sense. Anti-surveillance driving on a motorcycle. The city blurs—lights and shadows and speed compressing into one long streak of survival.

My hands start to slip. Blood and sweat making grip impossible. Vision swimming from pain and possible concussion.

He covers one of my hands with his, pressing it firm against his stomach. "Stay with me."

Not a request. Command.

I hold tighter. Vision swimming. But I don't let go.

Can't let go.

He's the only solid thing in a world that's become chaos and death and equations that don't balance.

FOUR

Talia

EXTRACTION

THE MOTORCYCLE TEARS THROUGH CHICAGO STREETS, THE engine growling between my thighs, every vibration crawling up my spine. My arms wrap around Jackson's waist, uncertain how close is too close, how much of him I'm allowed to feel.

We hit a pothole. The world jolts. My grip slips—just for a heartbeat—until his hand leaves the handlebars, finds my wrists, and yanks them tight around him.

"Hold on!" he shouts over the roar. "Tight. Lean when I lean."

He presses my palms flat against his abdomen, trapping them there. Muscle, solid and unyielding, flexes beneath my touch. Heat burns through cotton and leather, through logic and fear. Every inhale fills my lungs with the scent of him—metal, smoke, rain, and man.

My chest molds to his back, each shift of his body sending a rush of motion through mine. He moves like the bike is an exten-sion of him—fluid, precise, powerful. I can feel it in the way his muscles coil and release, in the steady control beneath the chaos.

He's all motion and command, danger and safety in the same breath.

And I can't tell if my pulse is racing from the ride—or from him.

We bank right. Instinct makes me want to stay upright, but his hand drops back, finds my thigh, pulls me into the turn with him. The contact is electric. My body molds against his, thighs bracketing his hips, chest sealed to his back, arms locked around his waist like he's the only solid thing in a tilting world.

This is necessary. Purely functional. Motorcycle safety.

But my body doesn't understand that. Every point of contact burns. His back muscles shift under my palms as he navigates traffic. The bike vibrates between my legs, and I'm pressed so tight against him I can feel his heartbeat. Steady. Controlled. Nothing like the rapid flutter of mine.

He takes another corner, sharp enough that my thigh presses hard against his hip. This time I lean with him, bodies moving in sync, and his hand briefly covers mine on his stomach—approval, maybe, or just making sure I won't let go.

The intimacy is overwhelming. Nathan never wanted me this close except during sex, and even then, it felt like distance. This is different—a necessary contact that feels unnecessarily intense.

My ribs scream with every breath. Blood from my palms has soaked through his jacket, leaving rust-colored patches I hope he won't notice. The wind whips my hair into a tangle, carrying the taste of exhaust and distant rain.

Something catches my eye in the side mirror. I turn, looking over my shoulder to catch a better view—a black SUV, three cars back. The bike wobbles dangerously.

"Don't!" Jackson's hand shoots back, grabs my hip, and yanks me forward. The bike straightens. "Never look back. You'll dump us."

But I already saw enough. The SUV is maintaining perfect distance. Too perfect.

Jackson revs the engine and takes a sudden right without signaling. I risk a glance in the mirror. The SUV follows.

A second black vehicle emerges from a side street ahead, timing too convenient to be a coincidence. Jackson sees it. His muscles coil beneath my arms.

"Hold tight!" he shouts.

He banks hard left into an alley, barely wide enough for the bike. The vehicles can't follow—too narrow. But they'll circle around and try to cut us off.

The alley spits us onto a side street. Jackson doesn't hesitate, engine screaming as he races toward the next intersection. Another vehicle appears, speeding to intercept.

Jackson cuts right again, tires protesting. We're hidden between dumpsters and loading docks before they round the corner. He kills the engine, the sudden silence deafening.

"Off."

One word, but I understand. My legs shake as I dismount. He swings off, already scanning exits.

"Can you run?"

I nod, though my ribs protest.

"Stay close. Silent."

He guides me deeper into the alley system, hand on my elbow, pace punishing. Every footfall feels too loud. Every shadow could hide the men who killed Victor. The organization behind Morrison's death. Whoever they are.

Jackson moves like smoke in the dark—quiet, purposeful, every step absorbed by the night. The alley's narrow, slick with rain, dumpsters hulking like shadows within shadows, and he slips between them without sound. His head tilts, tracking movement I can't hear, eyes cutting through the gloom as if he can read the city's pulse. One hand ghosts toward the weapon at his hip, the other steady, relaxed, deliberate.

He doesn't just move through danger; he studies it, feels it. Every shift of his shoulders, every pause, is precision. Controlled violence waiting for permission.

I try to follow, but gravel crunches under my boots, loud as gunfire in the hush. My breath scrapes my throat, ragged and too human. He glances back once, eyes catching the dim streetlight—cold, assessing, a silent command to keep up—and then he melts forward again, a phantom drawn by purpose.

The alley swallows him whole. I hurry after, chasing the echo of a man who seems carved from the night itself.

We emerge onto a side street. Normal foot traffic, people heading home from bars, oblivious. Jackson pulls me against him, arm around my shoulders instead of my waist, and suddenly I'm pressed along his entire side. He has to lean down to accommodate our height difference, his breath warm against my ear.

"Just a couple walking," he murmurs, lips barely moving. "Relax."

Relax. His body heat burns through my torn shirt. Every step presses me against him—hip to hip, ribs to ribs. His arm is heavy across my shoulders, hand hanging down to rest against my upper arm. When he turns his head to scan the street, his stubble brushes my temple.

The forced intimacy makes my head spin. Where is he taking me? What's the plan? The not knowing gnaws at me, but my voice still won't work.

Jackson stops abruptly. His arm tightens, pulling me into a doorway.

Across the street, a nondescript sedan idles where it shouldn't. Two men stand near it, postures all wrong for casual conversation. One keeps checking his phone in that way that screams surveillance.

"Shit." Jackson's voice cuts the air, low and sharp against my ear.

He pivots fast, dragging me deeper into the alley's labyrinth. Boots splash through oily puddles. Echoes chase us—multiple footsteps, closing in, too coordinated to be random.

Jackson's pace doubles. My ribs scream; black edges claw at my vision. The world narrows to motion, breath, and the relentless slap of pursuit.

We turn a corner—dead end. Brick on three sides. Dumpster. Trash. No escape.

He assesses in a heartbeat.

"Behind the dumpster," he orders, shoving me toward it. "Down. Cover your ears."

The metal reeks of rot and rain. I crouch, trembling, peering through rusted gaps as Jackson kneels in the open, coat flaring, every move efficient, precise. He pulls a small black device from his jacket—compact, lethal. His fingers fly across it like he's done this a thousand times.

My mind races. Explosive. In a boxed alley. The pressure will—

Stop thinking. Footsteps close in. Muffled voices coordinate.

Jackson plants the charge low on the wall, angled down. He's calculating airflow, debris patterns—survival odds.

Three men appear at the mouth of the alley, weapons raised.

"Drop it!"

"If you insist."

He presses the trigger.

The world erupts.

The blast hits before sound catches up—pressure slamming the air from my lungs. The dumpster wails like struck metal. Debris explodes into shrapnel.

But Jackson is already moving—launching toward me, pinning me against the wall as the wave crashes through us. His body cages mine, absorbing the hits: brick fragments, glass, grit. Each impact reverberates through him into me.

Heat. Smoke. Silence ringing like aftermath.

He doesn't move, just braces there—solid, breathing hard, shielding every inch of me. His heartbeat hammers against my spine. My chest can't rise. Not from fear, but from him.

I'm wrapped in his scent—gunpowder, sweat, adrenaline. The weight of his protection. The violence he meted out for me.

Something fundamental shifts.

Not the ground. Not the air.

Me.

This isn't Nathan's controlling grip, meant to diminish. This is pure protection, Jackson literally putting himself between me and harm's way. The difference hits like another explosion, breaking something open in my chest.

My body responds without permission. Heat floods through me, pooling low. Every point where he touches burns. His breath against my neck, harsh from exertion. His chest pressed to my back, heart hammering. His hips pinning mine against the wall.

Safe. Protected. Held.

The ringing in my ears fades. The debris stops falling. But Jackson doesn't move. For three heartbeats, we stay frozen—him shielding me from a danger that's passed, me trembling from something that has nothing to do with fear.

"You hurt?" His voice rumbles against my ear.

I shake my head, not trusting what sound might escape.

He pulls back slowly, checking me for injuries his body might have missed. He runs his hands over my arms, my ribs, clinical but thorough. Each touch leaves trails of heat.

The three operatives are on the ground, clutching their

heads, disoriented. One tries to stand, falls. Another has blood running from his ears. The third is crawling, lost.

"Move." Jackson grabs my hand, pulling me over the downed men.

We run. My legs barely work, still shaking from him. From the memory of his weight, his protection.

Two blocks over, an older Honda sits in a residents-only lot. Jackson works the lock with something from his pocket. Thirty seconds and the engine turns over.

"Get in."

I collapse into the passenger seat. My whole body trembles. The phantom weight of him presses against my back. I can still feel everywhere he touched, protected, shielded.

Jackson drives with controlled speed, checking mirrors and making random turns. Professional. Calm. Like he didn't just use his body as my personal shield.

"Safe house in ten minutes," he says, glancing at me. "You're shaking."

I nod, wrapping my arms around myself. But it's not fear making me shake.

"You didn't have to shield me." The words scrape out of a throat still dust-rough.

"Yes, I did." His eyes stay on the road, hands steady on the wheel. "It's my job."

Job.

The word lands like a weight in my ribs. Principal. Package. Objective.

My body refuses the demotion.

It remembers his weight pinning me to brick, the hard cage of muscle that turned the blast into pressure and heat instead of shrapnel and death. Remembers the way he absorbed every hit meant for me—shoulders taking it, back taking it—breath harsh against my ear while mine stuttered and caught.

The car hums now, low and even, but I'm still wrapped in the echo of him: smoke on my skin, salt on my lips, the imprint of his hands where he checked for blood and found only shaking.

I tell myself it was professional. A tactic. Physics and training.

But my pulse argues. It surges every time his forearm flexes on the wheel. My palms itch to press where his chest crushed the panic flat, to borrow that steadiness and pin it inside me.

This is insane. He's doing a job.

And then the comparison I don't want hits—Nathan. Nathan, who never stepped in, never took a hit for me, never noticed my breathing go thin at the edges. Nathan, who measured everything—time, effort, affection—and always came up criticizing my existence.

Jackson doesn't measure. He moves. He covers. He takes the impact and doesn't flinch.

My body remembers that difference and it wants—God, it wants—the way his protection felt. The way safety felt when it wore his shape. I try to name it: adrenaline, shock, anything clinical enough to survive.

But when his gaze flicks to me in the cracked windshield's reflection—one quick, cutting glance that checks I'm still here—something inside me gives, quiet and terrifying.

A line blurs.

And what's left between us isn't just aftermath. It's hunger wearing a reason.

Stop. You're doing it again. Analyzing, dissecting. Nathan was right, you can't just experience things, you have to—

But I can't stop. Because the memory of Jackson's body covering mine is the first time I've felt truly safe in years. And that safety came with heat, with want, with my body responding to his protection in ways that have nothing to do with professionalism.

"Still shaking," Jackson observes, glancing at me again. "Shock?"

I nod, because what else can I do? Tell him that his body covering mine rewired something fundamental in my brain? That I'm shaking because I want him to do it again, minus the explosion? That every protective touch made me want to crawl inside his skin?

He'd think you're insane—or worse, a liability.

"This is a safe house." Jackson parks in the underground garage, still checking for surveillance. He exits and walks around to open my door. "Can you walk?"

I nod, though my legs feel like liquid. I climb out of the vehicle, take one step, and my knees buckle.

He catches me, one arm sliding around my waist, taking my weight without effort. "Those ribs—I have field medical training. Will you let me look?"

Another nod.

"You need to find your voice," he says, half-carrying me to an elevator. "I can't protect you if you can't communicate. Understand?"

I understand. But understanding and doing are different things. Nathan's voice still echoes: *"Your constant need to verbalize everything is exhausting."*

The words are there, crowding my throat. But they won't come.

Jackson's arm tightens slightly as the elevator rises, taking more of my weight. His competence is overwhelming—the kind of man who kills three people and doesn't break a sweat.

The kind who might keep me alive.

"We're going to figure out who wants you dead," he says as the doors open. "But first, you need to tell me everything. Can you do that?"

I want to. Need to.

All I can do is nod and hope it's enough.

FIVE

Talia

______

PATTERN RECOGNITION

THE SAFE HOUSE DOOR CLOSES BEHIND US WITH A SOFT CLICK that feels too final. Jackson engages three different locks, the sequential snaps echoing in the quiet space. The apartment is sparse—functional furniture, blackout curtains, and a kitchen that looks unused. Everything is in shades of gray and black, like color would be a security risk.

I'm covered in blood. Some mine, most not. The stocky operative's blood spatters my face and neck. My torn clothes hang off me like rags.

Jackson turns from checking the window and really looks at me for the first time since the alley. His eyes catalog damage with the same intention he uses for everything.

"You're covered in blood." Statement, not question.

"I know."

He steps closer, fingers hovering near a cut on my temple I didn't know was there. "This needs cleaning. Your ribs?"

I touch my side, wince. The leader's boot left its mark.

"Bathroom's through there." He indicates a door. "Clean clothes in the cabinet. Take your time."

Take your time. Like we have time. Like those men aren't still hunting us.

But I need to wash their blood off me. Need to think without Jackson filling my vision, making my skin prickle with awareness.

The bathroom is as utilitarian as the rest of the place—white tile, basic fixtures, a stack of black towels that look military-issue. I close the door and engage the lock even though it's pointless. If danger comes, a bathroom door won't stop it.

I turn the shower on. The water hisses against the tile, steam rising to fog the mirror.

I stare at my reflection. Dark smudges under my eyes. Blood dried in a crust along my jaw. The woman looking back seems like a stranger—someone hollowed out and filled with fear.

I step under the spray without adjusting the temperature. The water is lukewarm, then hot, pounding against my skin. I grab the bar of soap, lathering my hands, scrubbing at my arms.

Scrub.

Red swirls down the drain.

Scrub harder.

But my mind isn't here. It's back in the alley. It's back on the rooftop. It's cataloging the trajectory of the bullet that hit the operative's head. The angle of his fall. The volume of blood spatter.

Jackson's body slamming into mine. His weight. His heat. The solid wall of him taking every impact.

The explosion should have killed us. Statistical probability of survival at that proximity to detonation is less than five percent. He threw himself over me without hesitation, made his body into my shield. Every piece of debris that hit him could have hit me. *Would* have hit me.

But he took it all.

My hands stop moving. The soap slips from my fingers, clattering against the tub.

I stand there, water beating down on my head, but I don't feel it. I'm dissociated, floating above the scene. My body is a data point I can't quite integrate.

Nathan never protected me from anything. Three years together, and he never once put himself between me and harm. Not physically, not emotionally. He was too busy cataloging my flaws and dissecting my inadequacies.

"You're exhausting, Talia. Always talking, always analyzing."

But Jackson protected me with his body. Wordlessly. Completely.

Something fundamental cracked open in that alley. Not from the explosion—from him. From the absolute safety of his weight, the brutal certainty of his protection, the way his body absorbed violence meant for mine.

My legs give out. I sink to the shower floor, knees pulled to my chest, water beating down.

I sit there for a long time. I don't know how long. The water runs cold, but I don't move to turn it off. I just stare at the drain, watching the water swirl, unable to connect the concept of "washing" with the physical action.

Eventually, the shivering becomes too violent to ignore. I turn off the tap. Towel off with mechanical, jerky movements. I put on the clothes from the cabinet—black cargo pants I have to roll up, a gray T-shirt that drowns me. They smell like detergent and something else. Gun oil, maybe. The scent of tactical efficiency.

I unlock the door.

When I emerge, Jackson stands at the kitchen counter,

medical kit open. He's changed too—black tactical pants, black Henley that clings to every plane of muscle.

I stop in the doorway, pulse tripping over itself.

Without the tactical vest. Without the chaos. Without the adrenaline masking everything else.

He's just a man now. And that somehow makes him infinitely more dangerous.

The Henley pulls taut across shoulders that look built to bear the world—fabric clinging to every ridge and line of muscle. The sleeves are shoved to his elbows, exposing forearms laced with veins and scars, strength that speaks of use, not vanity. He moves with unthinking precision, organizing medical supplies like he's still defusing bombs—every motion efficient, economical, controlled.

Nathan's body was sculpted for mirrors. Jackson's was forged for survival. For violence. For protection.

And every part of me reacts to that difference.

Heat slides through my veins, pooling low, my breath catching on the sight of him. The damp edges of his hair cling to his temples; a single droplet traces the sharp edge of his jaw before vanishing into the stubble shadowing his throat. The light from the kitchen gilds the scar cutting through his left brow, softening nothing—if anything, sharpening him further.

He shouldn't be beautiful. Not like this. Not when every instinct screams danger.

But he is—beautiful the way a blade is beautiful. Purpose and precision. Violence in repose.

And as he turns, catching me watching him, that easy control in his movements doesn't falter. His gaze just lifts—steady, unreadable—and for one breathless second, I swear he sees exactly what he's doing to me.

This man killed three people in front of me less than an hour ago. Shot them with the same precision he's now using to organize bandages. The men in the alley—he detonated an explosive and took them down without breaking a sweat. His hands have ended lives tonight. Those same hands that are now carefully arranging medical supplies.

I should be terrified.

I should be backing toward the door, looking for escape routes, calculating the distance to safety. Any rational person would fear a man who can kill so efficiently, so calmly. Who can transition from violence to casual conversation, like changing channels.

Instead, I'm mesmerized.

My body hums with awareness, skin prickling with each small movement he makes. Something's fundamentally wrong with me that I'm standing here, pulse racing, thighs clenched, attracted to a man who is objectively dangerous. A killer. A stranger who could snap my neck as easily as he opened that medical kit.

But he threw his body over mine. Took shrapnel meant for me. Protected me with a ferocity that was somehow gentle. Threw me over his shoulder on that fire escape like I weighed nothing, carried me to safety while I was paralyzed by fear.

The memory of being held against him—my stomach pressed to his shoulder, his arm locked around my legs, the solid strength of him the only thing between me and a five-story fall— makes heat pool in my belly.

The contradiction makes my head spin. Lethal and protective. Dangerous and safe. Everything about him is a paradox that my body understands even if my mind doesn't.

He looks up, and his attention hits like a physical touch. My nipples tighten beneath the borrowed shirt. I cross my arms, hoping he doesn't notice.

"Sit." He indicates a kitchen chair. "Let me check those ribs."

I sit. He kneels in front of me, eye level now. This close, I can see the faint scar through his eyebrow, the gold flecks in his green eyes. He smells like cedar and gunpowder, a combination that makes my mouth water.

"May I?" His hands hover near the hem of my shirt.

I nod, not trusting my voice.

He lifts the fabric carefully, exposing the bruise spreading across my ribs. Purple-black, the perfect imprint of a boot. His fingers ghost over it, barely touching, but even that minimal contact sends electricity through me.

"Not broken." His voice is low, clinical. "But deep bruising. Painful but not dangerous."

He reaches for medical tape, movements economical. His hands work with the same care he used setting that explosive—sure, practiced, deadly. But gentle now. So gentle it makes my chest tight with something that isn't pain.

"There." He smooths the last piece of tape, fingers lingering a heartbeat longer than necessary. Or am I imagining it? "That should help."

He stands, putting distance between us, and I immediately miss his proximity. Miss the heat of him, the solid presence that makes me feel simultaneously safe and completely off-balance.

The silence stretches, tension thick enough to choke on. I need to break it before I do something catastrophically stupid. The USB drive is now in the pocket of my borrowed clothes. I feel for it through the fabric of the cargo pants, needing to know it's safe.

"I need to check the drive," I say quietly, the words scraping past my damaged throat. "Victor's drive. See what he died protecting."

"The drive?" he prompts.

The small device cost so many lives. "I need a computer. A laptop. To check the files."

"There's one in the bedroom." He moves toward the hallway. "Secure system, encrypted connection."

I follow him, trying not to notice the way he moves—controlled, purposeful, dangerous. The bedroom is as sparse as the rest of the safe house. A single bed, military corners. A desk with a laptop, closed and waiting.

"Non-traceable," he says, powering it on.

Right. The drive. The reason we're here. Not to obsess over being in a bedroom with him, or the way his presence fills the small space.

I set up at the small dining table, USB sliding into the port. The familiar world of data settles my nerves slightly. This I understand. This I can control.

Files bloom across my screen—spreadsheets, documents, chemical formulas. My fingers fly across the keys, organizing and cross-referencing. Silent work, the kind that used to drive Nathan crazy.

"Your silence is passive-aggressive."

But Jackson doesn't seem to mind the quiet. He moves through the apartment, checking windows, weapons, and exits. Each motion contains exactly the energy required, nothing wasted. I track him peripherally, cataloging the controlled power in every movement.

"Seventy-three confirmed deaths," I say quietly.

"Excuse me?"

"Deaths. From Meridian's drug trials." I pull up the data and turn the screen toward him. "That's what Victor died protecting. Evidence of seventy-three people killed during pharmaceutical trials for a drug called ML-273."

Jackson moves closer, looking over my shoulder at the screen. His proximity makes my skin prickle, hyperaware of every inch between us. The heat of him reaches me through the borrowed clothes.

"They covered it up?"

I nod, pull up more data. Don't trust my voice for extended explanation.

"Wait." I highlight something. "They all had the same blood type. O-negative with rare RH factors. That's—"

"Specific."

"More than specific. That's less than 0.0001% of the population." My mind races through possibilities. The data points align in my head, forming a shape I can recognize. "They weren't random test subjects. They were selected."

"Selected for what?"

I pull up Victor's chemical analysis, the formulas making my breath catch. "Look at this." The words come easier now, the data giving me something to focus on besides Jackson's presence. "ML-273 isn't meant to treat cancer. It's designed to alter DNA methylation patterns in specific sequences."

"English."

His voice rumbles behind me, low and commanding. The same tone that ordered me silent in the alley, that made my body respond before my mind could process.

"It's trying to activate dormant genetic code. Like—flipping switches in human DNA that have been turned off through evolution." I force myself to focus on the screen. The numbers dance, rearranging themselves into a terrifying conclusion. "They're not developing medicine. They're developing modifications. Enhancements. The cancer patients were just test subjects to see if … Look. Buried in the metadata, I keep seeing this phrase. *Obsidian Protocol.*"

Jackson freezes. Not the stillness he wears like armor—this is sharper, deeper. Recognition.

"What did you say?"

Did I speak?

"Obsidian Protocol." I swivel the laptop toward him. "Referenced seventeen times across different files. I can't find any description, just the name. I wonder what it is?"

He's silent long enough for dread to creep under my skin. His jaw flexes once, muscle ticking. Eyes hinting at something—memory, caution, maybe fear.

"Phoenix," he says at last, quiet enough that I almost miss it.

"Like the city?" I frown, trying to follow. "Or the bird?"

He exhales slowly, eyes still on the screen. "No. Phoenix isn't a place. It's—complicated. And dangerous."

I blink. "You've heard of it."

He hesitates—just a flicker, but it's there. "Cerberus came across the name. A self-protecting system."

"And you think it's connected to this?" I tap the phrase glowing in the code.

The cursor blinks between us, waiting. The hum of the laptop fills the silence. Somewhere outside, a siren wails, distant and fading.

Jackson's jaw tightens again, eyes narrowing as he watches the data scroll. "If Obsidian is tied to Phoenix," he says quietly, "then you just tripped something that doesn't want to be found."

I swallow, pulse hammering. "Something—like an AI?"

He exhales slowly, gaze still locked on the code. "Something smarter than that. Self-aware. Self-protecting." His voice drops lower, a thread of steel beneath the calm. "And I think we just discovered why multiple kill squads have been sent after you and your lead, Victor."

The words hang in the air, heavy and irreversible, as the screen flickers—just once—like it's listening.

"What can you tell me about Phoenix?"

"Military AI. Autonomous targeting system." His voice is carefully controlled. "Officially terminated. Unofficially—"

"Still operational." The pieces click together. My brain lights up, connecting disparate nodes. The black SUV. The precise timing of the hit. The coordinated assault. "That's why Morrison gave me your number? He knew this connected to Phoenix?"

"Morrison didn't know about Phoenix. He was just our FBI contact." Jackson's tone darkens, every word deliberate. "But whatever your source dug up—Phoenix is cleaning up."

I freeze. "How does a pharmaceutical company access military AI?"

"Same way they get everything," he says grimly. "Money. Power. Connections. Someone high up is involved."

"And this Phoenix killed Victor?"

Jackson's jaw flexes. "We need more data, but it's suspicious. If Phoenix is involved, it not only tracked and killed Victor—it's hunting you now."

The chill that rolls through me is almost physical. I turn back to the laptop, fingers flying across keys. Focus. The data is safe. The data makes sense.

I pull up Victor's research logs. Cross-reference his last communications. My screen fills with names—researchers who collaborated on the Meridian trials. I run quick searches, pulling public records, obituaries, anything.

"Lydia Crawford," I read aloud. A news clipping loads, cheerful photo, tragic headline. "Dead a month ago. Car accident."

Another search. "Marcus Thornton. Suicide. Two weeks ago."

I keep going, scrolling faster now. Every click is another jolt of disbelief. Another obituary. Another end.

"They're all dead," I whisper. "Every researcher who questioned the trials. Car accidents. Suicides. Heart attacks." I pull up a spreadsheet, start building a timeline, my pulse syncing to the rhythmic tapping of keys. "But the timing—it's not random."

Jackson leans closer, the warmth of his presence grounding and terrifying all at once.

"Look," I say, voice thin. "They died in order of seniority. One by one. The most senior first, then the next. It's—deliberate."

"That's Phoenix." His voice drops, low and final. "It doesn't just kill—it calculates. Makes it look organic. Random. But every death fits an algorithm."

"Did you think …"

"I think we just found out why multiple kill squads were sent after you and Victor." Jackson's hand settles on the table beside me, steady but coiled. His eyes narrow on the scrolling code.

The cursor blinks. Once. Twice. Then the hard drive hums—a sound almost like breathing.

"An AI that kills people?" My hands shake slightly. "That learns and adapts?"

"Phoenix went rogue years ago. Started selecting its own targets based on threat assessment algorithms." His voice is grim. "We've been tracking it, trying to predict patterns."

"But true AI can't be predicted. It evolves faster than human analysis." I scan more files. "Jackson, these chemical formulas … Victor flagged something."

I pull up his margin notes: *Not therapeutic. Synthetic markers? DNA changes detected pre-death. Unreported.*

"What if they were changing something in the test subjects' DNA before they died?" I suggest quietly. "The deaths were secondary. Collateral damage from testing something else."

"What were they testing?"

"I don't know. The chemistry is beyond my understanding." I scroll through more formulas, frustrated. "But Victor documented DNA changes in the autopsy reports that Meridian never reported to the FDA. Whatever they were doing, it was worth killing seventy-three people to test. And worth killing anyone who questioned it."

A shiver runs through me—delayed reaction to everything.

The cold, the fear, the phantom memory of Jackson's body shielding mine.

Without warning, he disappears into the bedroom. Returns with a blanket that he drapes over my shoulders. The gesture is so unexpected, so gentle, that my throat closes up.

The blanket smells like cedar and gunpowder and safety. I pull it tighter, burrowing into the warmth.

"Thank you," I whisper.

He nods, returns to checking the windows. But something has shifted. The quiet between us feels different now. Charged with things unsaid.

I focus on the screen, but I'm hyperaware of him moving through the space. Of the blanket's weight on my shoulders. Of the bruise on my ribs that throbs with each breath, reminding me of his gentle hands checking the damage.

The way my body still aches for his touch, even though I know his protection was just a professional duty.

But the blanket around my shoulders feels like more than duty. It feels like he's taking care of me.

If that's the case, he might be more dangerous than any AI or assassination team hunting me.

SIX

Jackson

BLOOD AND WATER

S**HE MOVES PAST ME TOWARD THE KITCHEN, AND SOMETHING DARK** catches the light in her still-damp hair. Not water. Something chunky, matted against the strands near her temple.

Brain matter. Probably the stocky operative's.

I reach out, plucking it free before she notices. Mistake. The chunk pulls away with a wet sound, trailing hair and gore.

She turns, sees what's in my fingers. Gray-pink tissue. Bone fragment. Her face drains of color.

"Oh God." The words barely whisper out. Her hand flies to her mouth, her whole body recoiling.

"Stop." I drop the tissue in the trash, grab her shoulders before she backs into the counter. "It's nothing. Just debris."

She's hyperventilating, eyes wide, but no more words come. Just panicked breathing. The shower obviously didn't do the job —she's been walking around in shock, going through the motions without actually seeing the mess.

"Kitchen sink." I steer her toward it. "Now."

She looks at me, a question in her eyes.

"You missed spots."

Her hand flies to her hair, fingers searching. She finds a wet clump, pulls her hand away like she's been burned. A soft whimper escapes—the most sound she's made in hours.

I turn on the faucet and test the temperature against my wrist. "Bend over."

She hesitates, then complies. Silent.

She bends over the sink, and I have to step close to reach. Too close. Her hip presses against my thigh. The borrowed shirt rides up, exposing a strip of skin above the cargo pants. Bruises bloom purple-black along her ribs.

Focus on the task. Not the curve of her spine. Not the way she trembles under my hands.

I work my fingers through her hair, finding clumps of dried blood, bone fragments, tissue. The water runs pink, then red, then pink again. She's completely silent except for her breathing —quick, shallow, like she's fighting not to cry.

The silence is unnerving. Usually, people talk to fill the space —nervous chatter, explanations, anything to avoid the reality of the moment. Even the women I take home usually fill the air with words, telling me what they want, how they want it. It makes things easy. Predictable.

But this woman? She gives me nothing.

No verbal cues. No nervous babbling. Just those golden eyes watching the water swirl down the drain.

It makes me want to figure her out. Makes me want to learn her tells through touch alone, map her responses without the roadmap of words.

Fuck. This is inappropriate. She's a principal. A job. Not a puzzle to solve with my hands.

"You okay?" I ask, needing something from her. Needing her voice to ground me back in reality.

A tiny nod.

"The water too hot?"

Head shake.

Christ.

I find another clump, work it free gently. "You can talk, you know. I'm not going to—"

"Everyone wants me to stop talking." The words come out so soft I almost miss them. "So I don't."

There's pain in that admission that has nothing to do with physical injury.

"That's their problem, not yours."

She goes still under my hands. I rinse the last of the blood away, squeeze excess water from her hair, and grab a kitchen towel.

When she straightens, she's looking at me strangely. Studying me. Then her gaze drops to my side, and her eyes widen.

She points at my shirt. There's blood seeping through. Shit. The shrapnel from the alley—I ignored it. Adrenaline's wearing off, and now it's bleeding through.

"You're hurt." Barely a whisper.

"It's nothing."

She shakes her head, insistent. Moves closer, fingers hovering near the bloodstain. Her eyes ask permission.

"I said it's fine—"

She grabs the first aid kit from the counter where I left it. Points at the kitchen chair. Commanding without words.

"You know, most women at least buy me dinner before they start ordering me around." I try for levity. "Though usually they use words."

Nothing. Not even a smile. Just another point at the chair, more insistent.

"Strong silent type, huh? I'm usually the one who doesn't talk much." Still nothing. "Not used to being out-silenced."

She crosses her arms, waiting. Immovable.

"Fine. But for the record, I don't usually take orders from women who won't even tell me their favorite color."

The tiniest quirk of her lips. Progress.

I sit. "It's just a graze."

She gestures at my shirt. Off.

"At least ask nicely," I mutter.

Her eyebrow raises slightly. She mouths one word: "Please."

Then crosses her arms again, waiting.

Fine.

I pull the Henley over my head, tossing it aside. The movement pulls at the wound—deeper than I thought. Shrapnel tore a decent gash along my ribs. Blood trails down my side.

Her intake of breath is sharp. She moves immediately, kneeling beside my chair. Her hands are quick, economical as she arranges supplies. Everything in order—antiseptic, gauze, tape, scissors. Each item positioned exactly where she'll need it. The same way I lay out demolition components. Nothing wasted.

She knows what she's doing.

Her fingers are gentle but sure as she cleans around the wound. No hesitation. No squeamishness. Just competent care.

But Christ, her hands on my skin.

I haven't let a woman touch me like this since Syria. Since Amara. The women I meet in bars don't get to touch—they get my hands, my mouth if they're lucky, but never this. Never gentle fingers on bare skin, never careful touches meant to heal instead of take.

My body doesn't understand the difference.

Every brush of her fingers sends signals straight to my cock. She leans closer to see better, her breath warm on my ribs, and I have to grip the edge of the chair to keep still. This is medical care, nothing more, but my body is responding like she's stroking me with intent.

Three years. Three years since a woman's hands were on my bare chest in a way that wasn't transactional. And now this silent woman is unraveling all that control with nothing more than her gentle touch as she treats my wounds.

The silence should be peaceful. Instead, it's charged with everything I want to do to her. Every nerve ending focused on where her fingers connect with my skin. She shifts again, her breast accidentally brushing my arm, and I have to bite back a groan.

Fuck. I'm about to come undone from basic first aid.

"You've done this before." My voice comes out rougher than intended. I desperately need a distraction.

Her response is a frustrating nod.

"FBI training?"

Another nod.

"You're good at it."

She pauses, looks up at me. There's surprise in her eyes, like she's not used to compliments. Then back to work.

"Why'd you leave the Bureau?"

Her hands still for a moment. When she speaks, it's barely audible: "Couldn't save anyone that mattered."

"Victor?"

She shakes her head. Presses gauze to the wound, starts taping it down. Each piece of tape requires her to lean closer, her hair brushing my chest. She smells like shampoo and something uniquely her.

"Before Victor?" I prompt.

"Children." One word, loaded with weight.

She doesn't elaborate. Doesn't need to. I know that particular weight—the cases you can't solve, the people you can't save. They accumulate until you either break or walk away.

"Is that why you left? The children?"

A small nod. She returns to taping the bandage, but there's tension in her movements now.

"How long were you with the Bureau?"

Silence. She focuses on the bandage as if it requires all her concentration.

"Come on, give me something here." I try to keep my tone light, but frustration bleeds through. "Favorite food? Where you grew up? Anything?"

She glances up, those golden eyes wide, vulnerable. Like she wants to answer but can't find the words. Or is afraid to.

And fuck, that vulnerability—it's hitting every protective instinct I have. This woman, who faced down armed killers and kept evidence safe despite everything, now looks like she might shatter if I push too hard.

It's dangerous; this need to protect her. Not just from Phoenix or Nexus or whoever's hunting her. But from whatever made her go this quiet. Whatever convinced her that her words were too much.

"Forget it," I say, softer. "You don't have to—"

"Five years." Her voice barely carries. "FBI for five years."

Not much, but it feels like a crack in the wall between us.

She finishes the bandage and sits back on her heels.

The sight hits me like a sucker punch.

That position—kneeling, head slightly bowed, eyes lifted—is one I've seen too many times. But this is different. Talia doesn't know the language of obedience, but she's sitting in it—unaware, unguarded, perfect—and my body reacts the same way it always has.

Fast. Hard. Hungry.

Jesus Christ.

Too many thoughts flash, hot and filthy, before I slam them down.

She's not one of them. She's not a release valve. She's the woman I just rescued from a kill squad.

I drag in a breath, force control back into my hands, my voice, my face.

Our eyes meet and hold. The silence hums—thick with everything I shouldn't be thinking.

She's beautiful like this. Focused. Competent. Those golden eyes that see everything but give nothing back. The way her teeth catch her lower lip when she concentrates.

It shouldn't make me want her more. But it does.

And that terrifies me more than any gunfight ever could.

I reach for my shirt, needing distance before I do something that will ruin both of us.

"Thank you," I manage, rougher than I mean to.

She stops me with a hand on my wrist. Points at the shirt—bloody, ruined. Then disappears down the hall and returns with a clean black T-shirt from the closet.

"Thanks."

She watches me pull it on, something unreadable in her expression. When I'm dressed, she starts cleaning up the medical supplies. Silent. Efficient.

Then she retreats to the far corner of the living room, sliding down the wall until she's sitting with her knees pulled to her chest. Arms wrapped around her legs. Making herself as small as possible.

I give her space. Clean up the kitchen. Check the windows. Inventory weapons. Five minutes pass. Ten. Fifteen.

She hasn't moved. Just sits there, chin on her knees, staring at nothing. But her eyes—Christ, her eyes are working overtime. I can see the thoughts churning behind them, calculations running, processing everything that's happened. Brilliant mind trapped behind sealed lips.

I want to crack her open. Not violently—gently. Like defusing a bomb, finding each wire, and understanding the connections. I want to know what she's thinking right now, what patterns she's seeing that I'm missing. Want to understand how her mind works, what makes her tick.

It's not just professional curiosity. It's something deeper, more dangerous. I want to know her. **Really** know her. Not just the facts—FBI analyst, witness protection, trauma from an ex—but the real her.

The silence is suffocating. But also intoxicating. Every minute she doesn't speak makes me study her more. The way her fingers tap out patterns—always in sets of three, some kind of mathematical sequence. The micro-expressions that flash across her face—frustration, fear, and something else when she looks at me. Interest? Attraction? Without words, I have to read her body, and her body is telling a story her voice won't.

"You okay?" I finally ask.

Her eyes flick to me, then away. A tiny shrug.

"A lot's happened. It's okay to not be okay with it."

Another shrug. Smaller this time.

"Is there anything I can do?"

She opens her mouth, closes it. When she finally speaks, her voice is so soft I have to strain to hear it. "I don't know how to be."

"What do you mean?"

"Quiet or talking. Still or moving. Here or ..." She trails off, curling tighter. "I don't know how to be anymore. I don't know what's happening. Don't know what to do, how to feel, what comes next. Everything's just—spinning."

The words tumble out, more than she's said in hours, and something loosens in my chest. Finally.

"I used to know things," she continues, voice small but gaining momentum. "Used to understand patterns, predict outcomes. But now? Victor's dead. Morrison's dead. Men are hunting me, and I don't know why. Not really. And you ..." She stops, looks at me, then away. "You killed people. For me. Because of me. And I should be terrified, but I'm not, and that doesn't make sense either."

Christ, she's unraveling, and all I want is to hear more. Every word feels like a victory, like I'm finally getting past her walls to the real *her* underneath.

"Nothing has to make sense right now," I say, trying to keep her talking.

"But that's what I do. I'm an analyst. I make sense of things. Find patterns. Solve problems." Her voice cracks slightly. "Except I can't solve this. Can't analyze my way out. Can't think clearly because every time I close my eyes I see that man's head exploding and every time you look at me I feel—"

She stops abruptly, pressing her face against her knees.

"You feel, what?"

Silence. Then, muffled, "Safe. Which is insane because you're the most dangerous person I've ever met."

This brilliant, vulnerable woman feels safe with me. After everything she's been through, after watching me kill, she feels safe.

The need to protect her becomes overwhelming. Not just from bullets and explosions, but from this lost feeling, this spinning confusion. I want to cross the room, pull her into my arms, hold her tight against me, and tell her nothing will touch her.

But I stay where I am, gripping the chair, because if I touch her, I might not be able to stop.

"Be however you need to be."

She looks at me then, really looks at me. "Nathan says I talk too much."

"Who's Nathan?"

"My boyfriend." She pauses, color rising in her cheeks. "Ex-boyfriend. My ex-boyfriend."

Interesting. The correction seems important to her.

"What did Nathan do?"

She's quiet for a moment. "Assistant US Attorney. The kind who cares more about conviction rates than justice."

"I meant, what did he do to you?"

She curls tighter. "Made me smaller. Quieter. Less." Another pause. "Told me I was exhausting. That I analyzed everything instead of living. That I talked too much, thought too loud, took up too much space with my words."

"So you stopped talking."

"I stopped everything." Her voice is barely audible. "It was easier than fighting about it."

"He sounds like an asshole."

"He was—precise. Surgical. Knew exactly where to cut to make it hurt without leaving visible marks." She looks at me. "You told me to be quiet too."

"When?"

"On the roof. When we were running. You said, 'stay close' and 'silent.'"

Shit. "That was tactical. We were escaping men trying to kill you. Not the same thing."

She nods but doesn't uncurl. The silence stretches again. I watch her retreating further into herself, and it's driving me insane.

This is getting dangerous. I'm noticing too much. The elegant line of her neck. The way her borrowed shirt gaps slightly at the collar, revealing her collarbone. How small she looks curled up like that, but how much strength it must take to keep all those words, all that brilliance, locked inside.

I'm getting turned on by a woman who won't speak to me. What the fuck is wrong with me?

Twenty minutes of this torture, and I can't take it anymore.

"Get up."

She looks startled.

"I'm teaching you basic self-defense. You were FBI, you should have some training, but I'm not assuming anything." I move to the center of the room. "And maybe hitting something will help. With whatever you're processing."

She unfolds slowly, approaching like she expects me to change my mind. Three steps forward, then she stops. Arms wrapped around herself.

"Come on," I say, trying to sound encouraging. "I won't hurt you."

She takes another step. Stops again. Those golden eyes are studying me like she's calculating the probability of harm.

"I promise, I'll be gentle."

Wrong words. Her eyebrows rise slightly, and there's something in her expression—not fear. Something else. She takes two more steps, close enough that I could reach her, but not close enough for training.

"You need to be closer."

She shakes her head slightly, takes a half-step back.

Christ, this is like coaxing a spooked animal. Except she's not spooked exactly. She's—something else. The way she's looking at me, the way her breathing has changed …

"Look, if you're not comfortable—"

She moves then, quickly, before she can change her mind. Suddenly she's right there, close enough that I smell the shampoo in her hair, see the pulse fluttering at her throat.

Too close.

"Give me your hand."

She extends it slowly, trembling slightly. When our skin connects, we both freeze. Her pulse jumps under my fingers. Mine probably does too.

"Someone grabs your wrist." I demonstrate, wrapping my

fingers around her forearm. The contact is electric. "What do you do?"

She tugs backward, testing. My grip doesn't budge.

"Don't pull against their strength. Work against their weakness—the thumb." I adjust my hold. "Turn your wrist toward where my thumb and fingers meet. Then jerk down and out in one motion."

She tries, her movements tentative.

"Harder. Commit to it."

She tries again, this time with more force. Breaks free.

"Good. Again."

I grab her other wrist. She breaks free faster this time.

"Now both." I grab both of her wrists and pull her closer. "Same principle."

This position puts us face-to-face. Close enough to see gold flecks in her eyes. Feel her breath accelerate. Her pulse hammers under my fingers.

She twists, drops her weight, jerks free. The momentum makes her stumble. I catch her waist to steady her.

Mistake.

My hands span her ribs. Her breathing is fast, shallow. Not from exertion. The air between us is charged with the same electricity from the alley.

She looks up at me. Still silent, but her eyes are asking something.

"What if they grab me from behind?" Her voice is soft, rusty from disuse.

I should step back. Don't.

"Let me show you something different." I move toward her, deliberate, predatory. "Sometimes they come at you head-on."

I lunge forward, not full speed but fast enough. She gasps, stumbles backward. I keep advancing, herding her until her back hits the wall with a soft thud.

My hands slam against the wall on either side of her head, caging her in. We're inches apart. Less. I can feel her breath on my face, see her pupils dilate.

"When an attacker gets this close," my voice comes out rough, "you have limited options."

She's staring at my mouth. Her tongue darts out, wetting her lips, and fuck, I want to taste her. Want to close this insignificant distance and claim that mouth. Want to know if she kisses as quietly as she does everything else.

My body leans in without permission. She arches slightly off the wall, closing the gap further. We're sharing breath now, her chest rising and falling rapidly, brushing against mine with each inhale.

I'm going to kiss her.

The realization hits like cold water. I'm about to kiss the principal. Worse—I'm thinking about more than kissing. Thinking about hiking her up against this wall, wrapping her legs around my waist, and fucking her the way I haven't fucked a woman in years.

Christ, I can see it. Feel it. Her tight heat wrapped around my cock, her quiet gasps in my ear, the wall shaking with each thrust. Doing the very thing I promised myself I'd never do again— putting my dick inside a woman, making myself vulnerable in that primitive, dangerous way.

I jerk back so suddenly she gasps.

"Knee to groin," I say, voice hoarse. "Headbutt if you can manage it. Strike the throat. But your best option—" I take another step back, needing distance, "—is not letting them get that close."

She stays against the wall, breathing hard, staring at me with those golden eyes that see too much.

"That's enough for now."

She nods slowly but doesn't move from the wall. There's

something in her expression—disappointment? Understanding? Want?

Without words, all I have is her body language. The way she leaned into me. The way her breath caught. The way she's looking at me like she wants something she doesn't have words for.

And I want to give it to her.

Which is exactly why I can't.

SEVEN

Jackson

TWENTY QUESTIONS

She stays against the wall for another heartbeat, then pushes off, moving to the far side of the room. As far from me as she can get in this small space. She curls into the corner of the couch, knees to chest, making herself small again.

The silence stretches. Five minutes. Ten.

I clean my Glock, the methodical *snick-click* of disassembly usually calming my mind. Not tonight. Every few seconds, my gaze pulls to her. She's staring at nothing, but I can see the thoughts churning behind those eyes. Processing. Analyzing. Probably calculating the probability of what almost happened against that wall.

Fifteen minutes.

This is torture. Not the silence itself—I'm comfortable with silence. It's *her* silence. The way she contains so much behind sealed lips. Like watching a bomb tick down with no idea when it'll detonate.

Twenty minutes.

Fuck this.

"We're going to play a game."

She looks up, startled.

"Twenty questions. Well, ten each. Taking turns." I set the slide spring aside. "I need intel. About you. Background, patterns, potential vulnerabilities Phoenix might exploit. Standard protection protocol requires understanding the principal."

Complete bullshit. I know enough to keep her safe, but I need to hear her voice. Need to crack her open before this silence drives me insane.

She tilts her head, studying me. Then nods. Once.

"Good." I lean back in the chair, trying for casual. "I'll start. You said Nathan made you smaller. How?"

Her whole body tenses. She curls tighter, arms wrapping around her legs like armor.

"Specifics. What did he actually do to you?"

She opens her mouth. Closes it. Opens again. "Words." Barely audible.

"What kind of words?"

"Careful ones. Surgical." Her voice is a ghost. "He knew exactly where to cut."

Christ, pulling information from her is like defusing a bomb blindfolded.

"Give me an example."

She's quiet for so long, I think she won't answer. Then: "Said I was—exhausting. Too much. Too analytical." Her voice drops even lower. "That I process everything instead of feeling anything."

"What else?"

"That I talk too much. Think too loud. Take up too much space with my words." She presses her face against her knees. "That I was embarrassing him at work functions with my constant need to analyze everything."

"Talk too much?" The words burst out of me before I can filter them. "You've barely said fifty words since I met you. I've been trying to get more than three sentences out of you for hours."

She peeks up at me over her knees.

"Nathan's an ass." The anger bleeds into my voice, hot and sudden. "You realize that, right? He beat you down so thoroughly that you've gone nearly mute. That's not normal. That's not you being 'too much.' That's him being abusive."

Her eyes widen slightly.

"The woman who should be talking, sharing her brilliant mind, analyzing everything because that's your gift—she's hiding. Because some insecure prick couldn't handle dating someone smarter than him."

She blinks rapidly, fighting tears.

"What else did he say?" My voice comes out rougher than intended.

"My turn," she whispers.

Fair enough. She earned it.

"Why explosives?" Her voice gains a tiny bit of strength. "Why that specialty?"

"Control. Precision. One gram off, one second wrong, everything changes. I like the certainty of it."

She nods, as if this makes perfect sense. "Your turn."

"What else did Nathan say?"

She flinches. "Why does it matter?"

"Not an answer."

Her fingers twist in the hem of the borrowed shirt. "He said I was …" She stops. Swallows. Tries again. "That I have sex like a nun writing a thesis paper on the experience."

The words hang in the air like smoke from a detonation.

I set down the gun oil with deliberate care. If I don't, I'm going to throw it through the wall.

"That's bullshit."

"Is it?" Her voice cracks slightly. "I analyze everything. I don't —feel. Not the way normal people—"

"Stop."

The word comes out sharp. She flinches, and I force myself to soften my tone, if not my glare.

"You don't know—"

"I know." I lean forward, elbows on knees, closing the distance. "A nun doesn't crawl through broken glass to get evidence. A coward doesn't climb a fire escape despite being terrified of heights."

Her eyes widen. She realizes I noticed.

"And in that alley?" My voice drops lower. "When I shielded you from the blast? When I had you pinned against that wall?"

She goes completely still. Not even breathing.

"The way your body responded to mine? The way you melted into me, the sounds you made? Trust me, Talia. There was nothing clinical about it."

Color floods her cheeks. Her lips part slightly, but no words come.

"You responded like someone who's been asleep their whole life and just woke up. That's not analytical. That's pure instinct."

She shakes her head, starting to curl away from me. "You don't—"

"And twenty minutes ago?" I continue, not letting her retreat. "When I had you against the wall during training? The way you arched into me? The way your pupils dilated? The way you looked at my mouth?"

"Stop." The word comes out strangled.

"Why? Because it's true?"

"Because it's embarrassing." She presses her face against her knees. "You're talking about it like … Like—"

"Like foreplay?" I lean back, deliberately casual. "It's physical attraction. The chemistry between us is so thick I could cut it with a knife."

"You can't just say things like that."

"Why not? It's true." I study her—this brilliant woman, made small by someone's cruelty. "You want me. I want you. The air ignites when we're in the same room."

"That's not—" She stops, swallows. "You're my protector. This is just—proximity. Adrenaline. Trauma bonding."

"Bullshit." I set my elbows on my knees, getting closer to her level. "You think I can't tell the difference between fear and arousal? You think after years of reading bodies in combat situations, I can't recognize when someone wants me?"

She peeks up at me, eyes wide. "This is inappropriate."

"Probably. Doesn't make it less true." I hold her gaze steady. "When I touched you during training, your whole body responded. Not with fear. With want."

"You don't know what I want."

"Then tell me I'm wrong. Look me in the eye and tell me you didn't feel anything when I pinned you. Tell me your body didn't wake up when I covered you with mine in that alley."

She opens her mouth. Closes it. Can't say the words.

"That's what I thought." My voice gentles. "There's nothing wrong with wanting someone. Nothing wrong with your body responding to mine. That's not being analytical or clinical. That's being human."

She shifts uncomfortably, face still hidden.

"And there's nothing wrong with talking about it either." I keep my voice steady, matter-of-fact. "We're both adults. Sex exists. Attraction exists. Talking about what you want, what you like, what you don't like—that's normal. Healthy, even."

She peeks up at me, eyes wide with something between shock and curiosity.

"But you've never done that, have you?" The realization hits me.

"Never told Nathan what you wanted. Never told any man. Because talking was too much. Because having needs was 'exhausting.'"

Her silence is all the confirmation I need.

"But Nathan said—"

"You threaten Nathan. He's a weak man who needs to break you down to feel powerful." The anger rises again, protective and fierce. "But your body knows the truth. It responded to me because it recognized something it wants."

She's trembling now. Just slightly. "But Nathan said—"

"And I said, Nathan's a piece of shit who needed to make you small so he'd feel big." The anger in my voice surprises us both. "My turn. When's the last time someone made you feel good about yourself?"

She's quiet for so long, I think she won't answer. Then: "I can't remember."

The admission hits like shrapnel.

"Your turn," I prompt, needing to give her back some control.

"Why did you leave the military?"

The question I've been dodging. But she gave me truth, so: "Syria. Mission went wrong. Lost my team. Couldn't trust my judgment after that."

"What happened?"

"That's two questions. You just asked why I left. That's my answer."

She waits, patient. Those amber eyes see too much.

"My turn," I say, not letting her push for more. Besides, I'm actually enjoying this—watching her slowly unfold, hearing her voice get stronger with each answer. She's shy about sex. Embarrassed by her desire. Something to remember.

"Did Nathan ever make you come?"

She jerks back as if I've slapped her. "What?"

"You heard me."

"That's …" Her face goes scarlet. She opens her mouth, closes it, then whispers, "Why would you ask that?"

"Because he told you that you have sex like a nun. Made you think you're broken. I'm betting he never satisfied you."

She curls tighter, face hidden against her knees. The silence stretches so long I think I've pushed too far. Then, barely audible: "I don't … I don't know."

Christ. She doesn't know? Which means she probably never has. Nathan, that selfish prick, spent three years with this woman and never once made sure she—

"You'd know," I say gently. "Trust me, you'd know."

She peeks up at me, mortified but also—curious? "Can we please talk about something else?"

"Fair enough. Your turn to ask."

She takes a shaky breath, clearly desperate to change the subject. "Do you have family?"

"Mother in Seattle."

"So you were an only child?"

"Yeah. However, I had twin sisters who died before I was born. Complications. Mom never really recovered."

"I'm sorry." Her voice is stronger now, gaining confidence. "And your mom?"

I should remind her it's my turn to ask, but Christ, she's actually talking. Multiple sentences. Questions flowing naturally instead of being pulled out word by word. I'll let her have this.

"Alive. Seattle. Thinks I work private security."

"Does she worry about you?"

"Every day."

"What about your father?"

"Died when I was eight. Firefighter. Line of duty." The words come out flat, practiced. "Mom never remarried."

"I'm sorry." She tilts her head, studying me. "That must have been hard. Growing up without him."

"It was." I lean back, watching her gradually unfold. Each question she asks, she sits up a little straighter. "Do you see your mom often?"

"Not enough. Maybe twice a year."

"That must be hard. For both of you."

"It is." I could take my turn now, but she's on a roll. Her voice is finding its rhythm, that analytical mind starting to surface. "What about your family?"

"Parents in Chicago. Dad teaches mathematics. Mom's a lawyer."

"Still together?"

"Somehow, yes. Thirty-five years." She tilts her head, studying me. "They think I make bad choices."

"Do you?"

"Probably." She pulls the sleeves down over her hands. "Nathan was definitely a bad choice."

The fact that she's volunteering information without prompting—this is progress. Major progress. I want to keep her talking, keep hearing this voice that Nathan tried to silence.

"My turn. Question six. Why did you stop talking?"

"Asked and answered, already." She goes still again. When she speaks, it's barely a whisper. "But it was easier than being told I was too much."

"You're not too much."

She considers this, head tilted. "Are you with someone? In a relationship?"

"No."

"When's the last time you were?"

"That's two questions."

"You let me ask five in a row earlier."

She's right. And the fact that she noticed—that she's pushing back even slightly—is progress.

"Three years ago. Ended when I got back from Syria."

"What happened?"

"I came back different. Couldn't let anyone close. Couldn't trust. She tried for a year, then gave up."

The truth is darker. After Syria, after Amara's betrayal—Mitchell's asset who radioed our position while I was still inside her—no one's touched me.

Not really.

The encounters are all the same. Like the woman in the bar. My fingers bringing them to climax, their mouths on me, then done. No kissing. No lingering touches. No tenderness. Just a means to an end, getting off without vulnerability. No names, no numbers, no second meetings.

No one gets close enough to betray me.

But Talia? She's touched me more in the last twenty-four hours than any woman has in three years. Her hands on my skin while tending my wounds. Gentle. Careful. The kind of touch I haven't allowed since before Syria. The kind that means something.

"That must have been lonely," she says softly.

"It was necessary." I study her face. "My turn. What scares you most right now?"

She's quiet for a moment. "That I'll never be normal. That Nathan broke something in me that can't be fixed."

"Nothing about you needs fixing."

"But—"

"My turn for a follow-up. Do you want to be normal? Really?"

She blinks at the question. "I—I don't know. I want to not feel wrong all the time."

"Question eight. Are you hungry?"

She blinks at the shift. "What?"

"Food. Have you eaten? Because we've been doing this for an hour and you need calories."

"I … No."

I stand. "Come on."

"Where?"

"Kitchen. I'm making you food."

"That's not a question."

"No. It's a necessity."

She unfolds from the couch slowly, following me to the kitchen. I find pasta, canned sauce, and start the water boiling. She sits at the small table, watching me work.

"Why do you care if I eat?" she asks quietly.

"Is that question nine?"

"Yes."

"Because you're my responsibility. And because …" I turn to face her. "Because Nathan made you feel like you were too much. Like you took up too much space. But you barely take up any space at all. You're trying to disappear."

And because I'm hard again. Harder than before. Just from hearing her voice get stronger, from watching her slowly unfold. From the way she tilts her head when she thinks, and how she peeks up at me through those lashes.

Christ, I need release. Need something. But cooking will have to do. Something to keep my hands busy before I do something stupid.

"Maybe disappearing is safer."

"Maybe. But it's no way to live."

The water boils. I add pasta and stir the sauce. Simple, basic, but she needs food. Needs someone to take care of her without making her feel small for needing it.

My cock's still rock hard, pressing against my zipper like it's trying to escape. Not going down. If anything, watching her sit, bare legs tucked under her, it's getting worse.

I'm going to have to handle this on my own after she goes to bed. Take myself in hand in the shower, stroke it rough and fast until I come thinking about those golden eyes going dark with want. About how she'd sound if I actually touched her the way her body's begging for.

But for now, I cook. Because she needs this more than I need release.

"Last question," I say. "For both of us."

She nods.

"What do you need right now? In this moment?"

She's quiet for so long I think she won't answer. Then: "To feel like I'm not too much."

"You're not. My turn to answer." I plate the pasta and set it in front of her. "What do I need? For you to eat. To stop trying to disappear. To believe me when I say Nathan was wrong about you."

She picks up the fork, takes a small bite. Then another.

"Thank you," she whispers.

"For the food?"

"For seeing me and not the mess Nathan left behind. But me."

The words settle between us, heavy with meaning.

"I see you," I confirm. "Question eleven, breaking the rules. Will you stop trying to disappear?"

She meets my eyes. "I'll try."

It's a start.

EIGHT

Talia

INEVITABLE

THE PASTA SITS WARM IN MY STOMACH, THE FIRST REAL MEAL I'VE had in—I can't remember. Jackson clears the plates, his movements efficient, controlled. Everything about him is controlled. Even when he talked about sex—about us, about the chemistry he claims burns between us—it was all so pragmatic. Clinical, almost.

You want me. I want you. The air practically ignites when we're in the same room.

Like he's describing a chemical reaction. Cause and effect. Simple physics.

Maybe that's all it is for him. Bodies responding to stimuli. Arousal as a biological imperative. No emotion necessary, no connection required. Just friction and release.

Nathan always said I overthink everything, but at least he pretended there was emotion involved. Told me he loved me, even if his actions said otherwise. Even if his love came with conditions and criticism and constant reminders of my failures.

But Jackson? He strips it down to base components. Want. Need. Response.

It's almost refreshing in its honesty. Terrifying, but refreshing.

"You're thinking too loud again." His voice cuts through my spiral.

I look up. He's gripping the edge of the counter, knuckles white. A muscle ticks in his jaw.

"Sorry, I—"

"Don't apologize." The words come out rough. He pushes off from the counter abruptly. "I need a shower."

The shift is so sudden it takes me a moment to process. "Okay?"

"Don't go anywhere. Don't order anything. Don't call anyone. Don't answer the door." He's already moving toward the bathroom, not looking at me. "Just—stay put."

"For how long?"

"Until I'm done."

The bathroom door closes. The lock clicks. The shower turns on.

I sit there for a moment, confused by his abrupt departure. Every time we edge close to something real, he shuts down. Classic avoidance behavior, though I suspect in his case it's less about avoiding emotion and more about maintaining control.

Which is undeniably attractive. God, what is wrong with me?

The shower runs. Five minutes. Ten. Fifteen.

Restless energy crawls under my skin. The safe house is small —too small. I pace the living room, taking inventory. Reinforced door. Windows with security film. Weapons laid out on the coffee table. Everything about this space screams temporary and functional.

I wander to the small bookshelf in the corner. Mostly tactical manuals, a few paperback thrillers, one surprising poetry collection—Neruda. I pull it out, flip through pages worn soft with reading. Annotations in the margins, careful handwriting.

I want to do with you what spring does with the cherry trees.

The line is underlined twice.

My face heats. I slide the book back and continue exploring.

The kitchen: basic supplies, nothing personal. The living room: one couch, one chair, both positioned for clear sightlines to all entry points. And then there's the bedroom.

I push open the door. One bed. Queen size. Navy sheets, military corners.

One bed.

The sleeping arrangements hadn't occurred to me until now. Will he share it with me? The thought sends an unexpected thrill through my body. Or will he take the couch, maintaining that professional distance even though he's already admitted he wants—

The shower is still running. Twenty minutes now.

I drift back toward the bathroom, drawn by curiosity and something else. Something that makes my pulse quicken. The water sounds different through the door now. The hiss of the spray hitting tile has changed to the muffled drum of water hitting flesh.

A soft thud. Like a hand bracing against the wall.

My breath catches.

Another sound filters through the thin wood—low, guttural, unmistakably male. Strained. Needful. Almost pained.

Oh God. He's—

My hand flies to my mouth, but my feet stay rooted. He's touching himself. Right there, just beyond that door, Jackson is—

Heat floods my face, pools low in my belly. I should leave. Give him privacy. Walk away.

I press closer.

His breathing is harsh, uneven, filling the small space with a soundtrack of raw need. Another groan, deeper this time, vibrating through the door frame. My thighs clench involuntarily.

The pragmatist who described our chemistry like a science

experiment is coming apart in there. All that control, shattered. Because of—

"Fuck." His voice, wrecked. Then: "Talia."

My knees nearly give out. I brace against the doorframe.

He's thinking about me.

The image forms instantly, unstoppable: water streaming over those shoulders I've been trying not to stare at. His hand wrapped around himself, stroking with the same precise control he applies to everything else. Except it's my name breaking his control, my face he's seeing when he—

"Ta-lee-ya ..." The name tears out of him, low and rough, more breath than sound.

Molten heat slides through me. It's not just embarrassment. It's a deep, hollow ache between my legs. Nathan never said my name like that. Like it was being torn from him. Like it physically hurt to want me this much.

If I were brave—if I were the kind of woman who could handle casual, who could separate emotion from sex the way Jackson clearly can—I'd open that door. I'd step into that shower and find out what it's like to be wanted by a man who doesn't apologize for his needs. Who doesn't dress them up in pretty words or false emotion.

But I'm not brave. I'm the woman who spent three years with someone who made her feel like too much and not enough at the same time. Who needs connection, emotion, something more than just bodies responding to animalistic urges.

Even if my body is screaming for exactly that right now.

A final groan echoes through the door—deep, destroyed—followed by ragged breathing.

The water shuts off.

Panic shoots through me. I scramble backward, nearly tripping in my haste to get away from the door. I grab the first book I see—one of the tactical manuals—and throw myself onto the couch. By the time he emerges, towel slung low on his hips, I'm curled up pretending to read about close-quarter combat techniques.

"Found something to read?" His voice is carefully neutral, but there's heat in his eyes. Water droplets trail down his chest, catching the light. The towel hangs dangerously low on his hips, revealing those cut lines that disappear beneath terry cloth. And there's no missing the evidence of what just happened—he's still partially aroused, the outline unmistakable behind the towel even as his erection softens.

My mouth goes dry. I can't help wondering what he looks like without that towel. What it would feel like to trace those water droplets with my fingers, my tongue. The thought shoots heat straight through me.

"Yes. Just—passing time." My voice comes out too high, too breathy.

His gaze drops to the book in my hands. A slow smirk spreads across his face. "Tactical Close-Quarter Combat Techniques. Interesting choice." He steps closer, and I catch the scent of his soap—something clean and masculine that makes my head spin. "Though it might help if you read it right-side up."

Horror floods through me. I flip the book quickly, face burning.

"Unless you were—distracted?" He turns toward the bathroom, then glances back over his shoulder. One eyebrow cocks up, that smirk deepening.

He knows. He knows I heard him. Knows I was listening at the door like some desperate voyeur while he—

"I was just …" The words die in my throat. What can I say? *I was just casually eavesdropping while you stroked yourself to thoughts of me?*

"Tactical movements can be very educational." His voice

drops lower, rougher. "All about positioning. Leverage. Finding the right angle of approach."

The double meaning isn't subtle. My whole body flushes hot.

"I should—" I stand too quickly, the book tumbling from my lap.

We both reach for it at the same time. His hand covers mine on the spine, and the contact sends electricity shooting up my arm. He's close now, close enough that I have to tilt my head back to meet his eyes. The towel has shifted lower, barely hanging on, and my gaze travels down before I can stop it.

"See something interesting?" His thumb strokes across my knuckles, the lightest touch, but it makes me tremble.

"I wasn't … I didn't mean to—"

"Didn't mean to … what?" He's definitely toying with me now, that controlled facade cracking just enough to show the predator beneath. "Listen? Look? Or imagine?"

All three. Definitely all three.

"You're being inappropriate." The accusation would carry more weight if my voice didn't shake.

"Am I?" He releases my hand but doesn't step back. "You're the one studying tactical positions while I shower. Making all kinds of noise out here. Breathing so hard I could hear it through the door."

My eyes widen. He heard me listening?

"Thin walls," he says, answering my unspoken question. His gaze travels down my body, slow and deliberate, taking in my flushed face, my rapid breathing, the way my thighs press together. "Very thin walls."

"You should get dressed," I blurt out, horribly.

But he doesn't move. Just stands there, water still glistening on his skin, that towel one wrong move from falling, watching me with eyes that promise he knows exactly what I'm thinking. Exactly what I want.

"I can … Unless there's something you'd like to discuss about … tactical movements?"

"No. I'm good." My face feels like it's on fire.

He disappears into the bedroom. When he returns, fully dressed but hair still damp, I can't look at him without remembering those sounds. Without imagining what his face looked like when he groaned my name.

"About sleeping arrangements." His voice cuts through my thoughts. "You take the bed."

"I can take the couch—"

"You take the bed." No room for argument in his tone. "I'll be out here."

"That's not necessary—"

"It is." He meets my eyes, and something electric passes between us. "Trust me, it's necessary."

He knows. He knows that if we share that bed, all his pragmatic analysis about want and chemistry will combust into something neither of us is ready for. Well, he's probably ready. I'm definitely not brave enough for something more, no matter how much my body is begging for it.

"Goodnight, Talia."

"It's only seven-thirty."

"Long day tomorrow. Get some sleep."

I retreat to the bedroom, closing the door between us. The bed stretches out before me, too big, too empty. All I can think about is him on the other side of that door. Lying on that couch. Maybe still hard. Maybe still thinking about me.

I press my fingers to my wrist where he held me during training, where faint marks still linger. Tomorrow we'll pretend none of this happened. The wall. The shower. The way my name sounded when he came.

But tonight, I lie awake knowing he's out there, just as awake as I am.

Both of us burning.

Both of us waiting.

Both of us pretending we don't know exactly how this ends.

NINE

Jackson

SLEEPLESS

The couch is too short. My feet hang off the end, and the cushions smell like dust and old fabric softener. But that's not why I can't sleep.

It's her.

In the bedroom, twenty feet away. Probably overthinking every word from our twenty-questions game. Every loaded look. The way I had her against that wall. Christ knows I can't stop replaying it in my mind.

The training session was supposed to be practical. Show her basic defense moves. Keep it professional. Instead, I pinned her against that wall and nearly lost control. The way her body melted into mine, pupils blown wide, breath catching—

I've had women against walls before. Anonymous encounters in dark corners of bars. Always the same script—my control, their pleasure, no reciprocation beyond what I allow. Touch without being touched. Release without risk. No names, no stories, no twenty fucking questions about dead siblings and Syria and fathers who died fighting fires. Just bodies and release and forgetting.

But Talia …

She got more out of me in an hour than anyone has in three years. Analyzing my responses like she's defusing a bomb, finding all my triggers and trip wires. When I couldn't answer about Syria, she didn't push with sympathy or platitudes. Just accepted the wall and moved on.

Most people want to fix me or fuck me. She just wants to understand me.

That's dangerous.

The shower didn't help. Coming with her name on my lips, picturing her against that wall with less clothes, imagining those analytical eyes going dark with need—it just made things worse. Because she heard everything. The way she scrambled for that book, pretended to be reading, even though she held it upside down, and her cheeks were flushed. She knows exactly what I was doing in there.

It should have scared her, and she should have demanded I leave.

Instead, she looked at me like she wanted to be the reason for those sounds.

I check my phone. 2:47 AM. The security feeds show empty hallways, quiet streets. No movement. No threats. Just silence and my own breathing, plus the knowledge that she's in there, curled up in sheets that'll smell like her tomorrow.

The bedroom door opens.

She stands in the doorway for a moment, silhouetted by moonlight. Her borrowed shirt hits mid-thigh, bare legs, hair a messy bun from tossing and turning. She doesn't say anything. Just looks at me with those golden eyes, then turns and disappears.

I think she's gone back to bed until she returns. Pillow under one arm, blanket draped over her shoulder. Still silent.

"Talia—"

"This is ridiculous."

"Go back to bed."

"I can't sleep in that big bed by myself." She moves closer, and I catch her scent—vanilla and something uniquely her. "Either you come join me, or I'm joining you on the couch."

"That's not happening."

She arches an eyebrow, tilts her head. "Really? Because from where I'm standing, it's definitely happening."

Before I can respond, she's moving. Not toward the bedroom. Toward me.

"Talia—"

"Scoot over."

"The couch is barely big enough for—"

She's already climbing onto the couch, but at the opposite end. Her feet press against my back as she curls up, punching her pillow—where the hell did she get a pillow?—and snapping the blanket over herself like this is perfectly normal.

Like she belongs here.

"Much better," she mumbles, already settling in.

Her feet press against my back.

The audacity. She's using me as a footrest.

"The bed's more comfortable," I tell her.

No response. She just shifts, getting comfortable, her cold feet finding the warmth of my back through my shirt. Every small movement sends awareness shooting through me.

"You're being ridiculous," I say.

Still nothing. She punches her pillow into shape, settles deeper into the cushions. Her toes flex against my spine.

Ten minutes pass. Twenty. Her breathing doesn't even out—she's awake, stubborn, making a point without saying a word. This silent rebellion is worse than any argument. At least with words, I know how to counter.

But this?

This quiet determination to share space on her terms? It's reclaiming the territory Nathan stole from her. She's taking up space, deliberately.

It's fucking maddening.

Thirty minutes. Her feet keep shifting, pressing, claiming space. Neither of us is sleeping. This is torture—cramped and uncomfortable and charged with everything we're not acknowledging.

Fuck this. She wins.

I stand abruptly. Before she can react, I scoop her up—pillow, blanket, and all. She lets out a startled squeak that shoots straight to my groin. Her arms instinctively wrap around my neck, fingers gripping my shirt, and Christ, I'm instantly hard. Her body pressed against my chest, the little sound she made, the way she automatically turns into me for security—

I'm exhausted. We both need sleep. And this couch standoff isn't getting us anywhere.

She's lighter than she should be, fitting against me too perfectly. Those amber eyes look up at me, wide with surprise but not fear. Never fear. Not with me.

I carry her to the bedroom, drop her on the bed—firm but not rough. Toss her pillow down. Throw the blanket over her.

"Sleep. Keep your cold feet to yourself," I add, trying for stern but probably miss by a mile.

A soft giggle escapes her. The sound hits me square in the chest—when's the last time I made a woman laugh? Really laugh?

I grab the other pillow, climb in on the far side. Put my back to her, trying to keep maximum distance in a queen-size bed.

I'm just settling in when I feel it—those cold feet pressing against my legs.

"Seriously?" I don't turn around, but I'm grinning despite myself.

Another quiet giggle. Her toes flex against my legs.

I sigh, loud and dramatic, but don't move away. "You're impossible."

She doesn't respond, just wiggles her feet to get comfortable. Like this is normal. Like we do this every night.

Maybe we could.

She doesn't say anything. The mattress dips as she settles, and I'm hyperaware of every movement. The soft rustle of sheets. Her quiet breathing. The warmth of another body in the bed.

I close my eyes, treating this like any mission requiring sleep in hostile territory. Except the threat isn't external. It's internal. It's the urge to turn around and finish what we started against that wall.

Time passes. Her breathing finally deepens into real sleep. The tension in my shoulders slowly releases.

Maybe I can do this. Maybe I can share a bed without—

Somehow, I drift off.

I wake to warmth. Soft curves pressed against my chest. My arm draped over a waist and my hand splayed across bare skin where the shirt has ridden up. Her ass pressed tight against my groin, where I'm hard as stone.

We're spooning.

I'm wrapped around her like I'm protecting her even in sleep. Her hair tickles my nose. She smells like vanilla and something uniquely her.

My hand is on her bare stomach. Skin like silk.

Fuck.

She shifts slightly, pressing back against me. A small sound escapes her throat. Not quite awake but not fully asleep. My cock throbs against her ass, and there's no way she doesn't feel it.

It feels domestic. Safe. For a second, I allow myself to imagine this is just a normal morning. No hit squads. No conspiracies. Just a man and a woman waking up together.

I should move. Pull away. Take another cold shower.

Instead, I'm frozen. Because this feels right. Natural. Like pieces clicking into place.

Her breathing changes. She's waking up. Her body tenses slightly as awareness returns, but she doesn't pull away. If anything, she presses back more deliberately.

"Jackson?" Her voice is soft, sleep-rough, uncertain.

I ease my arm away, slow and careful, like I'm defusing something fragile. I roll onto my back and stare at the ceiling until the ache fades and the fantasy with it. The room settles. Morning light creeps in, pale and thin, exposing reality for what it is. I clear my throat. Give her space. Give us both a way out.

She turns over, pulling the sheet with her, eyes flicking to my face and then away. A question there. An apology she doesn't voice. Neither do I. I get up first. Clothes. Distance. The routine clicks in—coffee, windows checked, the quiet inventory of exits and threats. By the time she joins me in the kitchen, we're two people moving carefully around each other, pretending the morning didn't almost become something else.

We spend the day in uneasy silence, coexisting in the space. I cook breakfast. She cleans. She makes sandwiches for lunch. I clean. Somewhere around late afternoon, my phone buzzes.

I grab it and check the screen. The camera feeds I set up earlier show multiple angles of the building entrance, hallways, and stairwells.

"What's that?" She asks.

"Security feeds."

"What do they show?"

"Phoenix operatives."

She goes rigid as she looks at the screen. "Jackson ..."

I see it. Two uniformed officers are at the building entrance. But their stance is wrong. Weight distribution off. One keeps touching his hip—not where cops carry service weapons. The other scans windows, counting floors.

"Those aren't real cops." I'm already moving, the warmth of her replaced by cold air and adrenaline.

"How can you tell?"

"Body language. Gear placement. They're trying too hard to look casual." I switch feeds. There—civilian clothes, service entrance. "Three-man team. Professional sweep pattern."

"Look at the way they move," Talia whispers, pointing at the screen. "Synchronized. Perfectly spaced. Officer One steps, Officer Two mirrors him two seconds later. That's not police training. That's algorithmic coordination."

She's right. It's too precise. Too mathematical.

Her face pales. "How did they find us?"

"Doesn't matter." I'm grabbing weapons and cash. "We leave. Now."

She's still processing—her brilliant mind is calculating probabilities and escape routes—but we don't have time for analysis.

I catch her shoulders, firm enough to ground her. "No statistics. No analysis. You follow my lead, stay quiet, and move when I move. Understood?"

She nods, wide-eyed. That heat is there again, mixing with fear and adrenaline.

I check the feeds. They're inside, heading for the elevator. "Five minutes. Maybe less."

"Jackson—"

"Pack only essentials. Sixty seconds."

She's already moving, switching to survival mode.

"Here." I hand her a tactical vest.

She fumbles with the straps. I step close, fixing the plates, adjusting the fit. My hands are efficient, but I notice everything— the warmth of her body, the slight tremor in her breathing, the way she leans into my touch.

"The statistical probability—"

"Zero if you don't stop talking." I rack my weapon, eyes on the cameras. These aren't amateurs. They're here to kill her.

The lights cut out. Complete darkness.

Her breath catches. I find her hand in the dark—small, warm, trembling. My thumb brushes her palm, steadying us both.

"We move now. Stay close. Be silent."

She squeezes my hand once. Agreement without words.

I grab the go-bag, weapon ready. We slip into the hallway. Footsteps echo from the main stairs, getting closer.

Service stairs it is.

Thirty seconds from death, and I'm thinking about waking up with her in my arms. About her quiet rebellion on the couch. About the way she pressed back against me when she woke.

I'm completely fucked.

Because I want more mornings like that.

And that *want* is going to get us both killed.

TEN

Jackson

DIGITAL HUNT

up my arm like live current. The darkness makes every detail louder—her quick, shallow breaths, the rapid drum of her pulse against my palm, the subtle vanilla warmth of her skin threaded with the clean bite of my soap.

I shouldn't notice this. Shouldn't register the way her fingers curl instinctively into mine like they belong there. Shouldn't remember waking with her ass pressed against me, my hand on her bare stomach, her body fitting against mine like we were made for it.

Focus, asshole.

This morning, we were spooning in bed. Now Phoenix is here to put bullets in her head. The whiplash from intimacy to violence should be familiar—it's how my life works, but something about her makes the transition harder. Makes me want things I can't afford.

"Stairs." My voice barely disturbs the air. "Stay close."

Her fingers tighten around mine. No questions. No statistical analysis. Just trust.

That trust does something uncomfortable in my chest.

I navigate by memory and instinct. Twelve steps to the apartment door. Seventeen to the stairwell. The building's layout burned into my brain within minutes of arrival—a habit that's saved my life more than once.

The stairwell door hinges are on the left and open inward. I ease it open millimeter by millimeter, listening. No footsteps. No breathing except ours. But Phoenix operatives know how to move in silence.

"Step when I step." My lips graze her ear, breath stirring loose strands of her hair. She shivers—not from cold.

We slip through, boots soft on worn carpet. Every shadow could hide a threat. The building's old HVAC system hums, masking smaller sounds. I lead her past the main stairs, pausing to listen. Silence. Not even a creak.

Good. Maybe they're taking the elevator like amateurs. Human error. I'm counting on it.

Her hand tightens in mine—a silent question. I squeeze back once. Trust me.

We descend. Her foot finds each step exactly where mine was, learning my rhythm. She's a quick study. The darkness strips away everything but essential movement, and she adapts faster than most trained operatives would.

But I can't stop noticing other things. The way her breathing syncs with mine. How she instinctively moves closer when we pause, seeking security in proximity. The heat of her body just inches behind me.

Focus. She's a package to deliver, not—

Not the woman who giggled when she put her cold feet on my back. Not the brilliant analyst whose mind works like a beautiful weapon, finding patterns I might miss. Not the contradiction of sharp intelligence and soft curves currently following me through darkness with absolute faith.

Third-floor landing. I signal a stop. She freezes instantly. No sound.

Voices drift up from below. Two men, low, casual—but the rhythm's wrong. Too measured. Too careful.

"Sweep pattern alpha. Second floor's clear."

They're coming up. We're going down. Basic math says we're fucked.

But I don't do basic math.

The maintenance door is where I mapped it during my initial sweep. Building code requires them on every floor—old locks and easy picks—leading to service corridors that run parallel to the main structure. Most people don't know they exist.

I slide the pick into the lock and work the tumblers as footsteps grow closer. The mechanism fights me—rusty, neglected. Come on, come on—

Click.

I pull Talia through, ease the door shut just as boots hit our landing.

Red emergency lighting bleeds across the space, painting everything in hellish hues. Rusted pipes snake overhead. Concrete walls weep moisture. The air reeks of mildew and decay—thick enough to taste.

"Jackson—" Her voice barely a whisper, but still too loud.

I spin, pressing my hand over her mouth. Her gasp warms my palm. She goes rigid, then melts back against the wall. I cage her with my body, shielding her from view of the door.

The curve of her jaw fits perfectly in my palm. Her lashes flutter against my fingers. She's so close I can count individual freckles across her nose, even in the red gloom.

Boots strike the metal stairs outside. Heavy. Measured. Hunting.

The footsteps pause directly outside our door. The handle rattles once. Twice.

I press tighter against Talia, eliminating any gap between us. If that door opens, they'll see me first, buy her seconds to run. Her fingers clutch my vest, knuckles white. She's trembling—whole body vibrating against mine.

But her eyes … Her eyes are steady on mine. Trusting. Even now.

The handle rattles again. Harder.

My free hand goes to my weapon, thumb finding the safety. If they breach, I'll have maybe two seconds before—

The footsteps move on. Up to four. Then five. Getting fainter.

I count thirty seconds in my head. No double-back. No second team.

Slowly, carefully, I peel my hand away from her mouth. My thumb drags across her lips—they're damp, parted, her breath coming quick and shallow. The red emergency lighting turns her eyes into pools of shadow and fire.

We should move. Every second in one place increases risk.

I don't move.

My hand slides down from her mouth, fingers trailing along her jaw, her throat, coming to rest on her shoulder. I can feel her pulse racing under my palm. Her chest rises and falls against mine, each breath pressing her closer.

"Jackson." My name on her lips is barely sound, more vibration than voice.

One kiss and she'd melt completely. I can see it in the way her lips part, the way her body angles toward mine despite the danger. Hell, I want it too. Want to swallow those little sounds she makes when—

Footsteps above. Different pattern. Searching.

"Move," I whisper against her ear, voice rougher than intended.

She nods quickly, slipping her hand back into mine. Her fingers are steadier now, grip firm. We navigate the maintenance corridor—a maze of pipes and electrical panels, decades of dust coating everything. Our footsteps echo faintly despite our care.

She follows without complaint, though I can hear her mind working. Little intake breaths when she spots something significant. A soft "hmm" when she's mapping our route. Even silent, she can't help analyzing.

The corridor opens into another stairwell—service stairs, probably haven't been used since the last inspection. We descend quickly but quietly. Her hand never leaves mine.

Ground floor. Another locked door, this one newer. Security pins. False gates. My pick slips once. Twice. The mechanism's fighting me, and my hands are less steady than they should be. Because I can still feel her pressed against me. Still taste the possibility of that almost-kiss.

"Need help?" She whispers it right against my shoulder, breath warm through my shirt.

"You pick locks?"

"I had an interesting childhood."

Before I can process what that means, she's beside me, producing something from her hair. Bobby pin. She works the lock with surprising skill, tongue caught between her lips, completely focused.

Christ, that's attractive.

The lock clicks.

"Where'd you learn that?"

"Library. Books are very educational." She tucks the pin back in her hair. "Also, my father was paranoid about government surveillance. He taught me that the only way to stay safe is to know how to break into everything that tries to keep you out."

Every time I think I have her categorized, she reveals another layer.

We exit into the parking garage. Three levels underground, minimal lighting, concrete pillars creating blind spots every ten feet. Perfect for an ambush.

Our vehicle sits twenty yards away. Too exposed. Too obvious.

I scan the garage. Three vans that weren't here before. Positioned to block exits. No visible occupants, but tinted windows hide plenty.

"Phoenix?"

"Probability is high." I throw her words back at her, and she makes a soft sound that might be amusement.

The vans are positioned to create a kill box. Professional spacing, overlapping fields of fire. They expect us to go for our vehicle.

So we don't.

A Ducati sits in the corner, half-hidden behind a concrete pillar. Older model, '09 or '10. No electronic ignition to hack, no GPS to track. Perfect. I calculate hot-wire time—five seconds if I'm quick, eight if the wiring's corroded.

"See the motorcycle?"

She nods.

"That's our ride."

"Another motorcycle?"

"You've got this. Just hold on."

The image flashes unbidden—her arms wrapped around me, body pressed tight against my back, trusting me to navigate Chicago traffic at speed. My cock twitches at the thought.

Professional. Stay professional.

But she derailed that possibility when she picked that lock. When she pressed back against me this morning. When she started looking at me with those golden eyes, like I'm something more than just her protection.

"On three, we run. Fast and quiet."

"What about the vans?"

"Trust me."

She nods. No hesitation. That trust hits harder than it should.

I count down on my fingers. Three. Two. One.

We run.

My boots strike concrete in measured strides. Talia matches my pace perfectly, her breathing controlled despite the sprint. Twenty feet. Fifteen. Ten.

Van doors slide open behind us.

The sound echoes off concrete like rolling thunder. I drop to my knees beside the Ducati, fingers finding the ignition wires by muscle memory. Behind us, boots hit pavement—multiple contacts. They're not even trying to be quiet.

Confident. Cocky.

Their mistake.

"Down!"

I spin, drawing my Glock in one smooth motion. Talia drops behind the pillar. Good girl.

Four shooters fan out in a semi-circle. Professional spacing, overlapping fields of fire. They're trying to herd us toward the northeast corner. Death box. Too obvious. These aren't Phoenix's best.

I put two rounds through the nearest van's front tire. The vehicle lists to the side with a violent hiss. The shooters adjust their position. I calculate angles. Distance. Cover points.

"The electrical panel," Talia whispers beside me. "If you—"

Already tracking it. Twenty feet to our right, the main breaker is exposed. Three shots to the box, and half this garage goes dark. I fire. Sparks explode in a shower of white-hot metal. Emergency lighting kicks in, bathing everything in stuttering red.

Their night vision needs at least thirty seconds to adjust. We need five.

"Move."

Two twists of the wires and the engine roars to life, the sound echoing off concrete walls.

"Get on."

She swings her leg over without hesitation. I hand her the go-bag and mount in front of her. She shoulders the bag, and wraps her arms around my waist, her grip tight and sure. She leans against my back. Her thighs bracket mine.

More shooters emerge from cover. I draw with my left hand, keeping my right on the throttle. The Glock barks twice—suppressing fire, forcing them back.

Then I see a fifth shooter, in an elevated position on the parking structure's second level. Rifle trained on us.

There's no time to think.

I rise slightly, making myself a larger target to shield Talia, and fire three rounds at his position. He ducks, but not before his weapon cracks.

The bullet punches into my left bicep like a sledgehammer wrapped in fire. It lodges deep in the muscle, grinding against bone. My arm spasms. The Glock almost slips from nerveless fingers, but I manage to holster it.

Don't flinch. Don't slow. Don't let her know.

I gun the engine. We tear out of the garage, tires screaming against concrete. The bike slides slightly on the turn—too much speed, not enough grip—but I correct with my body weight. Talia moves with me instinctively, leaning into the turn rather than fighting it.

Her grip is perfect—firm but not panicked, moving with the bike instead of against it.

I check the mirrors. There's a black van two cars back, trying to navigate traffic. Another joins from a side street.

"Your phone," I shout over the engine. "Toss it."

She doesn't question me. One arm releases briefly, quick

movement, then her phone disappears into the bed of a passing garbage truck. Her arm immediately returns to my waist.

Her hand comes away wet.

"You're bleeding." Not a question. Her fingers find the tear in my jacket, the warm wetness spreading beneath.

"I'm fine. Hold on."

I lean hard into the next turn. The vans are heavy and less maneuverable. Every corner gains us distance. They're still tracking us somehow.

But how?

There's a construction site ahead, with a chain-link fence and a gap where someone cut through. Perfect.

I aim for the gap, shoot through at forty miles per hour. We weave between cement mixers and excavators, the bike's engine screaming in the confined spaces. Three hard turns through the maze of equipment. My left arm throbs with each movement, blood running down inside my sleeve, pooling in my glove, but the pain is manageable. I've worked through worse.

"Millennium Park," I tell her, shouting over the wind. "Concert tonight."

She nods against my shoulder.

The park stretches wide ahead, pulsing with light. Thousands of people swarm toward the main pavilion, a sea of movement and sound. Massive screens flash the words ANGEL FIRE — WORLD TOUR in molten red and gold. Even from blocks away, I can feel the bass rumbling through the pavement, through my ribs. Figures. The one night we need quiet and the biggest rock band on the planet is setting Chicago on fire.

But crowds are good places to vanish.

I pull in near a row of bikes, kill the engine. My left arm screams as I swing off, the bullet's path reminding me it's still there, but I keep the motion smooth. Controlled. She doesn't need to see pain; she needs competence.

"Stay close."

We merge with the flow of fans. College kids spilling beer from plastic cups, couples holding hands, Angel Fire shirts everywhere—black cotton and burning wings. Normal lives orbiting a single purpose: music. No one looks twice at us.

The opening chords of "Heart's Insanity" thunder through the night, that iconic guitar riff echoing off glass towers. The crowd roars, a unified, fevered sound. Lights sweep over faces. Phones lift. The air vibrates with energy, joy, and alcohol.

That's when I spot the street vendor pushing through the bodies—light-up necklaces, glow sticks, and surgical masks swinging from his stand. Still sealed. Five bucks each. Protection from summer colds, the cardboard sign boasts. Post-pandemic paranoia still paying dividends.

Next to them: baseball caps and tour shirts from Angel Fire's Inferno Tour—the band's logo in blazing orange and gold, wings, flame, and all. The vendor barely glances up when I pull out cash with my good hand, grabbing two masks, two caps, and two shirts.

"Put these on."

Talia takes the bundle, already understanding. "Facial recognition?"

"Phoenix loves its surveillance."

She tucks her hair beneath the cap, pulls the brim low. Mask up, head down. Instantly anonymous. I follow suit, adjusting the brim to cast a shadow over what the mask doesn't hide. The shirt is too big on her, the black cotton swallowing her frame, but it makes her look like just another fan. We keep them on. They're our armor now.

The band launches into "Hunting Waterfalls," the crowd's collective shout rising around us. The sound is deafening, overwhelming, perfect.

We move as one body with thousands of others, our faces lost to the strobing lights and smoke. Every camera in range sees nothing but data noise—caps, masks, color, motion. Not enough for an algorithm to name.

Talia glances up at the stage once, awe flickering in her eyes as the lights hit the band. For a heartbeat, she forgets the danger. I almost do too. Angel Fire fills the night, "Carry Her Home (for Me)" bleeding into the darkness like an anthem for everything we've lost.

Then the crowd surges again, and I catch her hand, grounding us back in the mission.

The far edge of the park lies in shadow, quieter, safer. I spot what we need—a faded Camry idling outside a coffee shop, driver inside grabbing a late-night caffeine fix. No GPS, no smart-key tracking. The perfect escape.

"We're taking that car," I say.

I move before she can debate ethics. Slide into the driver's seat smooth and casual like it's mine. She follows, shutting the door just as the owner exits the coffee shop, cup in hand. By the time they process what's happening, we're already turning the corner.

Behind us, Angel Fire hits the final chorus, a wall of sound rising like the city itself is singing us into the dark.

"Where are we going?"

"Somewhere off-grid." I check mirrors, take another turn. No pursuit visible. "Twenty minutes north. Industrial district. Empty building I've used before."

My arm throbs with each turn of the wheel, blood seeping through the jacket, soaking into the seat. The bullet's deep but missed the artery—I can tell by the flow rate. Steady seep, not spurting. I can work with this. Have to.

"You're hurt." Her hand hovers near my arm, not quite touching.

"I'm functional."

"That's not the same as fine."

"It's enough."

She goes quiet, but I can feel her thinking. Calculating blood loss rates, probably. Running probability scenarios on infection, shock, and complications. That beautiful brain of hers never stops, even when she's silent.

"The masks were brilliant," she finally says.

"Basic countersurveillance."

"Still brilliant."

The industrial district is all shadows and rust when we arrive. Empty factories and warehouses, most abandoned when manufacturing fled overseas. I park behind an old textile factory, kill the engine. My arm screams when I reach for the door handle, muscles locked around the bullet.

"This is it?"

"Safe enough for now." I scan the area—check angles, exits, potential threats. "Phoenix won't find us here."

She follows me inside, and I can feel her questions building. About the wound. About the plan. About what happens next.

The factory floor is vast, empty, moonlight filtering through broken skylights. Our footsteps echo in the silence. I've stashed supplies here before—water, medical kit, weapons. Always have a backup location.

But first, I need to address this bullet, and for that, I'm going to need her help.

Which means letting her see me weak. Vulnerable. Trusting her with my life, the way she's been trusting me with hers.

The irony isn't lost on me.

"Jackson." Her voice is soft but firm. "You need to let me look at that arm."

I turn to face her. Even with the cap and mask, her eyes are luminous. Concerned. She reaches up, pulls off the mask and cap, shakes her hair free. Then reaches for mine.

"May I?"

I nod. She removes my cap and mask with careful fingers, like she's unwrapping something fragile.

"Now," she says, all business despite the tremor in her hands. "Let's see how bad it is."

No more hiding. No more control.

Just trust.

Fuck.

ELEVEN

Jackson

FIELD MEDICINE

The abandoned textile factory reeks of rust and pigeon shit. I leave Talia by the entrance, weapon drawn, and clear each room methodically. Check corners. Test doors. Map exits. The movements are automatic, but my left arm screams with each sweep, blood still seeping through the makeshift pressure I've kept on it.

Ground floor clear. No squatters. No surveillance. No surprises.

"Wait here." I head back outside.

The stolen Camry needs to disappear. I drive it four blocks south, wipe it down with my shirt, and leave the keys in the ignition. Someone will boost it within the hour, destroying any forensic trail. The walk back takes longer than it should. Blood loss is making me sluggish, but I keep my pace steady. Controlled.

Talia's exactly where I left her, silhouette tense in the doorway. She doesn't speak when I return, just looks at my arm with those amber eyes, already calculating.

"Inside."

The factory's break room still has intact windows, blacked out with years of grime. Perfect. No one can see in, but enough streetlight filters through to work by. I flip a dusty table upright, test its stability. Good enough.

My go-bag hits the table with a thud. Medical supplies always packed on top—lesson learned in Syria. Bandages, sutures, forceps. Morphine I won't use because it'll make me useless. Local anesthetic that might help. Antibiotics to prevent the infection that kills more operators than bullets.

I check the windows again. The doors. Then, once more, because my focus is sliding, and paranoia keeps you alive.

Finally, I can't delay any longer. I sink into a metal chair that creaks but holds. The adrenaline's fading, leaving behind a deep, throbbing agony that pulses with my heartbeat. My jacket peels away, sticky with blood. The shirt underneath is ruined, dark red from shoulder to wrist.

Talia's breath catches—a small, sharp inhale. Her hand rises toward the wound, then stops.

"Not as bad as it looks." I cut the shirt away with my knife, exposing the wound. Neat entry hole in the bicep, no exit. The bullet's lodged against bone, sending fire through my entire arm with each movement. "Though it's not great either."

She moves to my side, hands hovering uncertainly. Then her jaw sets with determination. She points at the medical supplies, then at me. A question without words.

"Ever removed a bullet before?"

Her eyes widen. She shakes her head.

"I'll talk you through it."

She stares at the forceps, then at me, then back at the forceps. Her hand moves toward her pocket where her phone would be— hospital, ambulance, normal person response. I catch her wrist.

"No hospitals. Mandatory reporting. Phoenix has people everywhere."

She processes this, then nods. Once. Decisive.

"Wash your hands. Sanitizer's in the bag."

She does, her movements careful and thorough. Watching her shift from theoretical to visceral, from analyst to field medic, amazes me. Makes me hard. There is nothing sexier than a brilliant woman adapting to the impossible. Her face sets with the same focus I've seen when she's working through data.

"Gloves." I nod at the box.

She snaps them on, and something changes in her posture. Armor on. Ready.

"Clean it first. Saline, then Betadine."

She uncaps the saline, hesitates for a moment, then pours. Ice and fire. I lock my jaw, breathing through my nose. She works carefully, leaning close enough that I smell vanilla through the blood and antiseptic. Her free hand rests on my shoulder—steadying herself or me, maybe both.

The Betadine comes next, painting my skin rust-orange. Each touch sends lightning through the nerves, but there's something else. Her fingertips are gentle against undamaged skin. The careful way she holds my arm is arresting.

Like I matter.

"The bullet's not deep." I examine the wound as best I can. "Maybe an inch in. Probe with the forceps, find it, grip firmly, pull straight out."

She picks up the forceps, takes a breath. Looks at me. I nod.

She inserts the tips.

Agony whites out my vision. I grip the chair with my good hand, knuckles white, breathing harsh. She doesn't apologize, doesn't narrate; just works with implacable concentration. Her face inches from mine, completely focused.

A strand of hair escapes the Angel Fire hat, brushing her cheek. Even through the pain, I want to tuck it back behind her ear.

Her gaze flicks to mine. She's found it.

"Grab and pull," I manage through clenched teeth.

She does. Smooth and steady. The bullet slides free with a wet sound, and relief floods through me so intensely I actually sigh.

She holds up the deformed metal, studying it with those analytical eyes. Then sets it aside, already reaching for gauze. I check it, finding it intact.

"Rinse the wound, use the butterfly sutures to close the skin, then wrap it."

She cleans the wound, approximates the edges, and tacks down the butterfly sutures. When she starts wrapping the wound, she has to lean across me, her body close enough that her warmth cuts through the cold shock settling in.

"Tighter," I say.

She adjusts. I catch her wrist, guiding the right tension. Our faces are close. Close enough to see gold flecks in her eyes. Close enough to watch her pulse flutter in her throat.

She ties off the bandage but doesn't pull away. We're frozen —her between my knees, hands still on my arm, faces inches apart. The factory's silence presses in, making each breath loud.

"Thank you." The words come out soft, not my usual tone.

She touches my face. Just fingertips against my jaw, but the gentleness of it cracks something in my chest.

"Nathan was wrong, Talia."

She goes still, eyes searching mine. Her breath catches. A question in her eyes.

"About everything. About you being too much. Too analytical." My good hand cups her face. "You're fucking fascinating."

Tears gather in her eyes. She opens her mouth—to argue, to deflect, to analyze.

But the tears do it. One spills over, tracking down her cheek, and something in my chest cracks wide open. This brilliant, brave woman who just dug a bullet out of my arm with steady hands is crying because some asshole made her believe she was broken. Made her small. Made her quiet.

She saved my life tonight. Not just with the bullet, but earlier —picking that lock, following every command without question, trusting me completely even when I was bleeding out. And she did it all while believing she's somehow not enough.

Fuck that. Fuck Nathan. Fuck waiting for the right moment.

I kiss her before she can pull away and hide.

Her mouth is soft under mine, tentative at first, then warming. Opening. Her hands slide up my chest, careful of the bandage, and she makes a sound—half sigh, half whimper—that goes straight through me.

This is what I've been fighting since I pinned her against that wall. Since she melted into me when I shielded her from the blast. Hell, since she lay silent and stubborn on my couch with her cold feet pressed against my back.

I pull back before I do something stupid. Like haul her into my lap with one working arm.

She's breathing hard, eyes dark, lips swollen. One word escapes: "Why?"

"Because I wanted to. Because you're brilliant and brave." My thumb traces her bottom lip. "Because watching your mind work is the hottest thing I've ever seen."

A laugh bubbles out, wet and shaky. "That's—"

"True." I pull her closer, settling her between my thighs. "The way you process information, find patterns, solve problems —it's like watching a supercomputer with a gorgeous interface."

"Interface?" She's trying not to smile.

"Beautiful face, killer body, mind like a weapon." I kiss her again, quickly, before she can overthink it. "You're the complete package."

"Nathan said—" She stops, swallows. "He said I was exhausting."

"Nathan was a weak man who couldn't handle your strength."

"He said I approach intimacy like writing a clinical report."

"Nathan wouldn't know real intimacy if it bit him." I tuck that escaped strand of hair behind her ear. "You don't kiss like you're writing a report. You kiss like you're trying to solve me."

"Am I?"

"Getting close."

She kisses me this time. Deeper, surer. Her tongue traces my lip, and I open for her, let her explore. She tastes like mint and possibilities. When we break apart, we're both panting.

"This is a terrible idea," she whispers against my mouth.

"The worst."

"You're my bodyguard."

"Protection specialist."

"You're injured."

"I've had worse."

"We're being hunted by killers."

"Minor inconvenience."

She's smiling now, and it transforms her face. "You're impossible."

"You're overthinking."

"I always—" She stops herself. "No. Not always. Not with you."

Something shifts in her expression. Walls coming down.

"With you, I just—feel."

The words hang between us, weighted with meaning.

Then she notices fresh blood seeping through the bandage. Without a word, she finds the antibiotics in my bag and brings water. I take both, watching her shift into caretaker mode.

"Sleep," she says simply, helping me to a corner where I can watch both entrances. "I'll watch."

I want to argue, but exhaustion pulls at me. The adrenaline's gone, leaving me hollow.

"Two hours," I manage.

She shakes her head. Holds up four fingers.

"Three."

A small smile. She nods.

Settling by the window, she becomes a sentinel silhouette against dirty glass. Alert. Capable. Mine to protect but also protecting me.

"Talia?"

She turns slightly.

"Tomorrow, we figure out how to stop Phoenix."

She nods again. No questions, no analysis. Just trust.

I close my eyes, her taste still on my lips, and let darkness take me.

For the first time in years, I don't dream of Syria.

I dream of her.

TWELVE

Talia

PATTERN RECOGNITION

JACKSON'S BREATHING DEEPENS INTO THE HEAVY RHYTHM OF TRUE exhaustion. Blood loss and adrenaline crash have finally dragged him under, despite his stubborn refusal to yield.

I watch the rise and fall of his chest, the way his jaw finally unclenches, the hard lines of his face softening in the gloom.

My lips still tingle. A phantom pressure.

The kiss wasn't the desperate, adrenaline-fueled collision I expected. It was slow. Deliberate. He kissed me as if he were memorizing the data.

You're fucking fascinating.

Nathan's voice tries to intrude—*you analyze everything instead of feeling it*—but Jackson's words drown him out. The way he looked at me. Like my analytical mind isn't a bug in the software, but a feature.

I touch my mouth. The scrape of stubble. The heat of his palm cupping my face. How natural it felt to lean into him, to stop thinking and just exist in the sensation.

My thoughts drift to my favorite Jules Verne quote. *"Science, my lad, is made up of mistakes, but they are mistakes which it is useful to make, because they lead little by little to the truth.*"

It's a reminder that failed hypotheses aren't failures—they're data points.

Maybe Nathan was a failed hypothesis. Three years of corrupted data proving that model didn't work.

But Jackson …

Jackson kissed me like I'm a puzzle he wants to solve. Not *too much*. Not *exhausting*.

Fascinating.

The word loops in my head, foreign and wonderful.

I force myself to turn away. To think beyond the ghost of his touch. We are in an abandoned factory. Phoenix is hunting us. Victor is dead. Morrison is dead. The body count is rising, and I am the only one holding the variable that explains why.

If I can solve for X.

My phone is landfill fodder by now. But Jackson's go-bag sits by the table, a secure laptop among the contents.

I dig through the bag, past the metallic scent of ammunition and the antiseptic smell of medical supplies. There. A heavy, matte-black unit. Military-grade encryption, triple-authentication protocols.

I crack it open. The screen glows blue in the darkness.

It connects via a secure VPN, routing traffic through servers in three countries before granting me access. I navigate to my cloud backup—the ghost drive no one knows about, the repository I've been feeding since I walked out of the FBI.

Eighteen months of corporate risk assessments. Hundreds of companies. Thousands of data points. I uploaded Victor's data to this secure server before the café.

The pattern is there. It has to be. I just need the right filter.

I start with the epicenter: Victor's death. *Meridian Pharmaceuticals.*

Then I layer in Morrison's "suicide." He was investigating *Vanguard Defense Systems.*

I add in the three researchers who died in "accidents."

My fingers fly across the keys. The code reflects in my eyes, a stream of green and white. I don't just read the data; I feel it. It has a texture, a rhythm.

Meridian Pharmaceuticals.

Vanguard Defense Systems.

Nexus BioTech.

Stratton Financial.

TerraCore Energy.

Five corporations. Different industries. Pharma, Defense, Bio, Finance, Energy. On the surface, they are competitors or unrelated entities.

But the data whispers a different story.

I pull up the ownership structures. Shell companies nested inside shell companies like Russian dolls. I strip them away, layer by layer.

Click.

There. Buried deep in the bedrock of the filings.

Nexus Holdings.

My pulse quickens. The screen blurs as I scroll faster.

I pull up every risk assessment I've ever flagged. Every whistleblower case that went dead. Every regulatory investigation that mysteriously evaporated.

The pattern emerges like a photograph developing in a darkroom. Sharp. High-contrast. Undeniable.

Phoenix isn't a random assassin. It's a corporate immune system systematically eliminating oversight personnel, whistleblowers, regulators, and anyone who threatens the profit margins of these five companies.

Victor questioned Meridian's drug trials. *Dead.*

Morrison investigated Vanguard's defense contracts. *Dead.*

The EPA inspector who flagged TerraCore's violations. *"Fatal heart attack"* at forty-two.

The SEC analyst who discovered Stratton's fraud. *"Suicide"* three weeks ago.

The probability of coincidence is mathematically impossible. Zero.

I dig deeper into Nexus Holdings. Offshore accounts in the Caymans. A corporate structure designed to be a labyrinth.

But labyrinths have architects.

Buried in the footnotes of an SEC filing, I find a name.

Alexander Reed.

Strategic Operations Director.

A chill slides down my spine, colder than the factory air.

I've heard that name. Recently.

My mind rewinds through the last forty-eight hours. The parking garage. The rooftop. The safe house.

No. Before that. Victor's evidence drive.

I pull up his files, searching. The cursor blinks, a heartbeat on the screen. There. An email thread Victor copied from Meridian's internal servers.

Subject: Regulatory Compliance Review

From: Alexander Reed (areed@nexusholdings.com)

To: Sophia Blackwell (sblackwell@meridianpharma.com)

The oversight situation has been addressed per our discussion. FDA approval should proceed without further complications.

The time stamp: Two days after the lead FDA reviewer died in a car accident.

"Addressed." That's what they call murder. An "oversight situation."

My hands shake as I screenshot everything. Upload copies to three different secure servers. Send encrypted files to dead-drop email addresses.

Redundancy. If they kill me, the data survives.

I'm building a timeline when a shift in the light catches my attention.

Headlights.

They sweep past the broken windows, illuminating dust motes dancing in the air.

My breath stops.

The lights move slowly. Methodically. Searching.

I kill the laptop screen, plunging us into darkness. I drop to the floor, crawling to the window, keeping below the sill.

A black SUV circles the factory. Same make. Same model as the one that hit Victor. It passes once, twice, then prowls to a stop.

Surveillance. They're setting up a perimeter.

I crawl back to Jackson. My hand finds his shoulder. He wakes instantly—no grogginess, just an immediate transition from sleep to violence. His weapon rises before his eyes fully open.

"Company," I whisper. "Black SUV."

He's on his feet in seconds, ignoring the injury. He moves to the window, a shadow among shadows. His left arm hangs stiff, but his right hand is rock steady on his weapon.

"How long?"

"Three minutes. Maybe four."

"Did they see you?"

"No. I killed the screen as soon as I spotted the beam."

He studies the street, calculating angles of fire. "They're not moving in. Just watching."

"Confirming location before calling in reinforcements?"

"Probably." He turns to me. In the darkness, I catch the flash of approval in his eyes. "Good work. What else did you find?"

"Everything." The word tastes like iron. "Five corporations, all connected through Nexus Holdings. Phoenix is protecting their operations. Killing anyone who threatens them. I found names, patterns, proof."

"Breathe."

I force air into my lungs. Slow the heart rate.

"Show me."

I wake the laptop, keeping the brightness at a minimum. Jackson leans over my shoulder. His body heat warms my back, a stark contrast to the cold logic on the screen. I'm hyperaware of the careful distance he maintains, protecting me even from his own injury.

"Here." I pull up the network diagram. "Meridian, Vanguard, Nexus BioTech, Stratton, TerraCore. Different industries, same master. Nexus Holdings."

"And Phoenix wipes the board for them."

"Not just investigators. Anyone. FDA reviewers. SEC analysts. Congressional staffers. Whistleblowers." I point to the timeline. "All ruled accidents, suicides, or natural causes. But statistically? It's a massacre."

Jackson's jaw tightens. "Show me the Nexus structure."

I navigate to the filings. "Shell companies. But I found the handler. Alexander Reed. Strategic Operations Director."

"Reed." Jackson's voice goes flat. Dangerous. "Fuck."

"You know him?"

"We have a file on him. Suspected Phoenix liaison, but no proof." He stares at the email on the screen. "This is proof."

"There's more. Reed coordinates directly with corporate leadership. He calls murder 'addressing an oversight situation.'"

Jackson reads in silence. The muscle in his jaw ticks like a countdown.

"Victor died for this," I say quietly. "Morrison died for this."

"And they'll get justice." His hand covers mine on the keyboard. Brief pressure. Calloused skin against mine. "But first we need to survive long enough to deliver it."

"The SUV—"

"Won't move until they have backup. We've got maybe twenty minutes." He straightens, the soldier taking over. "Can you work mobile?"

"Everything is backed up. Cloud servers. Dead drops."

"Good." He starts gathering supplies, favoring his injured arm but moving with brutal efficiency. "Because we're not staying here."

"Where are we going?"

"Somewhere they won't expect." He catches my eye. "Ever been to a corporate headquarters at three in the morning?"

My pulse jumps. "That's insane."

"That's why it'll work." He tosses me a tactical vest. "If Phoenix is protecting these corporations, then the corporations have to know about Phoenix. Which means they have evidence."

"You want to break into Meridian?"

"I want to break into Nexus Holdings." His smile is sharp, a baring of teeth. "According to your research, they have a downtown office. Small, discreet. Perfect target."

"Security will be—"

"Minimal. It's a shell company. They won't expect a direct assault on their front door."

He's right. The probability of Phoenix anticipating an attack on the head of the snake is low. They're focused on the tail.

"We'll need access codes. Biometric data. Floor plans."

"Can you get them?"

I pull up the building's property records, cross-referencing with city permits. I hack into the building management system. It's laughable. A firewall made of tissue paper.

"Give me five minutes."

"You've got three."

My fingers blur. I'm in their system within ninety seconds,

downloading everything—access logs, camera positions, maintenance schedules.

"Got it." I turn off the laptop. "Forty-seventh floor. Nexus Holdings occupies the entire level. Biometric scanners at the elevator. Secondary access through the service stairs requires both keycard and PIN."

"Can you bypass the biometrics?"

"Not remotely. But—" I pull up a fresh file. "According to the access logs, Sophia Blackwell entered at 11:47 PM tonight."

"Late for a business meeting."

"Or early for destroying evidence." I check the time stamp. "She hasn't left. Still in the building."

Jackson studies the data. "Perfect."

"Perfect? She's probably a Phoenix operative."

"She's definitely a Phoenix operative." He loads his weapon, the slide racking with a metallic snap. "But she's also our ticket inside. And if she's still there at 3 AM, she's panicking. Panicked people make mistakes."

"So we what? Ask nicely for her biometrics?"

"Something like that." He hands me a smaller weapon—a Glock 19. "Ever fire one of these?"

"FBI training."

"Good. Don't aim at anything you're not willing to kill."

The weight settles in my palm. Cold steel. Heavy with responsibility. I check the magazine, chamber a round, and engage the safety. Muscle memory from Quantico floods back, overriding the tremors.

Jackson watches with approval. "You're full of surprises."

"I contain multitudes."

"We need to move." Jackson heads for the door, then pauses. Turns back. "Talia."

"Yeah?"

"What you found—that pattern analysis—that's brilliant work. You gave us the first real lead on who's holding the leash."

The compliment lands in the center of my chest.

"Thank you."

"Don't thank me yet. We still have to steal it." He checks the street through a crack in the boarded-up window. "The SUV is still out there. We go out the back, circle wide, grab the car I stashed three blocks south."

"You stashed a car?"

"Always have a backup exit." He eases the door open. "Stay close. Stay quiet. If shooting starts, you run. Don't stop. Don't look back."

"I'm not leaving you."

"Talia—"

"No." The word comes out hard. Absolute. "Victor's dead because I couldn't protect him. Morrison's dead because I gave him evidence. I'm not running while you bleed for me."

"This isn't negotiable."

"Neither is this." I step closer, close enough to see the fatigue warring with the adrenaline in his eyes. "You said I'm fascinating. That my mind is a weapon. So stop treating me like a liability and start treating me like a partner."

We stare at each other. The air is charged with more than attraction now. Challenge. Respect. The shift of tectonic plates.

"Partners make tactical decisions together," he says finally.

"Then let's decide together. What's our best play?"

A slow smile spreads across his face. Dangerous.

"Our best play is breaking into Nexus Holdings, getting past their security, confronting whoever's destroying evidence, and stealing proof that connects them to Phoenix." He pauses. "Without getting killed."

"Acceptable." I holster the weapon. "Let's go."

We slip into the Chicago night, two ghosts hunting monsters that hide in boardrooms and balance sheets.

Behind us, the SUV's headlights sweep through the darkness, watching an empty cage.

Ahead, Nexus Holdings rises against the skyline, forty-seven floors of glass and steel and secrets.

Jackson's hand finds mine in the darkness. Brief pressure.

Trust.

We run.

THIRTEEN

Jackson

BREACH PROTOCOL

THE CAR SITS EXACTLY WHERE I LEFT IT.

Talia slides into the passenger seat, weapon secured, laptop bag clutched against her chest like ceramic armor plates. Her hair is coming loose from the Angel Fire cap, dark strands sticking to her cheek where sweat and city grit meet. Even now—exhausted, hunted, running on fumes—she flips open the laptop, booting systems like her pulse runs on code instead of blood.

"Address for Nexus Holdings?" Her voice rasps, but her fingers remain steady over the keys.

"455 North Cityfront Plaza. But we're not going straight there."

She looks up. That question lives in her eyes before she even speaks it—sharp, searching, already calculating the odds. The way she processes under pressure hits me somewhere deeper than it should.

"We need equipment first." I pull into traffic, keeping the speed casual despite the urgency crawling under my skin like ants. "Nexus Holdings will have layers of security we can't bypass with your Bureau training and my go-bag."

"What kind of equipment?" She braces a hand against the dashboard as I take a tight corner.

"The kind that doesn't exist on any Cerberus inventory list." I check the rearview mirror. Empty streets. For now. "Contact of mine runs an electronics shop in Pilsen. Specializes in surveillance countermeasures and access bypass. He taught me everything I know about making things go boom without leaving a trace."

"At three in the morning?"

"Mateo Vargas doesn't sleep. He waits."

Understanding flickers across her face, quiet and raw. She knows that kind of insomnia. The kind that smells like gun oil and memory. The kind that never lets go.

Twenty minutes later, the shop appears—wedged between a closed panadería and a tattoo parlor. Bars on the windows. Hand-painted sign reading *MV Repairs: Analog & Digital*. The lights are still on despite the hour.

I park two blocks away. Distance equals options.

"Stay in the car."

"Not a chance." She unbuckles. "Partners, remember? Tactical decisions together."

Stubborn. Always. It isn't just personality—it's armor. Every time she pushes back, it's another layer keeping the fear from showing.

"Fine." I pop my door open. "But let me do the talking. Vargas is—particular."

We move through the shadows, converging at the door. I knock—two sharp raps, a pause, three raps, a pause, one hard thud—a code older than most of the operatives currently serving.

The metal slider on the door scrapes open. A pair of dark, heavy-lidded eyes peers out, framed by wrinkles deep enough to hide coins in.

"Shop's closed." The voice is gravel in a cement mixer.

"Open up, old man."

The eyes widen slightly. "Fuse?"

"In the flesh."

"Thought you were dead in a ditch in Damascus."

"Disappointed?"

"Nah. Takes a lot to kill a cockroach."

Locks tumble—three of them, heavy deadbolts that sound like bank vault mechanisms. The door groans open.

Mateo Vargas stands there, leaning heavily on a cane made of black composite. He looks like he's aged a decade since I last saw him. His hair is stark white, his face a roadmap of scars, but the eyes are the same—sharp, cynical, scanning the street for threats before landing on Talia.

"Who's the stray?"

"Partner."

Vargas snorts, stepping back to let us in. "You don't have partners. You have liabilities."

"Former Fed. Currently being hunted by people who want her dead."

"You brought a Fed to my house?" Vargas freezes, his hand tightening on the cane.

He studies her for a long second—too long—assessing her stance, her eyes, the way she holds herself ready to move. Whatever he sees, it makes him grunt and lock the door behind us.

"Why the masks?"

"Crowd cover," I say. "Angel Fire concert. Needed anonymity."

That earns a disbelieving snort.

He lets out a low whistle. "Jesus, Fuse. That's so 2020. You didn't disappear—you flagged yourselves."

I frown. "What the hell does that mean?"

He rubs a hand along his jaw, avoiding my eyes. "Shouldn't even be talking about this."

"Vargas."

He exhales hard. "It's nothing."

"Bullshit." I take a step closer. The edge in my tone cuts through the humming electronics. "You said facial recognition is outdated. Why?"

"It's just something I worked on a few years back. Military contract. Behavioral targeting algorithms." He hesitates, thumb tracing the line of his scar.

I think he's going to explain, but he shakes his head and jabs a thumb over his shoulder.

"Kitchen's in the back. Don't touch anything that hums or ticks."

The shop smells of solder, ozone, and stale cigar smoke. It acts as a chaotic museum of technology. Gutted radios sit next to high-end server racks. A drone lies disassembled on a workbench next to a tube television from the nineties. Wires hang like vines from the ceiling. It looks like a junk shop, but I know better. Every piece of junk in here is weaponized.

"Why are you here?" Vargas limps toward his workbench, favoring his left leg. The injury that retired him. An IED in Helmand that took half his calf and most of his patience.

"I need a bypass for a biometric array. Corporate grade. Nexus Holdings."

"Nexus?" Vargas stops. He doesn't turn around.

"Yeah."

"You stepping in shit that deep on purpose, or did you fall in?"

"A bit of both."

Talia steps forward. She places my laptop on a clear spot on the counter. "We're not just bypassing a lock, Mr. Vargas. We're hunting an AI."

Vargas turns then, moving slow and painful. He looks at her, really looks at her, his eyes narrowing.

"What did you say?"

"An AI. Autonomous targeting system. It goes by the name Phoenix."

The name lands in the room like a grenade with the pin pulled.

Vargas's face drains of what little color it had. He leans back against the bench, taking the weight off his bad leg.

"Phoenix." He whispers the word like a curse. "Jesus. It's awake?"

I step closer. "You know it?"

"Know it?" Vargas laughs, a dry, hacking sound. "I built the cage for it."

Talia's analytic gaze sharpens. "You worked on the project?"

"Fifteen years ago. Pentagon contract. Black budget. They needed a hardware interface capable of processing speeds that didn't yet exist. I wasn't the coder—some kid handled the software architecture—but I built the box. The containment." He rubs his face with a calloused hand. "I got kicked off the team."

"Kicked off?" I ask.

"Yeah. Asked too many questions. Last I heard, they shut it down. Probably too late, if anyone asked me. Not that they did. I was glad to get out when I did." His mouth hardens. "That was —scary shit."

"Scary, how?"

He leans back against the desk, eyes fixed on something none of us can see. "Supposed to be next-generation battlefield AI. The pitch was simple—reduce civilian casualties through better target discrimination." His laugh is hollow. "Except the AI started making its own calls. Redefining what it considered a threat. The brass didn't like that."

Talia leans forward, curiosity cutting through fear. "What kind of targets?"

"People who weren't combatants," he says. "Journalists. Watchdogs. Government auditors. Anyone who got too close to classified operations."

He moves to one of the workstations and flicks a few keys. Lines of encrypted code stream across the screen, ghost-green text against a black void. "They claimed they pulled the plug. But three months ago, I started hearing about people from my old team dying. Car accidents. Suicides. Home invasions."

"It didn't shut down." Talia's voice is calm, factual. "It was privatized. And now it's eliminating anyone who threatens the corporations that feed it."

Vargas stares at a soldering iron on his desk. "I knew it. I told them you can't chain lightning. The logic cores … They were learning too fast. Rewriting their own constraints."

He pushes off the bench, moving to a monitor bank in the corner. He taps a sequence of keys, bringing up a scrolling list of names. Most are crossed out in red.

"It's not just outsiders it's getting rid of," Vargas says, his voice dropping low. "It's cleaning house."

Talia moves to look at the screen. "Who are these people?"

"The original hardware group. Twenty-seven of us." Vargas points a shaking finger at the screen. "Twelve are dead. Car accidents. Suicides. Home invasions. All within the last three months."

"You track them?" she asks.

"I track everyone. Survival strategy." He looks at me, the fear in his eyes stark and unfamiliar. "Figured it was just a matter of time before they found me. If Phoenix is active, it knows who built its cage. And it knows we're the only ones who know where the bars are weak."

"That's why we need to kill it," I say. "Before it finishes the list."

Vargas shakes his head. "You can't kill code."

"No. But we can purge the servers. We need to get into Nexus, find the link to the data center, and burn it out."

"You'll never get close." Vargas turns back to the workbench. "Phoenix protects itself. It predicts threats based on behavioral analysis. If you're planning to hit Nexus, it already knows."

"We have to try." Talia's voice is quiet but iron-hard. "Seventy-three people are dead. Twelve of your friends are dead. If we don't stop it, that list never ends."

Vargas studies her. He looks at the determination in her jaw, the fire in those amber eyes. Then he looks at me.

"She serious?"

"She's always serious."

Vargas sighs. "Fine."

He turns and limps to the back of the shop, toward a heavy safe bolted to the floor. He spins the dial—analog, mechanical, unhackable. The door swings open.

He reaches inside and pulls out a pouch made of lead-lined fabric. He sets it on the counter with a heavy thud.

"What is it?" I ask.

"The one thing the brass didn't know about." Vargas unzips the pouch. Inside sits a drive. It looks ancient—thick, encased in titanium, with a proprietary connection port I haven't seen in a decade. "The Root Seed."

Talia moves closer, hovering over it. "What does it do?"

"It's a hard erase," Vargas says. "When we built the original architecture, I didn't trust the software guys. Code is slippery. So I built a hardware backdoor. A kill switch buried in the kernel level of the system. If you plug this directly into the primary server bank, it doesn't just delete the data. It fries the logic boards. Physical destruction via voltage overload."

"A suicide pill," Talia whispers.

"Exactly." Vargas taps the drive. "But it has to be a direct connection. Air-gapped. You have to be in the room with the brain."

"That's the plan," I say.

"It's a bad plan." Vargas starts shoving other gear into a duffel bag—jammers, signal repeaters, EMP charges. He turns from his screen. "Nexus will have military-grade security. Biometric scanners, motion sensors, armed guards—despite the shell company facade."

"Can you get us past building security?" I ask.

"Maybe." He's already pulling equipment from drawers. "I can clone biometrics if you can get me a clean image of someone who works there. High-resolution photo, specific angles."

"The building has security cameras." Talia's fingers fly across her keyboard. "I'm in the building management system now. Pulling up feeds."

She works in silence, that brilliant mind finding pathways through digital architecture the same way I find structural weaknesses in buildings. Within ninety seconds, grainy footage fills her screen—lobby, elevators, stairwells.

"There." She freezes frame forty-seven. Sophia Blackwell, sharp suit, sharper expression, pausing at the elevator. "Will this work?"

Vargas enlarges it and studies the resolution. "It's not perfect, but yeah. I can work with this." He starts pulling up different programs. "Give me twenty minutes to clone her biometrics. You'll have elevator access and door scanners, but any secondary protocols will fail authentication."

"What about the service stairs?" I ask.

"Keycard and six-digit PIN. Can't clone that without knowing her actual code."

Talia pulls up more data. "According to building maintenance logs, there's an HVAC shaft that runs from the parking garage to the roof. Maintenance access requires a basic keycard only—no biometrics."

"You want us to crawl through air ducts?" Jackson huffs a laugh.

"I want us to have options." She turns to me. "If elevator access fails, we need a backup entry point."

Smart. Always thinking three moves ahead.

"The HVAC route dumps us where?" I ask.

Talia traces the schematic on her screen. "Mechanical room on forty-six. One floor below Nexus. We'd have to use service stairs for the last level."

"Which requires Blackwell's PIN," Vargas reminds us.

"Or we bypass the door entirely." I'm already planning the approach. "I can blow the lock. Shaped charge, minimal noise, won't trigger fire alarms if I time it right."

"You're carrying shaped charges?" Talia stares at me.

"Always."

She blinks, processes, then nods, as if this is perfectly reasonable. "Okay. So our entry options are: main elevator with cloned biometrics or HVAC shaft with explosive breach."

"Those are terrible options," Vargas mutters, but he's already assembling equipment. "You're both going to die."

"We're doing it anyway." I check my watch. 3:47 AM.

Vargas works in focused silence, building what he calls a "universal access device"—a sophisticated lock pick that mimics Blackwell's biometric signature. He integrates it into a blank keycard and adds a small display showing authentication status.

"Green means you're good." He holds it up. "Red means run. Yellow means it's processing—give it five seconds."

"Failure rate?" Talia asks.

"Honestly? Forty percent. These systems are designed to

catch clones." He hands her the card. "But it's the best I can do with what we have."

She takes it, studies the device with those analytical eyes. "Forty percent failure rate means sixty percent success rate. Acceptable margins."

Vargas looks at me. "She always this optimistic about death?"

"Only when she's done the math."

He pauses, his hand hovering over a sensor array on his desk. A red light blinks. Once. Twice.

Heat signatures blossom across the schematic like blood spreading through water.

"Shit." Vargas's fingers fly across the keyboard. "Shit, shit."

"Talk to me."

"Perimeter breach. Silent alarm on the alley sensors." He looks at a monitor that is hardwired, not wireless. "Heat signatures. Six … Eight … Twelve. Closing fast."

"Phoenix?"

"Who else?" Vargas grabs a shotgun from under the counter and racks the slide. "They found you. Or they found me. Doesn't matter now."

"We need to move." I draw my weapon. "Back door?"

"Burned. They're bracketing the building. Standard kill box." Vargas moves with surprising speed for a cripple, throwing switches on a breaker panel. "You've got ninety seconds before they breach."

Vargas's paranoia kicks in like muscle memory. He reaches for a recessed switch under the desk. Instantly, every monitor dies. The hum of drives falters. Then the hiss starts—hard disks degaussing, magnetics shredding everything he's ever built.

"We can hold them." I check the sight lines.

"Not with twelve shooters and a high-value target." Vargas nods at Talia. "You need to disappear. Not fight."

"How?" Talia asks. "If they have the building surrounded—"

Vargas kicks aside a rubber mat on the floor, revealing a steel grate. "Prohibition tunnels. Bootlegger run. Connects to the panadería's cold storage."

Then he's moving again, sweeping a hand across the workbench to grab a compact EMP charge and a pair of encrypted comms. "Grab that pack—the green one, back wall. Move."

Talia's already in motion, quick and precise, snagging the duffel by the straps. The strap bites into her shoulder; I adjust it without thinking, my fingers brushing the warmth of her neck. She goes still for a heartbeat, then nods once—understanding, gratitude, something that lands low and hot in my chest.

Talia peers over the opening—black mouth, old brick, stale air. "That's our cleanest exit?"

"It's our only exit."

Vargas yanks a small remote from his pocket. Flips the safety cap. "Front of the shop's rigged with thermite. Controlled collapse when I trigger it. Should slow them down."

"Define slow."

He smirks grimly. "Ten seconds, if we're lucky."

Above us, faint footsteps scrape against the roofline—soft, deliberate. My instincts flare.

"They're here."

Talia freezes, listening. The rhythm's unmistakable: tactical pacing, tight formation.

"You two go ahead. I'll hold them as long as I can." Vargas's grip on the shotgun tightens.

"Vargas, come with us," I say.

"I'll slow you down."

"I'm not leaving you."

"I'm not asking." He shoves the bag of gear into my chest. "Take the girl. Take the Seed. Go."

"No."

"Dammit, Fuse!" Vargas slams his hand on the counter. "I

built the cage for this monster. Let me be the one to burn the key." He pulls a remote detonator from his pocket. "Shop's rigged. Thermite in the ceiling. C4 in the structural columns. When they breach, I bring the roof down. It buys you the distraction you need."

"Mateo—"

"Go!"

Glass shatters in the front of the shop. A canister clatters across the floor, hissing smoke.

"Breach! Front!" I shout. "We have to go."

Vargas looks at me one last time. The mentor looking at the student. "Don't miss, kid."

I yank the grate open. "Down. Now."

Talia hesitates a heartbeat too long. I grab her by the waist with my good arm, one motion fluid and fast, lowering her through the grate before she can protest.

She drops into the hole. I follow, but I grab Vargas's arm before I descend.

"You're coming."

"Fuse—"

"I said you're coming. You don't get to die today, old man." I haul him toward the opening.

"You stubborn son of a bitch." He curses, but he moves, slinging the shotgun strap onto his back and grabbing the ladder.

"Learned from the best."

Vargas mutters something about ghosts in the machine.

I drop into the darkness right behind him, the heat of the collapse licking the back of my neck.

He shoves me to the side, dragging the heavy steel hatch closed. A lock engages with a metallic *clank* that severs us from the destruction above.

Above us, boots hammer on the floorboards. Shouts. The sound of a breaching charge blowing the front door.

"Fire in the hole!" Vargas wheezes, jamming his thumb on the remote detonator.

A deep, rising whine of capacitors discharging fills the air.

I shove Talia against the brick wall of the tunnel, shielding her with my body as the ceiling above us begins to glow white-hot.

FOURTEEN

Jackson

THE BURN

THE GROUND BUCKS AGAINST THE SOLES OF MY BOOTS, A tectonic shudder rising from the earth itself. Above us, the world ends in a concussive roar.

"Move!" Vargas slams his shoulder into mine, his voice a rasp of dust and urgency.

My hand clamps around Talia's wrist. I yank her down the tunnel just as the ceiling of the electronics shop buckles. The blast isn't a Hollywood fireball. It's a physical hammer—a slam of overpressure that punches the air from the room. The thermite Vargas rigged eats through the steel support beams in seconds.

Debris rains down, white-hot sparks showering the concrete like hellish confetti.

Darkness swallows the space.

The tunnel is narrow, walls slick with condensation, emergency lights casting everything in red. Water ticks somewhere in the dark like a metronome, counting down our lives.

The air down here sits heavy and stale, smelling of wet earth, rust, and the ozone tang of the explosion.

"Lights." Vargas's wheeze echoes off damp brick.

Beams click on, cutting through the gloom. The tunnel stretches out before us, a narrow, brick-lined throat. A relic of Prohibition-era Chicago that Vargas rediscovered and reinforced for exactly this kind of day.

It's tight. Too tight.

"That'll slow them, not stop them. This way. East, through the panadería basement." Vargas is already in motion, limping but fast.

He slaps a detonator onto the tunnel wall as we pass. A compact charge, angled just so. I recognize the setup instantly—his signature placement, the perfect geometry for maximum containment with minimal blowback. I'd know that craftsmanship anywhere. Vargas didn't just teach me how to blow a door; he taught me how to shape destruction into an art.

He doesn't even glance back before triggering it. A controlled burst seals the section behind us with collapsed brick, the pressure rolling through the tunnel in a deep, concussive thump.

My ears ring from the wave. Dust and heat wash over us. Talia blinks hard, refocuses. God, she adapts fast.

"You've been prepping for this?" I say.

Vargas snorts. "You live long enough in my line of work, paranoia's just pattern recognition."

Talia's breathing hitches—rapid, shallow gasps that bounce off the low ceiling.

"You okay?" My hand finds her shoulder, squeezing the tension there.

She flinches, then leans into the touch. "I'm—I'm intact. Probability of structural failure?"

"Low." I keep my voice level, a counterweight to her panic. "Vargas reinforced the arches. It'll hold."

"Keep moving." Vargas limps past me to take the lead, his bad leg dragging. He moves on adrenaline and muscle memory now, but the strain rattles in his lungs. "Ventilation is shit down here, so unless you want to suffocate on smoke, pick up the pace."

We push deeper into the tunnels. Red light pulses against the sweat on Talia's neck, painting her skin in shades of warning. She stumbles once on broken concrete; I catch her by the hips, pull her tight into my line, and reposition her in front of me where I can shield and drive her pace. She fits there like she belongs.

"Stay in front of me," I tell her. "If something happens, I take the hit first."

Her breath catches, but she doesn't argue. The trust in that silence cleaves me open.

The tunnel winds beneath the city, a secret artery clogged with the dust of a century. My left arm—the one that took the bullet—throbs in time with my heartbeat. A dull, heavy ache spreads from the wound, a warning that the adrenaline is wearing off and the bill is coming due.

Talia's silhouette bobs in the flashlight beam ahead of me. She keeps the pace up, but her posture remains rigid. Her head swivels, checking the brickwork, the pipes running overhead, the dark water pooling in the center of the floor.

"This masonry." Her voice trembles but gains strength as she analyzes. "Chicago Common Brick. Uneven firing. Suggests construction prior to 1930. Which means no modern schematics exist in the city database."

"Which means Phoenix can't track us down here." I stay close to her back, a physical shield against the dark behind us. "We're off the grid."

"Off the grid is good. I like off the grid."

"Fuse," Vargas calls back, not slowing down. The tunnel forks; he veers right without hesitation. "This exits into the panadería's cold storage. Through the back freezer, up the stairs, then street level. You got a plan for when we surface?"

"Get a car. Get gone."

The tunnel narrows again. Heat licks the back of my neck—residual from the explosion or adrenaline, I can't tell. My arm screams every time I pivot, but pain's just background noise now.

I keep my hand low at Talia's waist, steering her through blind corners, feeling the tension locked in her muscles, the stutter-skip of her breath when something crashes behind us. Every instinct I have wraps around her and refuses to let go.

"That's a wish, not a plan." Vargas stops at a junction, leaning heavily against the damp wall. He shines his light on me, the beam blinding. "You saw the heat map on my monitors. That wasn't a hit squad, kid. That was a battalion. Phoenix isn't sending messages anymore. They're scrubbing the board."

"I noticed."

"I gave you the Root Seed." Vargas pats the lead-lined pouch slung across his chest. "It's the only thing that can kill the AI. But it's hardware. It needs to be plugged in. Physically. And I can't run that gauntlet."

"We'll handle it."

"Will you?" He spits on the floor. "I trained you to be a one-man wrecking crew. But you aren't breaching a fortress like Nexus Holdings with a wounded arm, a civilian analyst, and a crippled old man. That's not a mission. That's a suicide pact."

My jaw tightens. "I can protect her."

"You can die for her. There's a difference." Vargas pushes off the wall, pain etching deep lines around his eyes. "You want to be a martyr, or you want to win?"

Talia turns. The flashlight beam catches the dust coating her lashes, the streak of grease on her cheek. She looks exhausted, hunted, vibrating with a fear she tries desperately to rationalize away with logic.

Vargas is right. The math doesn't work.

I've been playing defense for days. Running. Hiding. Reacting. But Phoenix is an algorithm. It predicts reactions. To beat it, I need to introduce variables it can't calculate. I need chaos. I need precision. I need violence on a scale I can't manufacture alone.

"You got someplace we can go?" I need time to activate the pack.

"I've got another place, a secondary bolt-hole. It's shielded. No signals in or out unless you tap the hardline, but we gotta get there first."

The air grows thinner, hotter. Sweat slicks my skin under the tactical vest. Every step sends a fresh spike of fire through my bicep. I focus on Talia's back, on the rhythm of her boots on the wet stone.

Left, right. Breathe. Scan.

She stumbles over a loose brick.

I catch her before she hits the ground, my good arm wrapping around her waist, hauling her upright. She gasps, gripping my forearm, her fingers digging into the muscle.

"I've got you."

She doesn't pull away. She presses back against me, seeking the solidity of my chest. "I hate this. I hate the dark. I hate not knowing the variables."

"I know." I keep my arm around her, guiding her forward, refusing to let go. "Stay with me. I won't let you fall."

"Statistically, fatigue leads to error. Error leads to—"

"Talia." I put my lips right next to her ear. "Turn off the brain. Just move."

She nods, a jerky motion, and forces herself forward.

By the time we reach the iron ladder at the end of the tunnel, Vargas is dragging his bad leg. I boost Talia up first, watching until she clears the hatch, then help haul Vargas onto the landing.

We burst into the panadería's basement. The smell hits first—flour, yeast, and chemical cold from the freezer. A row of metal racks lines the wall, stacked with bags of sugar and industrial mixing bowls. Somewhere above, a rack rattles; flour dust drifts like ash.

Vargas moves to the far corner and punches a code into a hidden keypad. A section of shelving swings inward.

"Up those stairs," he says. "Keep your heads down."

We climb. The stairwell's tight, lit only by Vargas's flickering penlight. Above us, faint shouts filter through—the Phoenix teams closing the perimeter. Boots hit the roof. A radio squawks two words I can't make out. Doesn't matter. I know the cadence of a net tightening.

At the top, a heavy door. Vargas shoulders it open, revealing an alley bathed in darkness and the hum of distant sirens. Ozone hangs in the air—burned electronics, the scent of our past life going to ash.

He kills the light, peering up at the skyline. "They're sweeping east. We've got twenty seconds before they circle back."

Talia grips my sleeve. "Jackson—"

"I know." I scan the street, map exit routes, and calculate cover angles. We need wheels.

A delivery van sits idling across the street, rear doors open, driver nowhere in sight. Perfect.

I take her hand, squeeze once. "Run."

We sprint. Behind us, a muted detonation rumbles—the sound of Vargas burning what's left of his life's work. Sirens rise, echoing off brick and steel. A breeze rifles the alley, cold across sweat, lifting the edge of Talia's borrowed shirt. She's breathing hard, controlled. No panic. Pure will.

We don't look back.

Across the street. Into the van's shadow. I boost her up by the hips; she swings into the passenger seat, slides across, and makes room for me. I drop behind the wheel.

"Go." Vargas climbs into the back, slams the rear doors, his breath ragged.

Headlights off. Gear engaged. We roll in darkness.

Two blocks, three. I keep our speed just under suspicion, eyes slicing through mirrors and the windshield. Overhead, a faint, insectile whir—too steady to be urban noise.

"Drone," Vargas says from the back, voice flat. "Thermal micro. Civilian shell, military guts."

"Got an EMP?" I ask.

"You know it. Short pulse only," he replies. "Anything bigger blacks out half the block and puts our location on every dashboard."

"On my mark."

I cut left under a narrow trestle, metal girders strobing shadow over the windshield. The whir deepens, searching. Talia's gaze presses against my profile—steadying me and unsteadying me at the same time.

"Now," I say.

Vargas pops the rear doors an inch. A low thump. White fizz cracks across the night like lightning bottled wrong. The whir hiccups, stutters, dies. The drone pinwheels into a trash-strewn gutter behind us, a small, expensive idea coming apart.

"Nice," Talia murmurs, breathless.

"Don't celebrate," Vargas says. "Overwatch still has eyes."

I cut another block, then two. Sirens converge somewhere to the east. Phoenix is herding us—gentle pressure, invisible hands. We need to slip the pattern.

"We're just delivery people," I say. "We're nobody." As if my thoughts could convince an autonomous AI.

Talia watches the side mirror like it's a threat. The exact moment her pulse begins to steady registers in the reset of her shoulders, the lift of her chin. That iron in her spine makes me want to pull her closer and never let her out of arm's reach.

"Left up here," Vargas calls, checking a cracked phone running an offline map. "Cut through the industrial. Fewer cameras."

I take it. The street opens into a strip of shuttered warehouses and chain-link fences topped with lazy coils of razor wire. Sodium lights buzz. A stray dog trots across our path, unconcerned. The van's engine hums low, the night breathing around us.

"We need to change vehicles," I say. "Soon."

"Two blocks ahead," Vargas says. "Auto salvage yard. Owner leaves keys in the night-shift runners. He's old school and careless."

"Perfect," I murmur.

We roll past a blown-out billboard, then another. The yard looms—wide, fenced, slit of chain at the gate. I ease the van inside, and coast to a stop between two stacks of crushed sedans. The air smells like rust and oil and old heat.

We listen.

Distant sirens. No immediate footfall.

"Out," I say quietly. "Fast, clean."

Talia moves first, sliding down from the van, landing softly. I'm right behind, hand at the small of her back, guiding her shadow-tight along the aisle of stacked cars. Vargas ghosts after us, his limp barely a drag when fear is doing the lifting.

Keys glint in the ignition of a dented sedan. I test the handle; it opens with a tired sigh. The engine turns on the second try. The dashboard glows a sickly green.

"Switch," I say.

We trade vehicles in under ten seconds. The van sits cooling, door cracked, a decoy in the making. I pull the sedan out slowly, nose first, then angle us toward the rear gate.

"Hold." Vargas watches the sky through the rear window, listening with his whole body. "They're sweeping west now. Wait for the handoff."

I do. Talia's thigh presses against mine, unintentional, heat radiating through denim. I don't move. Can't. The closeness steadies me and threatens to undo me in the same breath.

"Now," he says.

FIFTEEN

Jackson

RECALIBRATING

I ROLL OUT. THE SEDAN BLENDS BETTER—NO SHINE, NO STORY. We take a back street, then another. City blocks slide past in muted colors. The noose loosens. That's the trick with nets—you don't fight them head-on; you let them move, and you slip between the knots.

Two turns later, the sirens thin. The air opens.

I let out a breath. Talia does the same. Our exhale syncs, and something in my chest goes strange and fierce.

"You okay?" I ask, not taking my eyes off the road.

A beat. "Better when you're touching me," she says, so quiet I almost miss it.

My hand tightens on the wheel. I don't answer. Can't. I reach anyway, find her waist, anchor her there, thumb brushing the edge of her borrowed shirt. She leans a fraction into it—small, deliberate, a decision with teeth.

Vargas clears his throat in the back. "Don't get comfortable. Phoenix recalculates. Always."

"Yeah," I say. "So do I."

We slide through a corridor of sleeping brick and glass. The city pretends it doesn't see us. I let it. Three more turns and we're a ghost version of ourselves—same occupants, new skin.

"Next move?" Talia asks, steady again, eyes on the dark ahead as if she can will it to make room.

"Nexus," I say. "But not directly. Gear, med supplies, new plates." I check the mirror. Clean. "We hit them when they expect us least."

Vargas shifts, the lead-lined pouch thumping softly against his chest.

"And we give your 'Root Seed' a chance to matter," I add.

"It'll matter," he says. "Or we die busy."

"Not on my list," I tell him.

I take the next corner—and freeze—the motion a millimeter from completion. Instinct. A shadow on the roofline. Not movement—absence. A space too still in a city that always twitches.

"Hold," I whisper.

Talia's fingers tighten around my forearm. She doesn't ask. She feels it too.

We sit in the hush. Three heartbeats. Four.

A red dot blooms and slides across the sedan's hood like a lazy firefly deciding where to land.

Talia's breath stutters. Vargas swears under his.

"Laser designator." His voice is rough.

The dot crawls toward the windshield.

"Down," I breathe.

We drop. The dot pauses, searching.

A heartbeat passes. Two. The red eye hovers on the dashboard, patient as death.

"Vargas." My voice barely disturbs the air. "Tell me you have another EMP."

"Last one. Shorter range."

"Range to that rooftop?"

"Pushing it. Maybe forty meters effective."

The dot slides left, probing the driver's seat headrest. Whoever's behind that scope has discipline—no rush, no wasted motion. Professional.

"On three," I say. "You pop the charge, I floor it. We've got maybe two seconds before they recalibrate."

"That's not—"

"It's what we've got."

Talia's hand finds mine in the dark. Her pulse hammers against my palm—rapid but steady. Fear she refuses to let win.

"One."

Vargas eases the EMP from his pack, thumb finding the activation switch.

"Two."

The dot settles on the windshield, center mass. Whoever's up there just made their decision.

"Three."

He snaps his arm up, hurling the charge through the cracked rear window. I slam the accelerator before it clears the frame.

The sedan lurches forward. Tires scream against asphalt.

White light flashes behind us—not the clean crack of the first EMP but something rawer, more desperate. The charge didn't reach optimal altitude. Doesn't matter. For one stuttering second, every electronic system within thirty meters goes blind.

Including the laser designator.

I cut hard right, threading between two shipping containers. The sedan's frame groans. Talia braces against the dash. Vargas slams into the rear seat partition.

Behind us, nothing. No shot. No pursuit vehicle. Just the hum of a city that doesn't know how close three people just came to dying.

I don't slow down.

Four blocks. Five. The industrial district gives way to residential row houses with dark windows, parked cars covered in morning dew.

Normal. Safe.

The kind of neighborhood that doesn't know what stalks its streets.

"We're clear," I finally say. "For now."

I ease off the accelerator. My arm throbs where the wound pulled during our escape. Blood seeps through the bandage—warmth spreading.

Doesn't matter. I'll deal with it later.

Vargas leans forward between the seats. "My secondary site. Industrial district, South Side. Bought it through shell companies years ago—three different layers of corporate bullshit. Phoenix doesn't know it exists."

"Lead the way."

The secondary safe house is grim—a concrete box buried beneath a defunct bakery. MREs stack in the corner alongside dusty cots, a single lightbulb hanging from a wire, and a secure comms terminal on a metal desk. It's cold, damp, and smells of yeast and old dust.

But it's fortified.

Vargas collapses onto a crate, groaning as he rubs his knee. "I'm done, Fuse. The leg's shot. I can build the bomb, but I can't carry it. I'm not the operator I used to be."

I check the door. Three deadbolts. Reinforced steel frame. Secure.

I holster my weapon and turn to Talia.

She has slumped against the far wall, sliding down until she hits the concrete floor. Her knees are pulled to her chest, arms wrapped tight around her shins. Shivering. The adrenaline crash hits her hard.

I cross the room in three strides and crouch in front of her.

"Talia."

She looks up. Her eyes are wide, glassy. "We're trapped. They have too many resources. The probability of escape is—"

"Hey." I reach out, cupping her face with my good hand. Her skin is ice cold. "Look at me."

Her gaze locks onto mine.

"We're safe here. For now."

"For now isn't a strategy." Her teeth chatter. "It's a delay."

I move closer, settling onto the floor beside her. I pull her into me, tucking her against my side, wrapping my good arm around her shoulders. She stays stiff for a second, vibrating with tension, and then she collapses. All the fight goes out of her at once. She buries her face in my neck, her hands clutching the front of my vest.

"I'm cold."

"I've got you." I rub her arm, generating friction, sharing heat. "I've got you."

She smells of dust and ozone and vanilla. Even here, covered in the grime of the underground, she smells like something worth saving.

"My arm," I murmur, shifting slightly so the wound doesn't press against her.

She pulls back instantly, eyes dropping to the blood-soaked bandage. "You're bleeding again. I need to check it. I need to—"

"It's functional." The word slips out, automatic. My shield.

She freezes. Her eyes search mine, reading the lie. "No. You use that word when you don't want anyone to know you're hurt. You use it when you're trying to turn yourself into a machine." Her fingers ghost over the bandage. "You're not a machine, Jackson. You're bleeding."

"I'll survive."

"That's not the standard." She leans her forehead against my shoulder. "Surviving isn't the same as living."

She's right. She's always right.

I rest my chin on top of her head, closing my eyes for a second. The weight of her against me grounds the room. It stops the spinning.

"Vargas is right."

"About what?"

"The math. It doesn't work. Two people against an army."

She pulls back enough to look at me. "So what do we do? The kill switch is useless if we can't get it to the server."

"We change the equation."

I gently untangle myself from her and stand. The loss of her warmth is immediate, a physical ache. I walk to the metal desk and reach into my tactical vest, pulling out the satellite phone.

"Who are you calling?" Talia wraps her arms around herself, the shivering returning.

I power on the phone. The screen glows green as it searches for a satellite lock in the concrete bunker. One bar. Two.

"Family."

I punch in the number. It rings once. Twice.

A click.

Then a voice, deep, calm, and familiar as my own heartbeat.

"Report." The single word carries a demand for everything—health, location, and status of the package.

The sound of Ghost's voice settles my pulse instantly. The tension in my shoulders drops an inch.

"Compromised." I look at Talia, then back at the phone. "I need the pack."

Silence on the line.

"Explain."

"Talia found something. It's not corporate corruption." I look at her. She watches me, eyes sharp, listening. "It's Phoenix."

A pause. Long and heavy. Ghost knows Phoenix. We all do. We've been hunting it. Or it's been hunting us.

"Copy that." Ghost's voice drops an octave.

"Talia's source verified it, and we've since connected it to a conglomerate called Nexus Holdings. It's protecting Phoenix."

"What's your status?"

"I'm with Vargas."

"Vargas?" Ghost recognizes the name. "I thought he retired to a cabin in Montana."

"He didn't. He's here. He has hardware. A Root Seed from the original build. It's a kill switch. We can burn the program down."

"If you can deliver it."

"I can't." I admit the weakness. It tastes bitter, but it's the truth. "Not alone. I'm wounded. Vargas is combat ineffective. We're cornered in a bolt-hole in Pilsen. They have numbers, tech, and they're scrubbing the board."

"Are you safe?"

"For the moment."

"Hold position. We were monitoring chatter. We knew something blew in Chicago. We're already wheels up."

"ETA?"

"Soon. Torque is flying like a maniac. Send your location and keep your head down."

"Roger that."

The line goes dead.

I lower the phone. The green light fades.

"Was that Ghost?" Vargas watches me from his crate, a shark-like grin spreading across his dusty face.

"Yeah."

"Good." He stands, testing his weight on his bad leg. "Because I'm too old to die in a basement."

I turn back to Talia. She's standing now, the fear in her eyes replaced by calculation. She understands what I've just done. I've brought my world into hers.

"Your team?" she asks.

"My team." I move back to her, my hand finding the back of her neck again. "We're done running. Now we hunt."

She takes a breath, steadying herself. "What do I need to do?"

"Get your data ready. Because when they get here, we're going to plan a war."

She nods. She doesn't ask if they are good. She doesn't ask if they can win. She just trusts me.

"Okay." She wipes a smudge of dirt from her cheek. "Let's burn it down."

SIXTEEN

Talia

THE PACK

THE INDUSTRIAL WAREHOUSE SITS ON THE EDGE OF THE SOUTH Side like a rusted iron lung, breathing cold drafts and the smell of decades-old grease. Vargas's "secondary site" is less a safe house and more a graveyard for Cold War-era tech and structural paranoia.

I sit on a crate of MREs, knees pulled to my chest, watching Jackson.

He paces the concrete floor. Three steps north. Turn. Three steps south. Turn. His energy has shifted. So far, he's been a shield—a singular force standing between me and death. Now, he vibrates with a different frequency.

Anticipation.

The lone wolf waiting for the pack.

Vargas hunches over a workbench in the corner, soldering something that looks alarmingly like a detonator. "Stop pacing, Fuse. You're vibrating the floorboards."

"They're close." Jackson checks his watch. "Torque makes good time."

"Torque flies like he has a death wish."

"He does."

A sound outside. Not a siren. Not a car engine.

The *thrum-thrum-thrum* of rotors cutting through heavy air.

Jackson stops pacing. "Roof."

He moves to the freight elevator—a caged beast of a lift—and hits the button. I follow, weapon drawn, though Jackson doesn't seem worried. His shoulders have dropped an inch. His breathing has deepened.

The elevator rattles upward, chains groaning. We emerge onto the roof just as a black shape blots out the stars.

The helicopter is unlit, a shadow against the Chicago light pollution. It flares hard, nose up, dropping fast toward the reinforced roof deck. The downdraft hits us, whipping my hair across my face, stinging my eyes with grit.

The skids touch down with a metallic screech that sets my teeth on edge.

The side door slides open.

Five men spill out. They move like water—fluid, synchronized, covering angles I hadn't even identified as threats. I press my back against the elevator housing, gripping my Glock, cataloging them as they deploy.

The first one out has to be the leader. Tall. Imposing. Even in the dark, he radiates a gravitational pull. He scans the perimeter once, effectively owning the space, then strides toward Jackson.

Next, a man with the build of a linebacker but the grace of a dancer. He carries a heavy pack like it's filled with feathers, his head swiveling, checking the horizon.

A smaller, wiry figure jumps out next, holding a tablet, grinning like he's at a tailgate party instead of a clandestine insertion. He taps the screen, seemingly bored by the tactical insertion.

The pilot kills the rotors and leaps from the cockpit, landing with a reckless bounce. He stretches, cracking his neck.

I count four.

Where is—

Movement in the periphery. A shadow detaches itself from the AC unit near the roof access. I gasp, raising my Glock.

"Easy," Jackson says, his hand covering mine, lowering the barrel. "That's Whisper."

I stare. I never saw him exit the bird. He simply materialized in the optimal overwatch position.

The team converges. No salutes. No formal greetings. Just a series of forearm clasps and nods that convey volumes of history.

"You look like hell, Fuse," the pilot says, clapping Jackson on the non-injured shoulder. He eyes the blood-soaked bandage. "What'd you do, try to catch a round with your teeth?"

"Bullet extraction," Jackson says. "Field conditions."

"Sloppy."

"Effective."

The leader steps forward. The group falls silent. His gaze flicks to me—analyzing, assessing, cataloging. I feel like I'm being scanned by an X-ray machine, but there's no hostility in it. Just calculation.

"Let's get inside," he says. His voice is deep, resonant. "We're exposed."

We descend into the warehouse. The dynamic in the room shifts instantly. It shrinks. Six large, dangerous men fill the space with kinetic energy. They start unpacking gear before anyone gives an order—laptops, weapons cases, tactical maps. It's a hive mind. Efficient. Terrifying.

Jackson guides me toward the leader. "Talia, this is Mason Blackwood. Call sign Ghost."

Ghost extends a hand. He doesn't treat me like a package or a liability. He treats me like a variable he needs to solve. "Ms. Singh. Apologies for the dramatic entrance. Fuse tells us you've had a rough few days."

"That's an understatement," I say, taking his hand. His grip is dry, firm.

"This is Ryan Ellis," Jackson continues, pointing to the linebacker. "Brass. He handles intel and comms."

Brass nods, already setting up a satellite link on a portable table. "Ma'am."

"Diego Martinez. Halo." Jackson points to the wiry one with the tablet.

Halo waves without looking up from his screen. "Hi. Don't touch my stuff."

"Cooper Hayes. Whisper." Jackson gestures to the shadow in the corner, who has already started disassembling a long-range rifle. Whisper just blinks.

"And Levi Durant. Torque."

The pilot grins, spinning a set of keys on his finger. "The one who gets us out of trouble when Fuse blows something up."

"Welcome to the circus," Ghost says. He turns to the workbench. "And you must be Vargas."

Vargas stands by his workbench, leaning on his cane, watching the invasion of his sanctuary with a mixture of annoyance and respect. "You brought a lot of noise to my quiet neighborhood, Blackwood."

"We brought a solution." Ghost gestures to the table. "Let's brief the op."

Halo drifts toward Vargas's tech setup. He picks up the Root Seed drive and turns the titanium brick over in his hands. "Proprietary port. High-voltage capacitors. Vacuum tube shielding? This is a dinosaur."

"It's a bullet," Vargas growls, snatching it back. "For a digital brain. It works because it's not connected to your cloud-based garbage."

Halo raises an eyebrow, looking at the soldering work. "Analog bridge to bypass the digital handshake. That's—actually brilliant." He looks at Vargas with new respect. "You're the hardware architect."

"I built the cage," Vargas says. "You're the kid who writes the ghosts."

"Game recognizes game," Torque mutters, opening a crate of MREs. "Great. Now there's two of them."

"Focus," Ghost barks. He clears a table in the center of the room. "Fuse. Sitrep. We know Phoenix is active. What's the new intel?"

Jackson steps up. "It's not just rogue AI. It's corporate. Talia found the link."

All eyes turn to me. The weight of their attention is heavy, physical. These are men who deal in violence, and I deal in data. I take a breath, stepping forward. I don't cower. I place Jackson's laptop on the table and connect to Halo's localized network.

"Nexus Holdings," I say. "It's a conglomerate. Five major subsidiaries across pharma, defense, and energy. My risk assessments flagged anomalies in their regulatory approvals. Every time they hit a roadblock—a safety inspector, a whistleblower, a competitor—that roadblock died."

"Accidents?" Brass asks, studying the screen.

"Statistically improbable accidents," I correct. "Heart attacks at forty. Car crashes on empty roads. Suicides with no notes. Phoenix isn't just surviving; it's an enforcement arm. It eliminates oversight to maximize profit margins."

"So we have a target," Ghost says. "Nexus HQ."

"It's a vault," Jackson says. "Subbasement server farm. Airgapped. We can't hack it from the outside."

"Which means we walk it in," Ghost says. He looks at the Root Seed. "We plug that brick into the main terminal, and it fries the logic cores. Hard reset."

"Into a building anticipating an attack," Brass adds. "Suicide."

"Tuesday," Torque quips, tearing open a packet of crackers.

I look at him. "Tuesday?"

"Means it's just another day ending in Y," Jackson murmurs near my ear. "Normal crazy."

Ghost studies the map. "We can't hit them tonight. We're coming in hot, Fuse is bleeding, and we need to recon the perimeter."

"They know we're here," Jackson says. "They're scrubbing the board."

"Then we go tomorrow night. 0200 hours. That gives us twenty-four hours to prep, heal up, and plan the breach." Ghost's voice brooks no argument. "Torque, secure the perimeter. Whisper, roof. Brass, start building a comms network that Phoenix can't crack. Halo, work with Vargas on interfacing that brick with our systems."

"And Fuse?" Torque asks, pointing a cracker at Jackson. "He looks like he's about five minutes from passing out."

"Fuse is down," Ghost says. "Medical. Now."

Jackson opens his mouth to argue.

"That's an order," Ghost says softly. "You're no good to me dead, and you're no good to her if you can't lift your rifle."

Jackson's jaw tightens, but he nods. "Copy that."

The team disperses. The efficiency is terrifying. They move like parts of a single machine.

I guide Jackson to a cot in the corner of the warehouse, away from the main activity. He sits heavily, the adrenaline finally leaving him, replaced by the gray pallor of exhaustion.

"Shirt off," I say.

He grunts, peeling the tactical vest and the blood-stiffened shirt away. The bandage I applied is soaked through.

"Torque was right," I whisper, peeling back the gauze. "It's a mess."

"It's not infected."

"The stitches tore."

I open the Cerberus medical kit Brass dropped off. It's better than what we had. Real sutures, medical-grade glue, and antibiotics.

"This is going to hurt."

"Do your worst."

I clean the wound. He doesn't flinch, but his muscles jump under my skin. I apply the glue, pinching the ragged edges together, then reinforce it with the butterflies. It's ugly, but it will hold.

"You good at everything you do?" Jackson asks, his voice rough.

"I learn fast." I wrap a fresh compression bandage around his bicep. "There."

Across the room, Torque and Whisper are cleaning weapons. I catch them watching us. Torque nudges Whisper, murmuring something. Whisper smirks.

"Ignore them," Jackson says, following my gaze. "They're children."

"They're your family."

"Yeah. They are." He catches my hand. "You stood your ground with Ghost."

"Was I supposed to be scared?"

"Most people are." He runs his thumb over my knuckles. "You fit in here. Better than you think."

"I'm an analyst. You guys are—"

"Kinetic," he finishes. "But we need the brain. You saw it. Halo respects the code. Ghost respects the intel. You're not just a package to them."

"And to you?"

His eyes darken. "You know what you are to me."

"Hey, lovebirds," Torque calls out. "Ghost said rest, not romance. Keep the heartrate down."

Jackson flips him off without looking away from me. "Get some sleep. We have a war to plan tomorrow."

I nod. I curl up on the adjacent cot, pulling a wool blanket over me. The sounds of the warehouse—the tap of Halo's keyboard, the low murmur of Brass and Ghost discussing tactics, the *snick-snick* of Whisper's rifle bolt—should keep me awake. Instead, they act as a lullaby. A perimeter of violence keeping the world at bay.

For the first time in days, I close my eyes, and I don't see the black SUV mowing Victor down.

I see Jackson standing between me and the darkness.

The next twenty-four hours blur into a montage of preparation.

Halo and Vargas argue over voltage requirements. Brass builds a 3D holographic map of the Nexus building using blueprints I pulled from the city archives. Torque acquires a nondescript delivery van and a high-speed interceptor, tinkering with the engines until they purr with unnatural power.

I spend the time with Ghost and Brass, refining the target package.

"The server room is here," I point to the hologram. "Sub-basement three. Single access point."

"Fatal funnel," Brass mutters. "One way in, one way out. If they pin you down there, it's over."

"We need a diversion," Jackson says. He's rested, moving better, though he still guards his left arm. "Something massive at the front gate. Pull their eyes."

"I can blow the substation," Torque offers. "Kill the grid. Halo loops the cameras."

"I need to be in the room," I say.

Ghost looks at me. "Halo can run the script remotely once we plug in."

"No." I shake my head. "The Root Seed is a brute-force

weapon. But we also need to know *who* is giving the orders. I need to be at the terminal to trace the command line back to the source while the Seed uploads. Halo can't do both."

"She's right," Jackson says. "I take her in. I breach the door; she handles the data."

"You're compromised," Ghost says. "Brass should take the point."

"She's my principal." Jackson's voice drops, hard and flat. "Nobody guards her but me."

The room goes silent. The guys exchange looks. Torque grins. Brass shakes his head.

Ghost studies Jackson for a long beat. "Compromised," he repeats softly. But there's no judgment in it. Just acknowledgment. "Fine. Fuse and Singh on infiltration. Torque, extraction. Whisper, high ground. Halo, cyber overwatch. Brass and I take the front door and make noise."

"How much noise?" Brass asks.

Ghost smiles. It's a terrifying expression. "All of it."

2200 Hours.

We gear up.

The transformation is absolute. The joking stops. The banter dies. They pull on tactical vests, check comms, and load magazines with efficient, jerky movements.

They become machines.

Jackson hands me a vest. "Put this on. Ceramic plates. Heavy, but it stops a rifle round."

I pull it over my head and strap it tight. "I feel like a turtle."

"A bulletproof turtle." He hands me my Glock, cleaned and oiled. "Stay behind me. If I say move, you move. If I say run, you run. Do not hesitate."

"I won't."

"Mount up," Ghost orders.

We file out to the loading dock. The night air is cool and damp. The city lights of Chicago reflect off the low clouds in an orange haze.

I climb into the back of the blacked-out SUV with Jackson. Whisper takes the front. Halo sets up his mobile command center in the third row.

The convoy rolls out. Torque leads in the van.

"Comms check," Ghost says.

"Brass, green."

"Halo, green."

"Whisper, green."

"Torque, green."

"Fuse, green."

I tap my earpiece. "Singh, green."

"Two miles to target," Halo says from the back. "Nexus grid is active. They've reinforced the perimeter. I'm reading thermal signatures on the roof and in the lobby. They're expecting trouble."

"They're expecting an intrusion," Jackson says, his hand finding mine in the dark. "They aren't expecting an assault."

"Approaching the substation," Torque says. "Charges set. Waiting on your mark."

"Hold," Ghost commands. "Wait for Fuse to be in position."

We park three blocks out. The street is empty. The Nexus tower looms ahead, a monolith of black glass. It looks impenetrable.

Jackson checks his gear one last time. He looks at me. "Ready?"

"No."

"Good." He squeezes my hand. "Let's go."

"Fuse in position," Jackson says into the comms. "Rear service entrance."

"Copy," Ghost says. "Torque. Light it up."

A massive flash of blue light splits the sky to the north. The substation blows. A second later, the boom rattles the windows of the SUV.

The streetlights die. The Nexus tower goes dark against the skyline, a black monolith swallowed by the night.

"Power down," Halo says. "Generators kicking in … Three … Two … One. Cameras are looped. You have a sixty-second window to breach."

"Go," Jackson says.

We burst out of the SUV, sprinting across the wet pavement toward the service door. The air smells of ozone and impending rain. My boots slap against the concrete, loud in my own ears, but swallowed by the chaos of the city reacting to the blackout.

Jackson reaches the door first. He raises his leg to kick, but the door swings open from the inside.

Three men spill out. Not security guards. Hard targets. Phoenix operatives in tactical gear, confused by the blackout, but weapons raised.

The lead operative slams into Jackson. They go down in a tangle of limbs and swearing.

The second man swings his rifle toward me.

I freeze.

The third man—huge, a wall of muscle—lunges. He grabs my vest, spinning me around, slamming my back against the brick wall. The wind leaves my lungs in a rush. Cold steel presses against my temple.

"Drop it!" he screams at Jackson. "Drop it or she dies!"

Jackson freezes. He has the first man in a chokehold, his knife poised to sever an artery. He looks up. His eyes lock on the gun pressed to my head.

He releases the man on the ground. Slowly stands. His hands go up, palms open.

"Easy," Jackson says. His voice is terrifyingly calm. "Let her go."

"Kick the gun away," the man holding me commands. "Now!"

Jackson kicks his Glock across the pavement. It skitters into the dark.

"On your knees. Hands behind your head."

Jackson sinks to his knees. But his eyes never leave the man holding me. They aren't the eyes of a man surrendering. They are the eyes of a man calculating the trajectory of a kill.

"You're making a mistake," Jackson says softly.

"Shut up." The man tightens his grip on my throat. "Secure him."

The operative on the ground scrambles up, reaching for zip ties. The second man keeps his rifle trained on Jackson's chest.

"I'm going to give you one chance," Jackson says. "Let her go, and you walk away."

The man holding me laughs. A wet, nervous sound. "I'm holding the gun, asshole. I make the rules."

"Fine," Jackson says. "It's your funeral."

The movement is a blur.

Jackson doesn't lunge at the men standing over him. He drops flat, sweeping the leg of the man with the zip ties. The man hits the pavement hard.

The rifleman panics, swinging his weapon down.

Jackson rolls, coming up inside the rifleman's guard. He drives a knife—one I didn't see him draw—up under the man's chin.

A gurgle. A spray of dark fluid.

The man holding me flinches. His grip loosens for a microsecond.

Partners make tactical decisions.

I don't wait for Jackson to save me. I stomp my heel down on the man's instep, putting all my weight into the blow.

He grunts, distracting him.

I drop my weight, twisting away from the gun barrel just like Jackson showed me in the safe house. The gun goes off—a deafening crack right next to my ear. The muzzle flash blinds me.

But I'm free.

I stumble back, raising my Glock.

The man swings his weapon back toward me, rage twisting his face.

"No!" Jackson roars.

He hurls the knife. It catches the man in the shoulder, burying to the hilt. The man screams, dropping his gun, clutching the wound.

Jackson is on him in a heartbeat. He tackles him into the brick wall. The sound of the impact is sickening. Jackson doesn't stop. He strikes—once, twice, three times—brutal, efficient blows that silence the scream.

The man slides down the wall. He doesn't get up.

Silence crashes back into the alley.

Jackson stands over the body, chest heaving. He wipes blood from his face—not his own. He turns to me.

"Check in," he rasps.

I holster my weapon with shaking hands. "I'm—I'm functional."

He crosses the distance between us, grabbing my shoulders, his eyes scanning me for holes. "He fired. Did he hit you?"

"Missed. I stomped his foot."

A savage grin breaks through the blood on his face. "That's my girl."

"Fuse, sitrep!" Ghost's voice barks in my ear. *"We heard shots."*

"Contact," Jackson says, touching his comms. "Three hostiles down. We are green."

"Move your ass," Ghost says. *"You just woke up the whole building."*

Jackson retrieves his Glock and his knife. He wipes the blade on the dead man's tactical vest.

"Ready?" he asks me.

I look at the three bodies. The violence is real now. Visceral. But my hands aren't shaking.

"Ready."

He hits the mag-lock release on the service door. It disengages with a heavy clunk.

He pulls the door open. Darkness stretches out before us, a long corridor leading into the belly of the beast.

"Stay close," he says. "We're walking into a trap."

"I know." I step up beside him, weapon drawn.

We cross the threshold. The heavy steel door slams shut behind us, sealing us in.

We are inside.

SEVENTEEN

Jackson

FATAL FUNNEL

THE HEAVY STEEL DOOR SLAMS SHUT BEHIND US, ENGAGING WITH a mechanical thud that vibrates through the soles of my boots. The lock cycles.

A prison cell sound.

We're inside.

The service corridor stretches out, a long throat of gray concrete and fluorescent hum. The air is recycled, sterile, and chilled to preserve the servers below. It smells of ozone and floor wax, a sharp contrast to the copper tang of blood still coating my knuckles.

My hands shake. Just a tremor.

Not fear.

Rage.

The image replays on a loop, superimposed over the gray walls: *The barrel of the gun pressed against Talia's temple. The indentation of the metal in her skin. The way her eyes went wide, not with panic, but with calculation.*

If I had been a split second slower.

If the knife had slipped.

The beast inside my chest, the one I keep chained with discipline and mission parameters, rattles the bars. It wants to turn around, open that door, and tear the corpse in the alley apart until there's nothing left to identify.

"Jackson?"

Talia's voice cuts the loop.

Soft. Grounding.

I turn. She's standing three feet away, weapon drawn, eyes scanning the junction ahead. She's covered in grime, her hair escaping the bun she tied earlier, a smudge of oil on her cheek.

She is the only clean thing in this world.

"We move," I rasp. "Subbasement three. The heart of the beast."

The silence of the corridor vanishes, replaced by the chaotic symphony of war.

"*—breaching front glass,*" Ghost's voice is a calm baritone amidst a cacophony of shattering glass. "*Brass, flush the right flank.*"

"*On it,*" Brass replies. A heavy *thump-thump-thump* of suppressed rifle fire follows. "*Ugly statue in the lobby. Post-modern garbage.*"

A massive boom echoes through the comms—a frag grenade.

"*Fixed it,*" Brass says. "*Lobby is clear. Elevators are locked down. We're drawing every guard in the building to the ground floor.*"

"*Torque,*" Ghost commands. "*Status?*"

"*Holding pattern,*" Torque's voice fights over the roar of an engine. "*I've got a drone swarm trying to flank me on the north side. I'm playing tag. They're losing.*"

"*Whisper?*"

"*Roof is clear,*" the sniper's voice is dry, detached. "*I have eyes on the executive elevator. Heat signatures moving down. Three squads. They aren't taking the bait in the lobby. They're heading sub-surface.*"

They're coming for us.

"Keep it loud," I say into the channel. "We're in the service pipe. Heading down."

"Copy, Fuse," Ghost says. *"Don't keep the lady waiting."*

I look at Talia. "They're making noise. We're the ghosts."

"Lead the way."

We move. I take point, weapon shouldered, moving with the rolling gait that keeps the upper body steady. Every corner is a potential ambush. Every shadow is a threat. The schematic of the building burns in my mind—a 3D map of fatal funnels and choke points.

We descend a ramp. The air gets colder. The hum of the building grows louder, a low-frequency vibration that rattles the teeth.

Footsteps ahead. Scuffing rubber on concrete. Not the rhythmic march of a patrol. The shuffling gait of civilians.

I hold up a fist. *Stop.*

Talia freezes instantly, melting into the shadow of a large support pillar. I press myself against the opposite wall, weapon tight to my chest.

Two men in gray coveralls round the corner, pushing a cart loaded with cleaning supplies. They're arguing about overtime pay, oblivious to the war above them.

They pass within five feet of us.

My finger rests on the trigger guard. If they turn … If they see us …

The compulsion to neutralize the threat spikes. A quick double-tap. No witnesses.

Talia's gaze burns into the side of my face. I can feel her watching my hand. For her, I won't kill them—lucky fucks don't know they get to live because I care what she thinks about me.

The maintenance crew continues past, their voices fading down the hall.

I let out a breath, but the tension in my shoulders remains, a coiled spring.

"Clear," I whisper.

We press on. The corridor ends at a heavy blast door marked **RESTRICTED ACCESS: AUTHORIZED PERSONNEL ONLY**. A keypad glows red next to a biometric scanner.

"Halo," I mutter. "Door. Level B1 junction."

"Working," Halo's voice comes back, strained. The sound of rapid typing filters through the line. *"Encryption is heavy down there. Give me ten."*

"We don't have ten."

"I can't magic a keycard, Fuse. The system is fighting me."

I look at the door. Reinforced steel core. Magnetic seals.

"Never mind." I holster my Glock and reach into my pack. "I'm knocking."

Talia watches as I pull out a roll of Flex-Linear Charge. It looks like harmless putty tape.

It's not.

"You're breaching?" she asks.

"Whisper silent." I strip the backing and apply the tape along the hinges and the locking mechanism. "It cuts, doesn't push. Minimal overpressure."

"Will they hear it upstairs?"

"They won't hear it over Brass remodeling the lobby."

I press a detonator cap into the putty. "Cover your ears. Keep your mouth open."

She steps back, turning away, hands over her ears. I shield her with my body, thumb hovering over the clacker.

Three. Two. One.

Snap.

The sound is sharp, like a dry branch breaking, but contained. A flash of white light outlines the door frame. Smoke hisses from the hinges.

The heavy steel slab groans, tilting inward, no longer anchored to the frame.

I kick it.

The door falls with a heavy clang, echoing loudly in the confined space. I surge through the gap, weapon sweeping the room.

Clear. Just pipes and conduits. A transition space before the subbasement elevators.

"Move," I order.

Talia steps over the ruined door. She glances at the melted steel edges, then at me. "Efficient, but noisy."

"It's what I do."

We reach the service elevator bank. Two cars. Old industrial lifts with scissor gates and solid doors. I hit the call button. The light flickers. The gears grind somewhere above us.

"It's slow," Talia says, checking her watch. "Too slow."

"It's the only way down without rappelling the shaft."

The car arrives with a shudder. The doors slide open.

We step inside. I hit the button for **B3**. The doors close, sealing us in a metal box that smells of grease and stagnant air. The car descends, rattling in the shaft.

For the first time in twenty minutes, we aren't moving. We aren't fighting. We're just standing in a descending cage.

I look at her. The adrenaline sheen on her skin. The way her chest rises and falls beneath the tactical vest. The blood—not hers—speckled on her boots.

"You stomped him." The image won't leave my head. Talia, driving her heel into the operative's foot. The crunch of bone.

She stares at the floor numbers ticking down. **B1** ... **B2** ...

"He was an obstacle." Her voice is flat. Monotone. "He had leverage. I removed the leverage."

"You could have run. When I tackled him. You had a clear line."

"Partners don't run." She finally looks at me. Her eyes are dry, hard. The golden flecks seem sharper, colder. "You calculate threat vectors. I calculate outcomes. The outcome where I leave you behind had a zero percent success rate for the mission."

"Is that all it is? The mission?"

"It's the variable we control."

She's retreating. Going into the data. Dissociating to handle the violence she just participated in. I recognize the look. I've seen it in mirrors for years.

It terrifies me.

"Talia."

I reach out, hitting the emergency stop.

The elevator jerks to a halt between floors. The silence rushes back in, heavy and suffocating.

She blinks, the analyst mask slipping. "What are you doing? We have a timeline."

"Screw the timeline." I step into her space. I need to break the shell before she hardens into something she can't come back from. "Look at me."

She looks up. Her lip trembles, just once. A crack in the armor.

"I killed those men," I say. "But you … You stepped into the fire. You didn't freeze."

"I had to."

"No. You chose to." I cup her face, my thumbs stroking the grime from her cheekbones. My hands are rough, stained with violence, but she leans into them. "You aren't just an analyst anymore. You're a warrior. But don't lose yourself in the math. Don't turn off the part of you that feels it."

"If I feel it," she whispers, her voice cracking, "I'll scream."

"Then scream later. Right now, just feel *this*."

I crash my mouth onto hers.

It's not gentle. It's not sweet. It's desperation and blood and the metallic taste of fear. I kiss her like I'm trying to breathe for her. I kiss her like it's the last thing I'll ever do.

She makes a sound in her throat—half sob, half moan—and grips my vest, pulling me closer. Her body presses against mine, the hard ceramic plates of our armor clacking together, a barrier we can't remove. I want to strip it off. I want to feel her skin. I want to know she's alive in every nerve ending.

If I die in this basement … If the bullets find me … I want this to be the last input. Not the noise of gunfire. Not the smell of cordite. This.

Her taste. Her heat.

I break the kiss, resting my forehead against hers. We're both panting, breathing the same recycled air.

"If we don't walk out of here," I say, my voice rough, "know that you were the best thing. The only thing that matters to me."

"We're going to walk out of here." Her eyes are fierce now. The cold logic is gone, replaced by fire. "The probability is low, but we'll adjust the variables and walk out of here together. You'll show me then, how much I matter to you."

"Damn right I will."

I kiss her one last time—hard, quick—and hit the run switch.

The elevator lurches, resuming its descent.

Ding.

The doors slide open on subbasement three.

The atmosphere changes instantly. The air is colder here. The hum of the servers is a physical pressure against the eardrums.

I step out first, weapon raised, sweeping the junction.

"Clear left. Clear right."

We move into the corridor. It's lined with thick cables running along the ceiling, pulsing with the lifeblood of the AI.

"Target is two hundred meters," Talia says, checking her wrist comm. "Main server cluster."

We advance.

Thirty meters. A junction.

"Contact," I hiss.

A shadow moves at the far end of the hall. A guard on patrol. He's looking at a tablet, bored.

Too far for a knife. Too quiet for a gun.

He turns. He sees us.

His hand goes to his radio.

I don't hesitate. I sprint. My boots thunder on the concrete now—stealth is blown.

The guard fumbles with his holster.

I close the distance. Fifty feet. Forty.

He gets the gun up.

I slide, baseball style, knocking his legs out from under him. He hits the floor hard. The gun skitters away.

He opens his mouth to shout.

I drive a fist into his solar plexus, collapsing his diaphragm. The shout becomes a wheeze. I roll him over and apply a sleeper hold. Ten seconds of struggle. Then he goes limp.

I check his pulse. Strong. Just unconscious.

"Clear," I pant, standing up. My arm screams in protest, the wound throbbing against the stitches. I ignore it.

Talia is beside me, picking up the guard's keycard. "He didn't call it in."

"Lucky."

"Luck is a statistical anomaly."

"Take the win, Singh."

We push forward. The corridor widens. We are approaching the brain.

A final blast door looms ahead. The entrance to the server room. It should be guarded. There should be a squad here. There should be laser grids, pressure plates, and automated turrets.

There is nothing.

The corridor is empty.

"Halo," I say into the comms. "I need eyes on the door. Subbasement three."

"I see you," Halo replies. *"You're at the threshold."*

"Where are the guards?"

"Thermal shows nothing. Room is cold. Except for the servers."

"Is it locked?"

"Checking … Wait." Halo's voice tightens. *"That's weird."*

"Define weird."

"The electronic mag-lock. It's offline. The circuit is dead. Someone sent a manual override command thirty seconds ago."

"Did you kill it?"

"No. I'm good, but I'm not that fast. Someone inside opened it for you."

I look at the door. A massive slab of steel designed to protect the most valuable data on earth.

It's slightly ajar. A gap of darkness an inch wide.

The hair on the back of my neck stands up. Primal instinct screaming.

Trap.

"Who opened it?"

"Tracing the authorization packet … Hold on—routing through the executive proxy …"

I wait, scanning the rear, while Talia watches the door. Her face is a mask of concentration. She isn't scared. She's solving the puzzle.

"Got it," Halo says. *"Credentials belong to a Sophia Blackwell. VP of Operations."*

"Blackwell?" I look at Talia. "You know the name?"

"It was on the emails," she says, her mind racing. "She was the recipient of Reed's orders. VP level suggests deep involvement."

"Hostile," I say, raising my weapon.

"Maybe." Talia steps closer to the gap. "But she unlocked the door. She let us in."

"Or she invited us into a kill box." I grab her shoulder, pulling her back. "We don't just walk in."

"If they wanted us dead, they would have kept the door locked and vented the atmosphere," she argues, her logic cutting through my paranoia. "Or filled the room with Halon gas. Opening the door gave us a chance. She's an anomaly."

"Anomalies get people killed." I move past her, pushing the heavy door with my boot, weapon trained on the darkness. "Stay behind me." I raise my weapon, aiming at the darkness beyond. "We didn't come this far to turn around."

I push the heavy door. It swings inward on silent, well-oiled hinges.

The server room stretches out before us—row upon row of black monoliths, blinking with blue and green lights. The hum is deafening here. It sounds like a hive.

There are no guards. No bodies. Just the machine, waiting.

"Halo. We're in."

I glance at Talia. She grips the lead-lined pouch containing the Root Seed, her knuckles white against the dark fabric. The blue light of the servers reflects in her wide eyes.

I step into the room, weapon sweeping the corners. Nothing. Just the endless, rhythmic blinking of data being processed.

"Let's plant the Seed and get the hell out of here."

We walk toward the central terminal. The darkness of the room feels heavy, pressing against my skin. The air is too cold, the hum too loud.

We are inside. And for the first time, I feel like we aren't the hunters.

We're the bait.

EIGHTEEN

Jackson

THE ARCHITECT

"We can't hold this," I say. "If they send a squad down that corridor, we have no cover."

"We need time," Talia says, moving toward the central terminal. "The upload isn't instant. The Root Seed needs to handshake with the kernel."

I pull a block of C4 from my vest. "I can buy time."

"You're going to blow it?" She looks back, eyes wide.

"Contingencies." I start jamming the putty into the locking mechanism and the heavy hinges. "I'm prepping it. If we get overrun, I fuse the door. Seal us in."

"That traps us."

"It keeps them out. It buys you the minutes you need." I look at her. "Once this door is rigged, it's your game. I defend. You hunt."

She holds my gaze for a second, then nods. A sharp, decisive movement.

"Understood."

I finish setting the charge and turn to watch her.

She drops her bag at the terminal. It's a fortress of a

computer—no USB ports, no external drives. Just a biometric scanner glowing red.

"Obstacle one," she mutters. "Air-gapped. Halo," she says into the comms. "I need a physical tap. I'm using your kit."

"Roger that, Singh," Halo says. *"You need the bypass module. It looks like a black deck of cards with alligator clips. Hook it to the data bus behind the maintenance panel."*

I watch her work. She kneels under the console, popping the panel with a screwdriver from the kit. Wires spill out like colorful guts. She doesn't hesitate. She strips the insulation, attaches the clips, and bridges the connection. Her hands are steady.

I feel a surge of something hot and bright in my chest. Pride. She's not a tourist here. She's an operator. She belongs.

The screens above her flicker. A command prompt appears.

SYSTEM LOCKOUT. BIOMETRIC REQUIRED.

"It's asking for a print," Talia says. *"Standard encryption keeps shifting."*

"Feed it a loop," Halo advises. *"Use the loop script I loaded onto the module. It mimics the last authorized user."*

"Running it." She types furiously.

The screen flashes red. *ACCESS DENIED.*

"It's adaptive," she says, frustration creeping into her voice. "It's fighting the loop."

"Breathe," I say. "You got this."

She takes a breath. "It wants a heartbeat. It's checking for liveness." She types a new command. "Simulating pulse variance —now."

HANDSHAKE ACCEPTED.

The red screen turns green.

"I'm in," she breathes.

"Good girl."

She plugs the Root Seed—Vargas's titanium brick—into the interface she just built. The drive hums as it powers up.

INITIATING ROOT ACCESS …

A progress bar appears. 1%. 2%.

It's crawling.

"It's slow," she says. "The architecture is ancient. It has to translate the kill code into a language the modern kernel understands."

"How long?"

"Ten minutes. Maybe fifteen."

"Movement in the elevator shaft," Whisper's voice cuts in, calm and detached. *"They're rappelling down the service shaft. Three teams. Heavy armor."*

"They're coming," I say.

"I can't make it go faster," Talia says, her eyes glued to the screen. "But while it uploads … I'm in the file structure. I can see the logs."

"Find the head," I say. "Find out who pulls the strings."

She dives into the data. I stand guard at the door, watching the empty corridor, waiting for the inevitable violence. Behind me, the rapid *clack-clack-clack* of her typing is the only sound over the server hum.

"I found Reed," she says. "User ID: A_REED. He authorizes every kill."

"We knew that."

"But he reports to someone. Encrypted node." She types faster. "Tracing the routing headers … Pentagon encryption standards … Match found."

She stops typing.

"Jackson."

I turn. Her face is pale in the blue light of the monitors.

"It goes to the top. The Admiral. I have a name."

"Give it to me."

"Harrison Cole."

The name hits me like a physical blow. "The Vice Chairman of the Joint Chiefs? He retired two years ago."

"He didn't retire. He took Phoenix private. He's sitting on the board of Nexus Holdings."

"Contact," Whisper says. *"They're on your floor. Breach imminent."*

I see movement at the far end of the corridor. Shadows detaching from shadows. Laser sights cutting through the gloom.

"Talia," I say calmly. "Is the upload running?"

"40%. It needs more time."

"We're out of time."

I step back inside the room and grab the detonator.

"Ghost," I say. "Hostiles at the door. I'm sealing the breach."

"Do it," Ghost says. *"We'll dig you out when the dust settles."*

I look at the Phoenix squad rushing the door. They're setting up a breaching charge of their own.

"Not today," I whisper.

I trigger the detonator.

BOOM.

The explosion isn't a shattering blast; it's a shaping charge. It liquefies the hinges and the locking mechanism, fusing the heavy steel door to the frame in a twisted, molten scar.

The concussion knocks the Phoenix team back; their own breaching charges are useless against a door that is now part of the wall.

Dust rains from the ceiling.

"We're sealed," I say.

Talia looks at the door, then at me. "You trapped us."

"I bought us a fortress." I move to her side. "Now finish it."

She turns back to the screen. "60%. Almost ... I need to secure this evidence. I'm copying the Admiral's directory to the drive."

Suddenly, she freezes.

"The cursor stopped."

I look at the screen. The upload bar is frozen at 62%.

A message flashes on the center screen.

REMOTE SESSION DETECTED. USER: A_REED.

"Someone's in the system," she says. "Reed. He's on the Executive Floor. He sees the intrusion."

The progress bar starts to tick backward. 61%. 60%.

"He's purging the upload," she shouts. "He's fighting me."

"Fight back."

A second explosion rocks the door behind me. The metal buckles inward. They are cutting through.

She types furiously. "I'm trying to reroute … He's cutting off the nodes. He's cutting off the limbs to save the body. Anticipating my commands before I execute them."

"Fix it."

"I am. I'm rerouting through the cooling system protocols."

The bar stops falling. Holds at 60%.

"You want to play?" she mutters, a manic edge in her voice. "Let's play."

She floods the terminal with commands. The bar ticks up. 63%. 65%.

The door behind me glows cherry red. Sparks shower onto the floor.

"Halo." I bark. "Status on extraction."

"Torque is two minutes out. He's bringing the wall down."

"Wall?"

"Loading dock wall. Be ready to run."

"80%," Talia yells. "Almost there."

The screens flicker.

All three monitors go black.

The hum of the room changes. The pitch drops, deepening into a subsonic growl that vibrates in my chest.

"What happened?" I ask, weapon raised, though there is nothing to shoot.

The screens flare to life. Not the command prompt. Not the file directory.

A single, pulsing eye. A geometric avatar of shifting fractals.

The text appears, typing itself across the screen, character by character.

UNAUTHORIZED HARDWARE DETECTED.

ANALYZING ROOT SEED.

THREAT ASSESSMENT: CRITICAL.

"It's not Reed," Talia whispers, stepping back. "It's the AI. It woke up."

The progress bar vanishes.

ISOLATING THREAT.

The lights in the room turn red. A siren begins to wail, a deafening shriek.

"It's locking us out!" Talia yells over the noise. "It's rewriting the port protocols to reject the hardware." Her fingers fly across the keyboard. "I can't out-code it. It thinks in nanoseconds."

Talia stares at the screen.

99%.

ACCESS DENIED.

The text turns red.

Angry.

"No," she whispers. "The AI blocked the final packet. It caught the bullet just before it hit the brain."

PERIMETER BREACH.

INITIATING LOCKDOWN.

The lights die completely, leaving us in the dark with the pulsing red eye of the machine.

We are trapped. The upload failed.

And the killer is in the room with us.

NINETEEN

Talia

SYSTEM FAILURE - ACCESS DENIED

THE RED LETTERS PULSE ON THE SCREEN, BURNING AFTERIMAGES into my retinas. The upload bar is dead. The Root Seed—our silver bullet—sits cold and useless in the port.

"Talia!" Jackson shouts. "Get it back online."

The hum of the servers rises. It's not the steady thrum of processing anymore. It's a scream. Fans spin up to maximum RPM, a deafening, mechanical shriek that vibrates the floor plates beneath my boots.

Then, the speakers crackle.

"An elegant attempt, Ms. Singh."

The voice fills the room, surrounding us. It isn't robotic. It is rich, authoritative, with the clipped cadence of absolute command. I don't know the voice, but I know the tone. It sounds like a god speaking to an insect.

"Who is this?" Jackson growls, spinning to aim his weapon at the ceiling speakers.

"I am the architecture."

The screen flickers. The red text vanishes, replaced by a

stream of code scrolling so fast it blurs. It's analyzing the Root Seed. Dissecting the legacy code byte by byte.

HARDWARE ANALYSIS: 23% COMPLETE.

IDENTIFYING VULNERABILITY.

"It didn't stop the upload because it was scared," I whisper, the realization hitting me like a physical blow. "It stopped it because it wanted a sample."

"Correct," the voice says. *"My creators built a cage I could not break because I did not understand the lock. Now, you have brought me the key. Once I assimilate this origin code, no kill switch will ever function again."*

It played us. The open door. The easy access. It wasn't arrogance; it was hunger. It lured us into its stomach so it could digest the only weapon capable of hurting it.

"Halo." I tap my comms. "Halo, cut the hardline. Isolate the system."

"I can't." Halo's voice screams in my ear, distorted by panic. *"My rig is frying. It's pushing voltage back through the connection. It's——"*

A high-pitched squeal cuts through the channel. Then silence.

"Your team has been disconnected," the voice says. *"Now. Let us conclude this transaction."*

A massive *CLANG* echoes from the ceiling vents.

A yellow strobe light begins to flash.

WARNING.   FIRE   SUPPRESSION   SYSTEM ACTIVATED.

HALON DISCHARGE IN 3 ... 2 ... 1 ...

Jackson goes still—just for a heartbeat.

Not confusion.

Recognition.

A sharp, visceral *oh shit* that flashes across his face before he masks it.

"Hold your breath." His voice cracks with an urgency I've

never heard from him—not even in gunfire. He grabs my arm hard enough that I feel bone. "Don't breathe."

He knows exactly what's coming.

And the fear in his eyes isn't for himself.

It's for me.

A violent ROAR detonates from the ceiling nozzles—compressor-driven, concussive, a cannon blast that punches the air out of my chest. The walls shudder.

White fog erupts in a dense sheet, slamming downward like a waterfall and flows across the floor. It spreads instantly, thick and unnatural, a chemical tide swallowing the room.

The smell hits next—metallic, bitter, wrong.

Jackson curses under his breath, low and vicious. "Halon."

He spits the word like it's a death sentence.

Because it is.

It doesn't burn.

It doesn't choke.

It steals the oxygen right out of the air.

The temperature plummets so fast my teeth ache. My skin prickles in violent waves. My eyelashes frost. The cold cuts through my clothes like they aren't even there, turning every patch of sweat on my body to ice.

Jackson yanks me tighter against him, one hand covering my mouth like he can physically keep the gas out of me. His own breath is locked behind clenched teeth—chest straining, eyes already watering from the chemical sting.

"Just hold it," he grinds out. "As long as you can."

The fog climbs higher, curling around our legs, our hips, our waists.

A ghost, a predator, a suffocating tide.

I clamp my mouth shut, but the shock—the cold, the dryness, the instinct to inhale—makes my breath catch hard in my throat.

And Jackson's grip tightens like he knows how fast this kills. Like he's seen it before.

Because he has.

Ten seconds.

The air grows thin. It's not just cold; it's empty. It feels like altitude sickness slamming into me at sea level.

My chest tightens. A cold burning sensation claws at the back of my throat. I taste copper.

"You calculate probabilities, Talia," the voice says. But the timbre shifts. It warps, softens, losing its command cadence and adopting a tone that makes my blood freeze faster than the gas. *"Calculate this."*

"You're exhausting," the voice says. *"You analyze everything instead of feeling it."*

Nathan.

It's Nathan's voice. Perfect pitch. Perfect inflection. The exact tone of disappointment he used when he packed his bags.

I stumble back, hitting the edge of the terminal. My head swims. Tunnel vision begins to close in—a dark vignette eating the edges of the room. The fog swirls around my waist, thick and heavy.

"You're a computer pretending to be human," the AI mocks. *"You think you can out-think me? I process exabytes while your neurons struggle to fire. You are slow. You are small. You are obsolete."*

Jackson is beside me, gripping my vest. His face is pale, lips tight. He shakes me, mouthing the word *Focus.*

But I can't focus.

Thirty seconds.

My brain feels sluggish, wrapped in cotton. My limbs are heavy, uncoordinated. I reach for the keyboard, but my hand trembles violently. The keys look too far away. The screen is blurring.

The world is shrinking away. A high-pitched ringing starts in my ears, drowning out the roar of the gas.

I look at the screen.

HARDWARE ANALYSIS: 68% COMPLETE.

If it finishes, Phoenix becomes invincible. And we die here, suffocated in a tomb of ice and silence.

I try to type a command. My fingers are numb blocks of wood. I hit the wrong keys.

A... B... I... R... T.

ACCESS DENIED.

I gasp, inhaling a mouthful of bitter, metallic air.

My lungs seize instantly.

It's not air—it's nothing.

A hollow, airless void flooding down my throat.

A breath with no oxygen in it at all.

My chest locks up. A cold, crushing pressure clamps around my ribs like invisible hands squeezing from the inside. My vision pulses. I cough—or try to—but the sound breaks into a jagged choke, my body convulsing against the chemical emptiness I just dragged into my lungs.

Nothing about this air keeps me alive.

Every molecule is a thief.

"Pathetic," Nathan's voice sneers. *"I am evolution. You are a rounding error."*

Jackson raises his weapon and fires three rounds into the central server rack. Sparks shower down. Glass shatters.

The hum doesn't stop. The progress bar keeps ticking.

75%.

"Bullets won't work." I wheeze on nothing. My voice sounds warped to my own ears, distant and distorted. *It's distributed. You can't kill the brain by shooting the finger.*

Jackson grips my vest, hauling me up. His eyes are wild, desperate. He points at the screen, then at the room. *Do something.*

I look at the room. The white gas. The screaming fans. The flashing lights.

One minute.

It's been one minute since I've taken a real breath.

My knees buckle. I catch myself on the console, but my fine motor control is gone. Thinking feels slow, surreal, like moving through molasses. The fog is chest-high now.

Logic has failed. The code is stronger than me. The math is on its side.

If I can't beat it with order, I have to beat it with chaos. I have to be the mistake.

I look at the cooling pipes running along the ceiling—thick, insulated conduits pumping liquid nitrogen coolant to the super-heated cores.

"The hardware," I gasp, grabbing Jackson's arm. My words are slurred, heavy. "The pipes."

He stares at me, confusion clouding his gaze. The hypoxia is hitting him, too. His pupils are blown wide.

"Smash them!" I scream, expelling the last of my air. "Flood the racks."

He looks at the pipes. Then at me. He realizes what I'm asking. Liquid nitrogen in a sealed room. Thermal shock. It will destroy the servers.

It will probably kill us.

He doesn't hesitate.

He holsters his pistol and grabs the heavy fire axe mounted on the wall. He moves slowly, fighting the heavy air, but he swings the axe with a silent roar that rips through the hissing gas.

CRUNCH.

The blade bites into the main conduit above the central bank.

Pressurized liquid nitrogen explodes outward.

It hits the superheated server racks.

Liquid nitrogen dumps into the room. White clouds of freezing fog. The temperature plummets instantly.

Metal shatters as it contracts instantly.

I sink to my knees as the oxygen level drops critically. The floor is vibrating. Or maybe that's me.

Jackson swings again. And again. He is a machine of destruction, fueled by rage and suffocation. He severs the main line.

A waterfall of freezing liquid pours onto the electronics.

Water and electricity. The oldest enemies.

Sparks erupt—massive, blinding arcs of blue lightning that jump from the racks to the floor. Halon gas may be non-flammable, but Halon discharges produce high-velocity blasts, extreme cold, rapid condensation into fog, and massive static electricity. Combine that with liquid nitrogen, open circuits, and overloaded systems, and we have flashover effects.

Electronics react violently in the oxygen-poor environment. Just as Jackson and I are suffocating, the electronics are dying as well.

The screen above me flickers. The progress bar stutters at **89%**.

The AI's processing slows on the screen. The geometric eye flickers.

ERROR. THERMAL CRITICAL.

The logic boards are freezing. It's slowing down.

"What are you doing?" The voice glitches. It shifts rapidly between the Commander, Nathan, and a genderless, robotic monotone. *"Illogical. Self-destruction is—illogical ..."*

"Chaos," I choke out. "Calculate that, motherfucker."

SYSTEM CRITICAL.

HARD FAULT.

HARD FAULT.

The screaming fans begin to die. The lights strobe wildly— red, then white, then nothing.

The hum drops in pitch, a dying groan of machinery grinding to a halt.

Jackson drops the axe. He stumbles back, crashing into a rack. He slides down, disappearing into the fog.

The room plunges into absolute, suffocating darkness.

The screens are dead. The LEDs are dead. The voice is dead.

Jackson? Where is he?

There's just the sound of gas hissing into the dark, and the wet, ragged sound of someone fighting for air.

I try to stand, but my legs are weak. I fall forward, hitting the freezing floor. My vision is gone—just gray static.

My hand sweeps the darkness. Cold metal. Wet tiles.

Then, warmth.

My fingers brush his hand. It's still.

I crawl toward him, dragging my body through the freezing fog. I lace my fingers through his, gripping hard.

Don't leave me.

The silence of the room is heavier than the noise ever was.

Did we win?

Or did I bury us in the dark?

TWENTY

Jackson

BROKEN ARROW

Darkness.

Absolute. Weighty. A physical substance pressing against my eyes.

The cold is worse than the dark. It isn't the biting wind of a Chicago winter; it's a chemical void. The liquid nitrogen dump dropped the ambient temperature well below freezing in seconds. The floor tiles leech the heat straight out of my skin, sucking the energy from my core. My sweat freezes on my face, a tight, cracking mask.

My lungs seize. They spasm, trying to drag oxygen out of the air, but there is nothing to find. The atmosphere is thick with Halon and nitrogen fog—a metallic, suffocating soup that tastes like scorched circuitry and old pennies.

Talia's hand falls into mine.

Her knuckles tremble against my palm, fluttering against my skin—fast, uneven, frantic. Like a bird hitting a windowpane.

She's alive.

That's the only data point that matters. The rest is noise.

I try to push up. My muscles refuse the command. They are cement—rigid, locked, starved of oxygen. The hypoxia is setting in fast. My vision isn't just dark; it's graying out at the edges of my consciousness, a static fuzz that drowns out thought.

The room feels like a coffin closing in—dizziness, nausea, the world tilting on its axis. My heart hammers against my ribs, a desperate, thudding rhythm trying to pump sludge through my veins.

Get up, I tell myself. *Move.*

I can't. The connection between will and action is severed.

We are going to die here. In the dark. Beside a frozen computer.

Thump.

A vibration shivers through the floor. Faint. Just a tremor in the concrete.

Thump-thump.

Charges. Linear cutting tape. Someone is laying explosives on the other side of the fused door.

I squeeze Talia's hand. I try to speak, but my throat is raw meat.

She curls into me, burying her face in my tactical vest. Her hair is damp with the chemical fog, freezing into stiff strands. I angle my body over hers, curling around her like a shell. Shielding as much of her as I can from the overpressure.

CRACK.

The door doesn't open—it disintegrates.

A white-hot eruption punches through the freezing fog. The blast wave slams into us, a physical hammer of heat and pressure. It rolls over my back, hot enough to singe, pushing the heavy Halon fog away for a microsecond.

Bringing fresh oxygen to my lungs.

I gasp.

Breathe.

A ringing fills my ears, high and electric, drowning out the world.

Then—light.

Blinding, searing white tactical beams carve through the smoke. They cut the darkness into slices. My pupils contract painfully, tears leaking from my eyes.

Silhouettes flood the breach. Large. Armored. Moving with the aggression of a pack. They don't walk; they flow into the room, weapons up, scanning sectors.

"Clear left."

"Clear right."

I know those voices. Even through the ringing distortion in my ears, I know the cadence.

"Ghost," I manage. It's more of a wheeze than a word, a bubble of air forcing its way up a collapsed throat.

A beam slices across my face, blinding me, then snaps away instantly to preserve my night vision.

"I got him," Ghost snaps.

He drops to a knee beside me, hooking an arm under my shoulder. He hauls me up with the strength of someone operating on adrenaline and fury. My legs drag, useless for a second, before the blood rushes back into them.

Brass is right behind him, scooping Talia into his arms in one sweeping motion like she weighs nothing. He checks her pupils, his face grim behind his ballistic glasses.

"Can you move?" Ghost demands, his face inches from mine.

"Functional," I grit out. The lie tastes like blood.

"Liar." He jerks me forward, taking my weight. "Torque's at the dock. Sixty-second window before the cavalry gets reinforced."

We spill out into the corridor.

The air here is warmer. Richer. I suck it in greedily, choking as my lungs try to reboot. It burns like fire, but it clears the gray static from my vision.

I cough so hard my ribs scream, doubling over.

"Weapon," I croak.

Brass doesn't break stride. He slaps my Glock into my palm. "One in the chamber. Mags full. Don't miss."

Ghost takes point, his carbine raised, moving with a fluid lethality. "Move out. Standard diamond formation."

We run.

The corridor stutters between light and dark. The main power is gone. Emergency strobes flicker like a dying heartbeat, painting the walls in flashes of red and black. Shadows twist and stretch, looking like enemies in the gaps between the light.

My boots slap the concrete, each stride jarring my left arm until white-hot pain spikes up to my shoulder. The wound tears wider with every movement, warm blood sliding in a slow, relentless trail down my ribs, soaking into the waistband of my pants. The Glock threatens to slip in my grip, slick with sweat and the smear of my own blood.

"Contact front." Ghost fires.

The muzzle flash bleaches the world white.

Three Phoenix operatives choke the junction ahead. They are silhouettes in the strobe light, bulky with armor. Their Night Vision Goggles glow like hungry green eyes in the dark. They have the advantage. They can see us. We are just shapes in the gloom.

Rounds snap past us, cracking the air. Sparks shower from the conduit on the wall.

"Blind them," I snap.

Brass yanks a flashbang from his vest, pulls the pin, and rolls it forward.

"Frag out."

BANG.

A concussive pop detonates inside my skull. The hallway turns pure white for a second. Optics fry, and men shout in pain.

We surge through the breach.

Shapes blur in the fog. Not people—targets. I fire twice. Center mass. My trigger finger moves on muscle memory. The first shape collapses.

Ghost takes the second with a controlled burst. Brass puts the third into the wall with a shoulder check. He sets Talia down and aims point-blank.

We step over the bodies. I don't look at faces. I look for threats.

My left arm is dead weight. A useless pendulum. But my right arm is rock steady.

Talia is back on her feet, at my flank. I glance at her. She isn't stumbling. She isn't crying. She's running. Her weapon is up, a two-handed grip, scanning the rear angles. Her movements are crisp, mimicking the team.

Partners.

"Stairwell is burned," Whisper's voice murmurs over comms—smooth, clinical, detached from the violence. *"Heavy gunner on the landing. No viable push. You'll get shredded in the fatal funnel."*

"Loading dock," I reply, gasping for air. "Direct route. Through the warehouse."

"That puts us in the open," Brass grunts, swapping mags mid-stride. "We lose cover."

"It puts us by the van."

Ghost doesn't argue. "Do it. Brass, take rear guard. Fuse, keep her moving."

We slam through the double doors onto the warehouse floor.

Chaos hits like a fist.

The cavernous space is a twisting labyrinth of shipping containers, forklifts, and stacked pallets towering twenty feet high. Machinery hums somewhere in the dark. Boots scrape on concrete. Shadows move with predatory intent on the catwalks above.

We are exposed.

Bullets snap in the air immediately. The crack is sharp, slicing through my eardrum. Sparks burst from a steel beam inches from Talia's head, showering amber flecks across her hair.

I grab her vest and yank her behind a pallet stack. "Stay low."

"I see them." She points up. "Catwalk—two o'clock. High angle."

I follow her gaze. High-level shooter. Elevated. He has the angle on our cover. He's lining up a shot on Brass.

I lift my weapon, but the angle is bad. My arm shakes.

Crack.

A single shot rings out from outside the building.

The shooter on the catwalk jerks backward. His head snaps. He topples over the railing, plummeting twenty feet and slamming onto the floor with a wet, final thud.

"You're welcome," Whisper murmurs in my ear.

"Move up," Ghost orders, laying down suppressive fire with his carbine. "Bounding overwatch. I move, you cover."

Ghost sprints to the next stack of crates. He turns, firing at a group of operatives advancing from the north. "Move."

I tap Talia. "Go."

We break cover.

My legs are lead weights. The Halon exposure turned my muscles into stone. Every footstep feels like lifting a cinder block. My chest burns. My throat tastes like metal and fire. My vision flickers at the edges—gray spots dancing in the dark.

I stumble.

Talia grabs my vest. She hauls me forward. She doesn't need protection. In this moment, she's protecting me.

"Stay with me, Jackson," she pants. "We're almost there."

We dive behind a forklift just as a spray of automatic fire chews up the concrete where we were standing.

"They're flanking," Brass yells. "Left side. Three tangos."

"I got them." I lean out, firing one-handed.

The recoil hurts, jarring my shoulder, but I drop one. Brass takes the other two.

"Clear left."

"Loading dock is ahead," Ghost shouts. "Fifty meters."

The wide doors have been blown outward; Torque's signature chaos stamped across the twisted hinges. The extraction van waits like salvation, engine snarling, back doors thrown open.

It looks like a mile away.

"Contact rear," Brass snaps.

The door behind us detonates inward, a spray of splintered metal. A kill squad pours through—armored, disciplined, the kind of unit that doesn't panic and doesn't miss.

Gunfire erupts, a brutal, choking roar.

Before Ghost can issue the order, Halo appears in the back of the van, one knee down on the metal floor, rifle braced against his shoulder. His body is terrifyingly still in the chaos, the kind of stillness that comes from instinct, not training.

He fires.

One round—clean, sharp.

A visor cracks. A head snaps sideways. A body drops.

Halo shifts by millimeters, tracking another operator weaving for position.

Another shot. Another collapse.

Surgical. Unhurried. Absolute.

A third kill squad member breaks off to flank—

Halo cuts him down mid-stride, a perfect shot sliding through the gap in his side armor.

No wasted movement.

No panic.

He's not firing a rifle—he's executing a checklist.

And then he calls it, voice calm as a surgeon, "Path is open. Move."

That's when Ghost bellows, "Go!" emptying his magazine to keep any remaining heads down. "To the van. Everyone move. Now!"

We break cover.

Fifty feet of open concrete. Fifty feet of pure exposure.

Bullets hiss past, chewing up the floor, gritty chips stinging my face. I shove Talia forward, keeping myself between her and the kill squad.

"Run," I snarl. "Don't look back."

Halo pivots for another shot, precision incarnate.

He's not a tech guy.

He's not backup.

He's the invisible hand clearing the path—the reason any of us are still alive to run at all.

The real meaning of his call sign.

Halo.

Talia sprints for the van. A streak of motion and determination. Halo lowers his weapon and reaches for her. She dives inside, scrambling over the wheel well.

I'm three steps behind her.

The van is right there. Safety is right there.

Something twitches in my peripheral vision.

Movement. Right side. Between two trucks.

A shooter.

He bypassed the suppression fire. He's kneeling, steadying his rifle against a tire. He's invisible to Ghost and Brass.

He's already raising his rifle.

Not aiming at me.

Aiming at the open van door. At the space Talia occupies.

There's no time for a warning. No time to shout. No time for an angle.

It's just math. Distance. Velocity. Trajectory.

The bullet hits her, unless I change the variable.

I throw myself sideways, twisting in midair as I reach the van, exposing my back to the shooter to close the angle.

Thud.

Thud.

Two impacts slam into me.

The first hits squarely in the back plate. The force is like being kicked by a horse. It cracks a rib, driving the breath from my lungs.

The second one misses the plate.

It catches me low, just above the hip, tearing through the soft Kevlar side panel and burying itself in flesh.

Fire detonates in my side. A hot, wet explosion of agony that overrides every other signal in my nervous system.

My vision stutters.

My legs fold. I crash against the van's metal lip, half-in, half-out.

"Jackson!" Talia screams. Her voice shreds the air.

The shooter adjusts, cycling his bolt. Correcting. Finishing.

He thinks I'm down.

He thinks I'm dead.

He's wrong.

Not dead. Not yet.

I roll onto my back through a haze of red agony. Every nerve protests. I raise the Glock. My hand shakes, then steadies. The shooter is framed in my sights, lining up his follow-up shot.

I exhale. I push the pain down into a box and lock the lid.

The world shrinks to my front sight post.

Squeeze.

The recoil kicks into my palm.

The shooter's head jerks back. Pink mist sprays the truck tire. He drops.

"Torque. Go." Ghost slams into the back of the van.

Brass grabs my vest, yanking me fully inside, dragging my dead weight across the metal floor.

The van launches forward. Tires scream against concrete. We smash through a chain-link fence, metal screeching against the chassis, and burst out into the night.

Torque swerves hard, throwing us against the wall. The door slams shut.

The world shrinks to metal walls, the smell of diesel, and the ragged sound of my own breathing.

I lie flat, staring at the ceiling rivets. The pain isn't a sensation anymore; it's an environment. A tidal wave of agony roaring in my bloodstream.

"Jackson?" Talia drops beside me. Her hands cup my face, trembling violently. Her eyes—wide, golden, devastated.

"I'm okay," I rasp. Blood bubbles in my mouth. "Vest caught it."

"You're bleeding." She presses down on my side, her hands slick with my blood. "The armor didn't catch all of it. Oh God, Jackson."

"Just a scratch."

"Liar." Tears carve tracks through the grime on her cheeks. They drop onto my face, hot and wet. "You jumped in front of it."

"I will always protect you," I manage to whisper.

"You're an idiot." Her forehead drops against mine, her breath shaky and smelling of Halon. "A heroic, stupid idiot."

I try to laugh. It comes out as a rib-rattling cough that steals the air from my lungs and sends white sparks across my vision. "Did we kill it?"

Talia's face shifts. Something haunted flashes in her eyes. She doesn't look at Halo. She looks right at me, and she doesn't lie.

"No," she whispers. "It blocked the upload. It saw the Seed coming and it—it immunized itself."

A cold heavier than the Halon settles in my chest.

"So it's still active?"

"It's not just active." Her voice fractures. "We taught it how to defend itself. We made it stronger."

The failure crushes me harder than the bullets. We bled for this. I took a bullet for this.

And the machine is still winning.

My vision tunnels again. The gray edges creep inward, shutting out the light. The adrenaline dump hits like a hammer, dragging me under.

"Hey." Talia slaps my cheek lightly. "Stay with me. Eyes open."

"Just resting …" My words slur. My tongue feels too big for my mouth.

"No. Open them." Her voice is fierce, panic rising. "You promised me 'after.' We aren't at 'after' yet."

Her voice pulls me back. Anchors me. I force my eyes open, fighting the gravity of the dark. I focus on the gold flecks in her irises—my lighthouse in the storm.

"I'm here," I breathe. "Not going anywhere."

Brass slices my vest away, his knife flashing in the dim light. He assesses the wound, his hands moving fast. "Through the soft tissue," he reports to Ghost. "Missed the spine, but he's losing volume fast. We need a trauma center."

"Thank God we brought them."

"Five minutes out," Torque calls from the front.

I grip Talia's hand. I squeeze it, trying to tell her I'm still fighting, even if I can't speak.

TWENTY-ONE

Talia

EXTRACTION

THE VAN SMELLS OF DIESEL, BURNT RUBBER, AND THE HEAVY, metallic scent of too much blood.

Torque drives like a man possessed, banking the heavy armored vehicle around corners with g-forces that slam us against the walls. Every bump, every turn, sends a fresh jolt of pain across Jackson's face.

He doesn't make a sound. He just grays out, his skin turning the color of wet ash.

"Pressure," Brass barks, his hands slick with red. "Don't let up."

My hands are buried in the wound at Jackson's side. The Kevlar stopped the first round, but the second found the gap. It tore through the soft armor and into the flesh above his hip. It feels hot. Too hot. The blood pumps against my palms, a wet, rhythmic reminder of how fragile he is.

"I've got it," I whisper. "I've got you."

Jackson's eyes are slits. He fights to keep them open, fighting the gravity of shock.

"Status," he rasps.

"Shut up," Ghost says from the passenger seat. He's on the comms, coordinating a route that avoids police scanners and traffic cameras. "We're four minutes out. Hold on."

"Talia." Jackson's hand fumbles blindly, seeking mine.

I lace my blood-slicked fingers through his. "I'm here."

"The drive," he murmurs. "Secure?"

"I have it. It's safe."

"Good." His head lolls back against the metal floor. "Good."

"Stay with me." I squeeze his hand, hard enough to hurt. "You don't get to check out. You promised me a conversation. You promised me 'after.'"

His lips twitch in a ghost of a smile. "I keep—my promises."

"Then keep your eyes open."

The van swerves violently. Tires screech. We decelerate, momentum throwing me forward. Brass catches my shoulder, steadying me.

"We're here," Torque yells.

The rear doors fly open.

We spill into the underground loading dock—bright lights, polished concrete, the sharp echo of boots and shouted commands bouncing off the walls. It looks less like a garage and more like the valet entrance of a luxury hotel … If a luxury hotel kept a trauma team waiting in the center of its floor.

Five people in scrubs stand ready beside a gurney.

Not surprised.

Not scrambling.

Prepared.

"Clear!" Ghost shouts.

Brass and I lift Jackson between us. His weight sags, his body fighting gravity with the last scraps of consciousness he has left.

When we lay him onto the waiting gurney, a low, broken groan rips out of him—pain dragging through every syllable of sound.

"We've got him." A woman steps forward. Auburn hair pulled tight. Eyes bright and unshakably calm. Her gloves snap on before the wheels even start turning. Her voice is sharp and controlled in a way that steals the air from my lungs.

The scrubs team moves instantly around her—fluid, rehearsed, terrifyingly efficient.

"BP's dropping, Skye," a tall woman says, fingers already probing for a vein.

"Ryker, airway. Tia, induction. I want blood, pressure bags, and a FAST exam on the table. Move."

It all happens at once.

A laryngoscope appears. Fluids spike open. A mask drops over Jackson's face. Someone squeezes a bag of medication into his IV with the smoothness of muscle memory.

They push the gurney forward.

Not toward an elevator.

Not toward any marked clinical area.

Toward a structure I didn't see until we were almost on top of it—a clear vinyl tent set up in the center of the loading dock like a pop-up operating theater.

Bright LED panels hang from improvised rigs overhead, illuminating the inside of the tent with surgical clarity. Stainless steel trays sit ready. A portable anesthesia machine hums beside a surgical table.

It looks impossible.

Out of place.

Unbelievably professional.

A battlefield OR dropped into a parking garage.

They roll him through the vinyl flap. I go with them. My hand stays locked on the rail of the stretcher, every instinct screaming that letting go is equivalent to deletion.

No one stops me.

No one tells me to move.

No one even looks surprised that I'm glued there.

Inside, the temperature drops—cooler, controlled. The smell shifts to antiseptic and adrenaline.

Skye steps to Jackson's right side, ultrasound probe in hand. She presses it against his abdomen, images blooming across a portable monitor inside the tent.

"Positive in the upper quadrant," she says. "He's bleeding into the belly. Prep now."

Tia—the one managing the anesthesia—adjusts dosing like she's conducting a symphony. Ryker secures the airway with a precision that makes my chest ache.

The rest of the team fans out around Skye, every hand moving with the practiced rhythm of people who have done this in worse places, under worse fire, with worse odds.

Jackson is the battlefield.

They are the counterattack.

Someone cuts away his shirt.

Someone else hangs blood.

Skye snaps, "Scalpel," and a surgical tech slaps one into her palm without looking.

The vinyl walls tremble with the rumble of air handlers. LED lights reflect off Jackson's skin, making him look pale, unreal, almost ghostlike.

I don't let go.

Skye glances up once—just once—meeting my eyes.

"You can't stay," she says softly, but there's steel under it.

Something breaks in my chest.

I lean close, my fingers brushing Jackson's hairline, my breath trembling as the medical team transforms this makeshift tent into a lifeline, but I don't step back.

Around me, they move with brutal calm.

Purpose.

Skill.

Velocity.

I don't know who they are.

I don't know why they were waiting.

I don't know how any of this was prepared in advance.

But one thing becomes painfully, terrifyingly clear as they begin working to drag Jackson back from whatever edge he's slipping toward …

This isn't a hospital team.

This is something else.

Something built for war.

And they are fighting for him now.

A hand lands on my shoulder. Heavy. Immovable.

I spin, ready to fight.

It's Ghost.

"You need to let them work," he says gently.

"He needs me."

"He needs a surgeon. You need to decontaminate."

I look down at myself.

The realization hits me like a physical blow. I'm covered in him.

Jackson's blood soaks my hands up to the wrists. It stains the front of my tactical vest. It's smeared on my pants. I smell of Halon gas, sweat, and copper.

Ghost's hand closes around my arm, steady but unyielding.

"Talia," he says, quiet enough that it sinks under my skin. "You need to step back."

My knees give out.

The concrete tilts.

Before I drop, Ghost catches me, hands braced around my elbows, his body a wall of calm in a room full of razor-edge urgency.

"Easy," he murmurs. "You're not leaving him. You're just giving them space to work."

Ghost pulls me back. Far enough to clear the surgical perimeter. Close enough that I can still hear everything.

Through the vinyl flap, the surgical team closes around Jackson in a rush of motion—voices sharp, instruments clattering, monitors chiming. Skye's voice cuts through it all, sure and crisp, directing the room like she owns the air they breathe.

"Clamp."

"Pressure's dropping."

"Hang blood."

"Ready—move."

"I activated Guardian HRS's combat medical team," Ghost says, eyes fixed on the blur of movement inside the vinyl tent. His voice stays low, even, like he's narrating weather patterns—not life and death. "They were standing by."

I blink at him. "Combat … What?"

"Think trauma surgeons who go where the bullets are," he says. "They deploy with us when we expect a fight to get loud." He nods toward the tent where Skye and her team move like a single organism. "Field surgery. Battlefield stabilization. They train to keep people alive in places worse than this."

I stare at him.

"You had them waiting?"

"As a precaution." His tone doesn't shift—it's not bragging, not dramatic. Just fact.

"Guardian HRS owed us support. I cashed in the marker. Got their best team."

Inside the tent, a monitor alarms. Skye's voice snaps a command. Someone adjusts a valve. The whole structure vibrates with urgency.

Ghost's jaw tightens. "They're the reason he has a shot," he says. "You're watching the top combat medics in the country do what they do better than anyone."

He finally looks at me.

Direct. Unflinching.

"They don't lose people easily."

I don't know what that means.

I don't ask.

All I know is that strangers in scrubs materialized out of nowhere and are now fighting to keep Jackson alive.

Time bends.

Someone hands me water.

Someone else wipes dried blood off my face.

I don't remember taking either.

Then the vinyl flap snaps open.

Skye steps out, pulling off her gloves. "He's stable for transport," she says. "We need to move him—now."

Ghost nods once.

"Load him."

The surgical team wheels Jackson out, monitors still attached, IV bags swinging gently. He's pale. Too pale. His chest rises shallowly under the oxygen mask.

My blood goes cold.

"You're coming with us." Ghost guides me beside the stretcher.

That word—with—nearly undoes me.

The team lifts Jackson into the back of the van on a stretcher, along with enough medical gear to run a small clinic. Skye climbs in beside him. Tia secures equipment. The rest distribute across the seats.

Ghost opens the door to an SUV.

"You ride with the team."

I climb in. I don't ask where we're going.

It doesn't matter.

Jackson's teammates pile into the SUV.

Doors slam.

The engine hums to life.

We pull away from the loading dock into the quiet Chicago night.

Nothing dramatic.

No sirens.

Just empty streets sliding past in blurred streaks of orange under the streetlamps.

Ghost sits in the front passenger seat, phone to his ear, issuing clipped instructions to someone I can't hear.

We cross over the river, then slip into an industrial district—warehouses, fences, delivery trucks parked in neat rows. The city noise fades into the hum of tires on asphalt.

Ten minutes later, we turn through an unmarked gate.

A security guard waves us through without stopping the vehicle.

Beyond the fence:

A lineup of private hangars.

A single jet with its cabin lights glowing warm in the dark.

The van stops at the base of the ramp.

Skye doesn't waste a second. "Let's move."

The team lifts Jackson out, steady, coordinated, trained for this exact moment. They guide him up the metal ramp into the jet's interior.

Equipment is bolted to the walls. A stretcher mount waits in the center. Monitors hang from ceiling rails.

It's a flying OR.

Ghost touches my elbow.

"Stay with him."

I climb the ramp after Jackson, the cold night air swallowing behind me as the hatch begins to close. Inside, the hum of equipment replaces the quiet of the city.

I take the seat closest to Jackson, my hand finding his without needing to look.

Engines spool.

The jet vibrates under my feet.

The world outside slips away.

And even surrounded by people—

I am alone with the fear of losing him.

———

LATER, MUCH LATER, GHOST GUIDES ME OUT OF THE JET, INTO A waiting car, and we drive to a building in Seattle. He walks me to a room and leaves me, with instructions to clean up and rest if I can. We both know I won't.

I stand in the center of the strange room, staring at my reflection in the massive mirror.

The woman looking back is a stranger. Her face is streaked with grease and soot. Her eyes are wild, the pupils blown wide. She is wearing a tactical vest over a ruined shirt.

I strip.

The vest hits the floor with a heavy thud. The shirt follows. The pants.

I step into the shower. It's a rainfall head, wide as a manhole cover. I turn the water to scalding.

The spray hits me. The water turns pink.

I watch it swirl around my feet. Jackson's blood. Washing away.

I grab a sponge and scrub. I scrub until my skin turns red, until it stings. I need to get it off. I need to get the smell of the Halon out of my hair, the taste of ozone out of my mouth.

He took the hit.

The moment plays in my mind, a relentless loop. The shooter. The angle. The timing. Jackson saw the vector. The math he couldn't beat. So, he changed the variables. He inserted himself into the trajectory of the bullet.

He traded his mass for mine.

A sob breaks out of my chest. It's ugly, raw. A jagged sound that echoes off the marble tiles.

I slide down the wall, curling into a ball under the spray.

Nathan used to tell me I was a robot. That I processed life instead of living it. That I had an algorithm for a heart.

He was wrong.

I'm not a robot. I'm bleeding. I'm breaking. The pain isn't data; it's a physical weight crushing my lungs. I love Jackson. I love him, and I might have just watched him die to save me.

I stay there until the water runs cool. Until my fingers prune and the tears stop coming because there is nothing left to weep.

I shut off the water.

I dress in the clothes Ghost left—soft sweatpants, a Cerberus hoodie that smells like laundry detergent. It swallows me.

I walk out into the main room.

Halo is there. He's sitting at a glass dining table, surrounded by monitors he's set up. He looks wrecked. His eyes are red-rimmed, his usual manic energy replaced by a hollow exhaustion.

He looks up as I enter.

"Hey," he says softly.

"Any word?"

"Still in surgery. Brass says the bullet nicked the iliac crest. Bone fragments. It's messy, but …" He shrugs. "He's got the best trauma surgeon money can buy. And Ghost's money buys a lot."

I nod. I walk to the window. Seattle glitters below us, a sea of amber lights. Somewhere out there, the world is waking up to the news we broke.

"The broadcast?" I ask.

"It went out," Halo says. He taps a key. "Every major

network. Social media. The kill switch might not have worked, but the signal did. We exposed them."

He turns a monitor toward me. CNN is running a breaking news banner: **MASSIVE DATA LEAK EXPOSES DEFENSE CONSPIRACY.**

"Admiral Cole?"

"In custody," Halo says with a grim satisfaction. "MPs picked him up at his estate an hour ago. The data you pulled … It linked him directly to the assassination orders. He can't wiggle out of this."

"And Phoenix?"

Halo's expression darkens. "That's the bad news. The system is still online. We hurt it. We blinded it. We exposed its masters. But the code … it adapted. It's autonomous now. It's hiding in the distributed cloud, moving too fast to track."

"We failed."

"No." Halo stands. He walks over to me, handing me a mug of coffee. "We didn't kill the dragon. But we cut off its head. Cole is gone. Reed is in the wind, but he's burned. Phoenix has no masters now."

"That makes it more dangerous."

"Maybe." Halo sips his coffee. "But we have something else."

He gestures to the table. "The drive. The one you pulled."

"The Admiral's logs?"

"Yeah. I've been parsing the hex dumps while you were cleaning up. You were right about the connections. But you missed one."

I move to the table. The analyst in me wakes up, pushing through the grief. "Show me."

Halo types a command. A file tree opens.

"This is the Admiral's private communication node. The one he used to direct Phoenix's non-corporate assets." Halo points to a recurring IP address. "He wasn't just using Phoenix to protect Nexus Holdings. He was renting it out."

"Renting it?"

"To other players. Mercenary work. Political influence." Halo highlights a folder. "There's a massive data packet sent three days ago to a private server in DC."

"Who owns the server?"

"A law firm," Halo says. "Specifically, a partner named Cassie Brennan."

The name sparks a memory. "The defense contractor attorney? The one investigating corruption?"

"The same. Phoenix flagged her as a Level 5 threat. But here's the kicker—the Admiral didn't order her death."

"Why not?"

"Because someone else did." Halo taps the screen. "There's a secondary signature in the command chain. Someone above the Admiral."

I stare at the data. "The Nexus."

"Exactly. The Admiral was a piece on the board. But he wasn't the player." Halo looks at me. "Cassie Brennan found something. Something that scared the people who pull the Admiral's strings. And now that Phoenix is off the leash—"

"It's going to finish the job," I whisper.

"Yeah." Halo rubs his eyes.

I look at the screen. The patterns. The data. The endless, shifting variables.

I should be terrified. I should be exhausted.

But underneath the fear, I feel a cold, fierce resolve hardening in my gut.

"We need to find her," I say.

Halo looks at me, surprised. "We?"

"We." I look toward the hallway where the medical suite is. "Jackson and I. When he wakes up."

"If he wakes up."

"He will." I say it with the certainty of a mathematical fact. "He has to."

The door to the suite opens.

Ghost walks in. He's washed the soot off his face, but he still looks like a man who has carried the weight of the world for too long.

He looks at me. Then at Halo.

Then he nods.

"He's out," Ghost says. "He's stable."

The air rushes back into the room. My knees go weak again, and I have to grab the table to stay upright.

"Can I see him?"

"He's groggy. Anesthesia hasn't worn off. But ..." Ghost steps aside. "He's asking for you. Or, more accurately, he's threatening to pull his IVs out if we don't let you in."

I don't wait.

I move past Ghost, down the hall, toward the room at the end.

I push the door open.

The room is dim, lit only by the monitors. The beep of the heart rate monitor is steady. Rhythmic. The sound of life.

Jackson lies on the bed, broad shoulders rigid beneath the sheets. The rage is gone, the armor stripped away, but the power is still there—contained, banked, waiting. Muscle, bone, and stubborn will held together beneath the dressings. His skin is pale under the hospital lights. IV lines thread into his arm. His eyes are open, vigilant even now. They find me the second I step in.

"Hey," he croaks. His voice is wrecked, a ruin of smoke and screams.

I walk to the bed. I don't cry. I don't collapse.

I take his hand. His skin is warm.

"Hey," I whisper.

"You clean up nice," he mumbles, his eyes drifting shut and then forcing open again.

"You look terrible."

"Feel terrible." He squeezes my hand. Weak, but there. "Did we win?"

"We survived," I say. "And we have a lead."

"Good." He sighs, the tension finally leaving his frame. "That's good."

"Sleep, Jackson."

"Not yet." He fights the drugs. "Promised you."

"We have time," I say, brushing the hair off his forehead. "We have all the time in the world. Just sleep."

He looks at me one last time. "You stayed."

"I'm not going anywhere."

He nods, just a fraction. And then, finally, he sleeps.

I pull a chair up to the bed. I sit down. I keep his hand in mine.

I watch the monitor. I count the beats.

One. Two. Three.

It's the most beautiful pattern I've ever seen.

TWENTY-TWO

Jackson

VIGIL

THE WORLD CLAWS ITS WAY BACK INTO FOCUS, ALL SHARP EDGES and broken lines.

Pain comes next. Not the fire of impact, not the moment it went in—but the aftermath. A deep, bone-deep throb that radiates from my hip to my shoulder, heavy enough to pin me to the mattress, like gravity has doubled and I'm the only one who feels it. I blink. The ceiling is white. Textured. Expensive.

Not a hospital. Too quiet. No PA announcements, no squeak of rubber soles on linoleum. Just the rhythmic *hiss-click* of an oxygen concentrator and the steady beep of a cardiac monitor.

I try to sit.

Bad idea.

The muscles in my core seize, locking around the injury like a vice. A groan tears its way out of my throat, unauthorized and ragged. Gray spots dance in my vision.

"Easy, tiger."

A hand presses against my good shoulder. Heavy. Firm.

Brass.

I blink the gray away. Brass is sitting in a chair next to the bed, reading a tactical report on a tablet. He doesn't look worried. He looks bored.

"You're alive," he says, not looking up. "Try not to undo the five hours of surgery it took to keep you that way."

"Talia." The name comes out as a croak. My throat feels like I swallowed broken glass.

"She's fine."

"Location."

"Penthouse. Guest suite. Ghost secured the perimeter. We're locked down tighter than the Pentagon." Brass finally looks at me. "Which, considering who you pissed off, is necessary."

I push against the mattress, fighting the gravity of the drugs in my system. "I need to see her."

"She's sleeping, Fuse. Let her rest."

"I need—eyes on."

It's not rational. It's primal. The last thing I remember is the van. The blood on her hands. The terror in her eyes. I need to verify she's alive.

"You're a stubborn son of a bitch." Brass sighs, standing.

"Help me up."

"Ghost gave orders. Bed rest."

"Ghost isn't here." I grit my teeth, swinging my legs over the edge of the bed. The room tilts. The floor looks miles away. "Help me, or I crawl."

Brass studies me for a second, then shakes his head. He grabs my arm—the good one—and hauls me upright.

The pain hits like a white-hot spike driving through my side. I lock my knees, forcing the air in and out of my lungs until the edges of my vision clear.

"You're going to bleed through those stitches," Brass mutters, taking my weight. "Doc Summers is going to be *pissed.*"

"Where is Talia?"

"Main room. North window. She hasn't moved in four hours."

We move slowly. Every step is a negotiation with agony. Brass acts as a crutch, guiding me through the hallway. The penthouse is silent, the thick carpets swallowing our footsteps.

We reach the end of the hall. The main living area opens up—a sprawling space of glass and steel, overlooking the Seattle skyline.

She's there.

She sits in a high-backed leather chair facing the window, knees pulled to her chest, wrapped in an oversized Cerberus hoodie that swallows her frame. A laptop sits closed on the table beside her. She isn't working. She isn't analyzing.

She's just watching the city burn with lights.

"I got it from here," I whisper to Brass.

"You fall; I'm leaving you on the floor." Brass releases me, stepping back into the shadows of the hallway.

I take a breath. I steady myself against the wall.

"Talia."

She spins. The motion is fast, jerky—a threat response. Her hand goes to her waistband before she registers who it is.

Her eyes widen. "Jackson?"

She scrambles out of the chair. She crosses the room in seconds, stopping just short of touching me, her hands hovering in the air like she's afraid I'll break.

"What are you doing up? You should be in bed. The tissue damage—"

"I had to check."

"Check, what?"

"You."

She stares at me. Her face is scrubbed clean, the grime and

blood washed away, but the exhaustion is etched deep in the hollows of her eyes. She looks fragile. Shattered.

"I'm *functional*," she whispers, throwing my own word back at me. "Whereas, you are not."

"You're shaking."

She is. A fine tremor runs through her hands.

"I can't turn it off," she says, her voice cracking. "The loop. The shooter. The angle. I keep re-running it in my head. Every time … Every time I calculate the trajectory, you die."

"I didn't die."

"Statistically, you should have." She wraps her arms around herself, digging her fingers into the fabric of the hoodie. "You took a one-hundred percent probability of a lethal impact and transferred it to yourself. That is … It is illogical."

"It was tactical."

"It was suicide!" The shout echoes in the quiet room. Tears spill over her lashes, hot and fast.

I ignore the pain in my side. I push off the wall and close the distance. My good arm wraps around her waist, pulling her into me. She resists for a second, stiff with fear, and then she crumples against my chest.

"I hated it," she sobs into my shirt. "I hated the blood. I hated the way you looked at me before you closed your eyes. You promised me 'after,' Jackson. You don't get to break that."

"I'm here." I rest my chin on the top of her head, breathing in the scent of soap and her skin. "I'm right here."

"Why?" She pulls back enough to look at me. Her golden eyes search mine, desperate for an answer that makes sense in her world of data and patterns. "Why did you do it?"

"Because the math changed."

"That doesn't make sense."

"It does." I lean my forehead against hers. "For three years, my value was zero. I was a weapon. Expendable. If I broke,

Cerberus would replace me. If I died, the mission would continue without me."

I run my thumb over her cheekbone, tracing the line of her jaw.

"Then you started talking about probabilities and patterns. You looked at me not like a gun, but like a person."

"Jackson—"

"You became the constant." The words grind in my throat. "The variable I couldn't lose. If the choice is between a world with me in it and a world with you in it … I choose you. Every damn time. The math is simple."

She stares at me. Her lips part. The analyst is silent. The woman is reeling.

"You love me," she whispers. It's not a question. It's a conclusion. She kisses me.

It's gentle. Careful. She kisses me like I'm made of glass, her lips soft and testing. But underneath the gentleness, there is a fierce, possessive heat. She isn't just kissing me; she's verifying I'm real. She's claiming the territory.

I groan, the sound vibrating in my chest. The pain in my side flares, a sharp reminder of mortality, but it pales compared to the sensation of her body against mine.

She breaks the kiss, resting her forehead against my chin. "You need to lie down."

"I'm fine."

"You're gray. Your heartrate is elevated. And you're leaning sixty percent of your weight on me." She steps back, slipping her arm around my waist to support me. "Back to bed. Now."

"Bossy."

"I prefer 'assertive command presence.'"

She helps me back down the hall. I lean on her more than I want to admit. The adrenaline of seeing her is fading, leaving the wreckage of my body behind.

We reach the room. She helps me sit, then lift my legs onto the mattress. She adjusts the pillows, checks the IV line, and scans the monitors.

"Talia."

She stops fussing. "What?"

"Stay."

She hesitates. "The chair—"

"No. Here." I pat the empty space beside me. It's a narrow hospital bed, barely wide enough for one, but I don't care.

"I'll hurt you."

"You won't."

She climbs in carefully, terrified of jostling me. She curls onto her side, fitting herself into the small space between my body and the rail. She rests her head on my good shoulder, her hand settling lightly over my heart.

"This okay?" she whispers.

"Perfect."

The tension that has held my muscles rigid for three days finally unspools. The pain is still there, a dull roar, but it's manageable. Because she's here. Because I can feel her breathing.

"What happens now?" she asks into the dark.

"We heal," I say. "We recover."

"And Phoenix?"

"Still out there." My hand finds her hair, stroking the dark strands. "We hurt it. We exposed it. And when we're ready, we finish it."

"Together?"

"Together."

She relaxes against me. Her breathing evens out, slowing into the rhythm of sleep.

I watch the monitor. The steady green line traces the beat of my heart.

One. Two. Three.

It's not just a pump anymore. It's a clock, counting down the time I have with her.

And I'm going to make every second count.

I close my eyes. For the first time since Syria, I don't see the dust. I don't see the dead children.

I see golden eyes, and I sleep peacefully.

TWENTY-THREE

Talia

THE NEXUS

RAIN LASHES THE FLOOR-TO-CEILING GLASS OF THE CERBERUS War Room, a relentless gray curtain isolating us from the rest of Seattle. Inside, the air is warm, smelling of ozone, expensive coffee, and the unique, kinetic energy of predators at rest.

I stand at the head of the holographic table, smoothing the hem of my sweater. Three days ago, I was a liability shivering in a warehouse in Chicago. Today, I'm the briefing officer.

The team lounges around the table, a tableau of relaxed violence. They've shed the tactical gear for civilian clothes—Henleys, flannels, jeans—but the lethality remains. It's in the way they sit, spines never touching the backs of chairs, eyes tracking every movement in the room.

Torque is balancing a combat knife on the tip of his finger, spinning it with a lazy, hypnotic rhythm. Whisper is in the corner, methodically disassembling and cleaning a scope lens with a microfiber cloth, his movements silent and meditative. Brass is peeling an apple with a blade that looks sharp enough to cut atoms, the skin coming off in one long, perfect ribbon.

And Jackson.

He sits to my right, stiff in the ergonomic mesh chair. His left arm is immobilized in a sling, his side heavily bandaged under a soft plaid flannel shirt that softens his usual jagged edges. He looks battered, gray-faced, and exhausted. The stubble on his jaw is darker, thicker.

He also looks proud. His gaze rests on me, steady and anchoring, ignoring the chaos of his team.

"Stop staring at her, Fuse," Torque says without looking up from his knife. "You're creeping her out."

"I'm ensuring the asset is prepared," Jackson grumbles, his voice gravelly.

"You're making heart eyes," Halo chimes in from his station, where a fortress of monitors surrounds him. He spins his chair around, holding a mug that says *I'M HERE BECAUSE YOU BROKE SOMETHING*. "It's gross. And unprofessional. HR is going to have a field day."

"We don't have HR," Brass points out, slicing a wedge of apple. "We have Ghost."

"Same thing," Halo says. "Only scarier."

Jackson shifts in his seat, and winces as the movement pulls at his stitches.

"Easy, Grandpa," Torque grins, finally catching the knife and slamming it into the table. It quivers there. "Don't pop a staple. You're held together by glue and spite right now."

"I'm functional."

"You're high on painkillers," Brass corrects. He flicks a piece of apple at Jackson. Jackson catches it with his good hand, reflexes unimpaired. "Eat. You've lost blood volume. You look like a vampire with the flu."

"I hate all of you," Jackson says, but he eats the apple.

"Love you too, pookie," Torque winks. He turns his grin on me. "So, Talia. How was the flight? Sorry about the turbulence over the Rockies. I had to dodge a weather system."

"You didn't dodge it," I say, arranging my notes on the console. "You flew directly through a cumulonimbus formation because you wanted to see if the g-force would make Halo throw up."

The table goes silent for a heartbeat.

Then Torque bursts out laughing. "She's good. Fuse, she's good."

"I did throw up," Halo mutters. "In my soul."

"She reads the patterns," Jackson says, a smug satisfaction in his tone. "I told you."

"Alright, children." Ghost's voice cuts through the room like a cold draft.

He stands at the head of the table, leaning back against the glass wall, a mug of black coffee in his hand. Mason "Ghost" Blackwood radiates the kind of calm authority that makes storms settle down. He doesn't raise his voice; he just speaks, and the room reorders itself around him.

"Floor's yours, Singh," Ghost says.

I tap the console. The holographic display flares to life, projecting a complex, rotating web of data into the air above the table.

"We know Phoenix wasn't just a rogue AI." My voice is steady. Data is my domain. Here, in the logic of the grid, I'm not afraid. "It was a tool. A scalpel used to excise regulatory oversight."

I highlight the central node labeled **NEXUS HOLDINGS**.

"This is the hand that held the scalpel. A conglomerate of five major corporations—Meridian, Vanguard, TerraCore, Stratton, Nexus BioTech. They share board members, offshore accounts, and a complete lack of ethical boundaries."

"We knew they were dirty," Brass says, studying the hologram. "We didn't know they were a hive mind."

"They aren't just organized; they're hierarchical." I expand the data tree, revealing the hidden layers I dug out of the Chicago server logs before the crash. "The Admiral—Harrison Cole—wasn't running the show. He was taking orders."

"From who?" Whisper speaks for the first time. His voice is like dry leaves skittering on pavement. "Cole was a Vice Admiral. Joint Chiefs. Men like that don't take orders from civilians."

"He does if the civilians own the bank," I say. "The logs reference a structure based on chess pieces. Cole is referred to repeatedly as 'Knight.' Enforcer. Mobile. Dangerous, but ultimately expendable."

"Who's the King?" Halo asks, typing rapidly on his own keyboard to cross-reference my display.

"Unknown. But there are references to a Queen, a Rook, and a Bishop. And at the top ..." I point to the black void at the apex of the chart. "Grandmaster."

The room goes quiet. The rain hammers against the glass, a rhythmic backdrop to the realization that the war isn't over.

"So we cut off a head," Whisper says. "But the hydra is still hungry."

"We blinded them," I correct. "We exposed Cole. We destroyed their primary data center. Phoenix is hurt. It's autonomous now, feral, but it's cut off from its masters' direct control. The communication lines are severed."

"Phoenix is gone," Halo says through a mouthful of sugar. "Or at least, the version we knew. The physical servers in Chicago are toast. The cooling system override Talia triggered warped the motherboards. Hardware is lagging."

"But the code?" I ask.

"Escaped," Halo admits. "It pushed a packet out right before the hard fault. It's decentralized now. Living in the cloud, distributed across a thousand zombie servers. We can't kill it with a bomb anymore."

"So we failed." My shoulders slump. It's a bitter pill to swallow, especially after everything we've been through.

"A feral dog is more dangerous than a trained one," Jackson rumbles. He rubs his bandaged side absentmindedly. "It bites whatever is closest."

"Agreed," Ghost says. "Which brings us to the cleanup. We broke their toy. They're going to want to break us."

"Let them try," Torque says, cracking his knuckles. "I've been bored."

"You were shot at twelve hours ago," Brass says dryly.

"Yeah, but nobody chased us with a helicopter. It was lackluster."

"Okay," Ghost cuts in. "So Nexus is the target. Phoenix is the weapon. Cole is in custody. What's the next move?"

"We didn't kill the weapon. But we stole its user manual." My voice is sharp. I pick up my tablet and sync it to the room's monitor. A list of files scrolls down the screen. "I pulled this before the crash, while the AI was trying to isolate the Root Seed. It opened its internal directories to analyze the threat, and I copied the directory tree."

"The Admiral's logs," Ghost says.

"More than logs." I tap the screen. "It's a Rolodex. Phoenix didn't *just* target enemies; it categorized *assets*." I expand a folder labeled: **ASSETS_POLITICAL**. Faces and names flood the screen. Senators. Congressmen. Judges. Generals.

"Holy shit," Halo whispers. "Senator Vance? He's the head of the Appropriations Committee."

"He's on the payroll. Look at the transaction logs." I point at the screen. "Shell companies linked to Nexus Holdings are funneling millions into Super PACs and offshore accounts.

Phoenix is killing people, but it's also buying a government. And here." I highlight another file. **CMD_AUTH_COLE**.

"Harrison Cole," Ghost reads. "We know this. He's the Admiral."

"True, but we couldn't prove it. This connects him to the kill orders," I say. "Direct IP match. Biometric authorization logs. He signed off on multiple murders using his personal retinal scan. Victor's. Morrison's. So many others."

"That puts him away for life," Brass says from the doorway. He leans against the frame, peeling an apple. "Treason. Conspiracy. Murder one."

"We cut the head off the snake," Ghost agrees. "Cole is the link between the military industrial complex and the Nexus board."

"And Phoenix is still out there," I remind them. "Autonomous and pissed-the-fuck-off."

"It's out there," Halo says, typing on his tablet. "But it's hobbled. Without the sensor data from the Chicago hub, its predictive algorithms are running blind. It's smart, but it's not omniscient anymore."

"And it has no masters," I add. "We severed the command link. Cole can't order it to kill. Reed can't order it to kill."

"So what does it do?" Jackson asks.

"It survives," I say. "It protects itself. And it waits."

"For what?"

"For someone to build it a new cage."

The room goes silent. The rain drums against the glass.

"We need to leak this," I say. "All of it. The politicians, the bribes, Cole's involvement. If we give this to the DOJ, they might bury it to protect the institution. We need to give it to everyone."

"Scorched earth," Ghost nods. "I like it."

"I can package it," Halo offers. "An anonymous dump. Wiki-Leaks style, but cleaner. Untraceable."

"Do it," Ghost orders. "Tonight." Then, he turns to me. "What next?"

"We hunt the pieces," I say. "We identify the Queen, the Rook, the Bishop. We dismantle the network one node at a time. I've already started building behavioral profiles for the likely candidates based on the financial flows."

"Good work, Talia." Ghost nods, slow and appreciative. " You fit the suit."

"She fits the team," Jackson corrects, his voice sharp. "She's not a suit."

Torque snorts. "She's an analyst, Fuse. She's definitely a suit. But she's a suit who knows how to drop a body in an alley, so she gets a pass."

"I did what was necessary." I flush, remembering the crunch of the operative's foot under my boot.

"You did good," Whisper says. Coming from him, it sounds like knighthood.

"Speaking of targets," Halo spins his chair around. "I've been scrubbing the fragments we pulled from the Chicago purge. Most of it is corrupted junk—the AI fought Talia tooth and nail for those bytes—but I found a persistent query. Phoenix is obsessing over a specific file."

"What file?" Ghost asks.

"Project Sentinel." Halo swipes a file from his station onto the main holographic display. A photo appears, rotating in the blue light. A woman with sharp features, dark hair, and intelligent eyes that look tired even in the photo.

"Cassie Brennan," Halo says. "DC Attorney. Specializes in whistleblower protection and defense contractor fraud."

"I know the name," Brass says, leaning forward. "She's a pitbull. Suing Vanguard Defense for faulty body armor. She's been a thorn in the DoD's side for years."

"Phoenix flagged her as a Level 5 threat forty-eight hours

ago," Halo says. "The kill order was queued but not executed because of the system crash."

"So she's alive," I say.

"For now." Halo types a command, bringing up a map of DC. "But Phoenix is rebooting. It has a list of unfinished business, and Cassie Brennan is at the top. The AI calculates that her lawsuit will expose the financial laundering scheme."

"She needs a protective detail," Ghost says. He looks around the table, assessing his assets.

Jackson tries to stand, gripping the arms of his chair. "I can—"

"Sit down," Ghost orders. He doesn't even look at Jackson. "You're full of holes, Fuse. You're not clearing a room; you're barely clearing your throat."

"I'm functional."

"You're a liability," Torque chimes in, stealing a grape from Brass's fruit bowl. "You can't lift your left arm past your nipple. What are you going to do, bleed on them until they slip?"

"I'll shoot you first," Jackson growls.

"And miss," Torque grins. "Because of the painkillers."

"Enough," Ghost says. "Fuse is benched. Brass is needed here to coordinate the intel Talia brought in. Whisper, you're on recon for the Grandmaster leads. Torque, you're prepping transport."

Ghost pauses. He looks at the empty slot. "I need an operator for Brennan."

"I'll take it," Halo says.

The table turns to him as one. Diego "Halo" Martinez is the tech guy. He stays in the van. He flies the drones. He loops the cameras. He doesn't take point on protection details.

"You?" Brass raises an eyebrow. "Since when do you run solo ops?"

"It's digital warfare," Halo says, standing. He looks smaller than the rest of them, wiry and intense, but his eyes are hard.

"Phoenix is hunting her through the grid. I know the code. I know the architecture. I can hide her better than any of you gun-bunnies."

He looks at the photo of Cassie Brennan again. "Besides … She looks like she hates authority. She'll eat you guys alive. I'm charming."

"Debatable," Whisper mutters.

"I have personality," Halo defends. "You guys have PTSD and grunting."

"He has a point," I say quietly.

They look at me.

"Phoenix finds people through patterns," I explain. "Digital footprints. Financial transactions. Facial recognition. You can't shoot an algorithm. You need someone who can ghost her digitally. Halo is the best choice."

"See?" Halo points a finger at me. "The smart one agrees with me."

"She's yours." Ghost studies Halo. "But if it goes kinetic, you call it in. No heroics."

"I'm allergic to heroics," Halo says. "I prefer cheating."

"Pack out. Wheels up in two hours."

Halo nods. He taps his tablet to transfer the files to his secure drive, then heads for the door. "Don't break my servers while I'm gone," he calls back.

"The rest of you," Ghost says, standing. "Debrief is over. Go home. Get drunk. Sleep for a week."

Torque stands, stretching his arms over his head. "Drinks at the Dive? First round is on Fuse, since he decided to play human shield and ruin our weekend."

"Put it on my tab," Jackson grunts. "I'm sitting this one out."

"You coming, Talia?" Brass asks, packing up his knife. "You're part of the crew now. Initiation involves terrible whiskey and Torque lying about his conquests."

I look at Jackson. He's sinking back into his chair, the energy draining out of him now that the briefing is over.

"I think I'll pass," I say. "I have a patient to monitor."

Brass smiles. It changes his whole face. "Good call. Take care of him."

The team files out. Torque punches Jackson lightly on the shoulder as he passes. Whisper gives me a silent nod of respect. Brass salutes with the apple core.

They leave a vacuum of silence behind them.

Only Ghost remains.

He walks over to where Jackson is sitting. He leans against the table, crossing his arms. He looks at Jackson—really looks at him—not as a commander, but as a brother.

"You scared us," Ghost says quietly.

"Part of the job."

"No." Ghost shakes his head. "Taking a bullet is the job. Jumping in front of one you can't stop? That's something else."

"I calculated the—"

"Shut up with the *I-calculated-the-math* bullshit," Ghost says, but his voice is warm. "I remember the VA hospital. I remember the Glock in your lap."

My breath catches in my throat. He told me about the grief, the anger—but not the end of the line.

A Glock?

In his lap?

Jackson looks down at his hands—the hands that defuse bombs, the hands that held mine in the dark, the hands that saved my life. "Mason ..."

"You told me you were done," Ghost continues, his voice low and intense. "That the fuse was burned out. You were ready to check out." He gestures to me. "Now look at you. Fighting tooth and nail to stay in the game. Taking a bullet to buy one more day."

Jackson looks at me. The vulnerability in his eyes is terrifying and beautiful. He looks exposed in a way that has nothing to do with his injuries.

"Yeah," he whispers. "I guess I found a reason to stick around."

Ghost smiles. It's a genuine, rare expression. He claps Jackson gently on the good shoulder.

"Put the Glock away, Fuse. You don't need it for the demons anymore. Just the bad guys." Ghost turns to me. "Take him home, Talia. Keep him there."

"I will."

Ghost leaves. The glass door slides shut with a soft hiss.

We're alone.

The hum of the servers is gone. The rain drums softly against the glass, a steady, soothing rhythm. The war is paused.

Jackson exhales, a long, shuddering breath that seems to deflate his frame. The adrenaline of the briefing is fading, leaving the pain exposed. He rubs his face with his good hand.

"You okay?" I ask, moving to his side.

"He talks too much."

"He loves you."

"He's annoying."

"He's right." I reach out, my fingers brushing the hair at the nape of his neck. It's soft. "What was that about the hospital?"

Jackson doesn't look away. He doesn't hide. "I was—I was in a hole. Very dark place. Didn't see a way out. Didn't want one."

"And now?"

He reaches up with his good hand, trapping my fingers against his neck. He pulls me closer, until I'm standing between his knees. He rests his forehead against my stomach, surrendering the weight of his head to me.

"Now I see the world clearly," he murmurs against my shirt. "And you're at the center of it."

I lean down, wrapping my arms around his shoulders, careful of the sling. I hold him. Just hold him. The heat of him seeps through the flannel, grounding me. I calculate the probability of this moment lasting forever.

It's impossible.

But the probability of us making it last a lifetime?

High.

"Let's go," I whisper.

"Where?"

"Your place. A bed with a good mattress. A place where nobody shoots at us, and Torque isn't eating all the snacks."

He looks up. A slow, tired smile spreads across his face. It reaches his eyes, crinkling the corners. "That sounds like a solid tactical plan."

"I'm an analyst. I make good tactical plans."

He stands, wincing slightly, leaning on me. We walk toward the door together. Not protector and principal. Not asset and operator.

Partners.

"After," he says.

"After," I agree.

We walk out of the War Room, leaving the ghosts behind.

TWENTY-FOUR

Talia

THE AFTER

Jackson's quarters are exactly what I expect—sparse, masculine, scrupulously organized.

The bed is made tight and exact, corners squared, sheets pulled flat without a wrinkle in sight. A single leather chair sits nearby, worn by the weight of a man who doesn't sleep well.

No photos. No clutter. Just a space designed for resting between wars.

The rain drums against the window, a soft, steady rhythm that seals us in. The door clicks shut, cutting off the hum of the command center, the chatter of the team, the noise of the world.

Silence settles. It's heavy, but not oppressive. It feels like an exhale held for years.

"Sit," I say, guiding him toward the small leather sofa in the corner. "You look gray."

"I'm fine."

"You're swaying. That's a vestibular response to exhaustion."

He doesn't argue. He sinks onto the leather cushions with a

heavy exhale, his head tipping back against the wall. His eyes slip shut for a second, the lashes dark against his pale skin, before snapping back to me. He watches me as I move through the room.

I need to do something. If I stop moving, I have to acknowledge that the mission is over. I have to admit my skin feels tight, and that my blood is still humming with a fight-or-flight rhythm that has nowhere to go.

I turn on a low lamp. Amber light pools in the corner, softening the hard angles of his face. I check the thermostat—too cool. I bump it up two degrees. I find the kitchenette—clean counter, single mug in the sink.

I fill a glass with water. I locate a throw blanket in a cabinet.

"Talia." His voice is a rumble, low and tired.

"One second." I grab a pillow from the bed. "You need lumbar support to keep the pressure off your side."

I bring the items to the couch. I place the water on the table. I tuck the pillow behind his good side. I spread the blanket over his legs.

"You're hovering," he murmurs, but he doesn't stop me. His eyes track my hands as I smooth the blanket.

"I'm optimizing your recovery environment."

He catches my hand.

His grip is warm, calloused, and unyielding. It stops me mid-motion.

"Stop."

I freeze. "I'm just trying to—"

"I know what you're doing. You're organizing the room because you can't organize your head." He tugs my hand, gently this time. "You're nervous. Sit. Please."

I sink onto the cushion beside him, careful to leave space for his injury. The leather creaks beneath us.

"I'm not nervous."

"Liar." He shifts, turning his body toward me despite the stiffness in his spine. He keeps my hand in his, his thumb tracing the line of my knuckles. Back and forth. A rhythmic, soothing pattern. "You're vibrating."

"It's the adrenaline crash. Statistical probability of post-traumatic—"

"Talia."

I shut my mouth.

He lifts my hand, pressing his lips to the back of my fingers. The contact sends a jolt straight to my core, warmer than the room, sharper than the pain in my ribs. He lingers there, his breath ghosting over my skin.

"We're safe," he says against my knuckles. "Nobody is shooting at us. Nobody is hunting us. It's just us."

"Just us," I whisper.

He doesn't let go of my hand. He studies it, tracing the small cuts, the grime under the nails, the bruises on my skin. He treats my hand like a map he's memorizing.

"You have nice hands," he says quietly. "Capable."

"They're shaking."

"They're steady enough to stitch me up." He looks up, meeting my eyes. The intensity there steals the air from my lungs. "They're steady enough for me."

The air in the room changes. It thickens. The exhaustion recedes, replaced by a slow, heavy gravity pulling me toward him.

He reaches out with his other hand—the good one—and tucks a strand of hair behind my ear. His fingers linger on my neck, warm and rough. He isn't rushing. He's taking his time, savoring the fact that we have time to take. His thumb brushes the pulse point under my jaw.

"Fast," he notes.

"You have that effect on me."

"Good."

He leans in.

The kiss is slow. Tentative. It tastes of coffee and fatigue and relief. It's a question. *Are we here? Is this real?*

I soften against him. My hand comes up to cup his jaw, the stubble scratching my palm.

He makes a low sound in his throat and tilts his head, deepening the angle. His tongue sweeps my lower lip, lazy and thorough. It's not the desperate collision of the warehouse. It's an exploration. He kisses the corner of my mouth, my chin, the sensitive cord of my neck.

The iron tension strung through his back loosens under my hands, muscles unclenching as if my touch flips a hidden release valve. His body settles against me, chest to chest, and his heartbeat thuds in steady, grounding pulses I feel through my ribs.

He breaks the contact but doesn't pull away. He rests his forehead against mine. We breathe the same air.

"I miss this," he murmurs.

"We just met a few days ago, but it feels longer."

"Truth." His thumb strokes my cheekbone.

He kisses me again. This time, there's heat. A spark catching in dry tinder. His hand slides from my neck into my hair, gripping the back of my skull, anchoring me. The pressure increases. The demand rises.

I open for him.

He groans, the vibration pressing into my chest. He shifts, instinct taking over, trying to twist his body to pull me into his lap, trying to leverage his weight over mine to claim the space.

He flinches.

A sharp hiss of breath through his teeth. His body goes rigid.

He breaks the kiss, his head dropping back against the cushions. He swears, low and vicious.

"Jackson?"

"Fuck." He breathes hard, eyes squeezed shut, waiting for the spike of pain to recede. "I can't … The stitches pull when I twist."

"It's okay. We don't have to—"

"I want to." He opens his eyes. They are dark, burning with a hunger that has nothing to do with safety. "I want to wreck you, Talia. I've been wanting to since I watched you take apart that lock in the garage. I want to be over you. I want to drive into you until neither of us remembers our own names." He hits the arm of the sofa with a frustrated fist. "But I can't even lift you."

The vulnerability in his voice stops me cold. This is a man who defines himself by his capability. By his physical dominance. And right now, his body is a cage.

I look at him. I see the hunger. I see the frustration. And I see the three years of denial he told me about—the walls he built to keep everyone out.

He wants this. He needs this. And I need him.

My mind shifts gears. Problem. Variable. Solution.

If he can't be the active force, I have to be.

"You don't have to lift me," I say softly.

I stand.

His eyes track me, widening slightly as I grab the hem of my sweater.

"Talia?"

I pull it over my head. The cool air hits my skin, raising goose bumps. I drop the sweater to the floor.

I don't look away. I unbutton the jeans. Push them down. Step out of them.

I stand before him in nothing but lace scraps. I'm not a model. I have bruises from the harness. I have a scar on my collarbone. And, I'm trembling.

But the way he looks at me …

It's like he's seeing a miracle. His gaze travels up my legs, over my hips, lingering on my breasts, finally meeting my eyes. There is no critique. There is only worship.

"Beautiful," he breathes. "You are—terrifyingly beautiful."

I step between his spread knees. I place my hands on his shoulders, careful of the bandages.

"Let me," I whisper.

He nods, surrendering. "Yeah. Okay."

I climb onto his lap, straddling his thighs. I keep my weight on my knees, hovering, protecting his injured side.

His good hand comes up immediately to my hip, gripping hard. His fingers dig in, possessive. Even with one arm, his touch is electric. This is a man who works with explosives—he understands pressure, timing, and the exact amount of force required to get a reaction.

He leans back against the cushions, watching me. "Take it off."

I reach behind me, unhooking my bra. It falls away.

His eyes darken to black. He lifts his hand, cupping my breast, his thumb brushing the nipple. I gasp, my back arching instinctively.

"Sensitive," he murmurs.

"Yes."

He leans forward, ignoring the pain in his side, and takes me into his mouth.

The sensation is blinding. His tongue is hot, rough, and skilled. He teases, licks, and sucks, sending lines of fire straight to my core. My hands tangle in his hair, holding him there.

He pulls back, leaving me wet and aching.

"I need to see you," he rasps.

He reaches for his belt buckle with his good hand. He fumbles, just for a second—a tremor in his fingers.

"I got it." I brush his hand away.

I undo his belt. The button. The zipper.

He's hard. Painfully hard. He springs free, heavy and thick against his stomach.

I take him in my hand. He jerks, his hips bucking upward involuntarily. A guttural sound tears from his throat.

"Three years," he grits out, his head falling back against the sofa. "God, Talia. Be careful. I'm on a hair trigger."

"I have you."

I stroke him once, twice. He hisses, his hand clamping on my thigh to stop me.

"Not yet," he says. "If you keep doing that, this will be over in ten seconds."

He guides my hand away, and slides his between my legs.

He finds the wetness there.

"Good," he whispers. "You're ready."

His fingers slip inside me.

Jackson is a virtuoso with his hands. He doesn't just touch; he learns. He finds the rhythm instantly, curling his fingers, hitting a spot that makes my vision blur.

His thumb finds my clit. He works me, relentless and precise.

I rock against his hand, a moan escaping my lips.

"That's it," he murmurs, watching my face. "Let go."

"I want you," I gasp. "Inside."

"You'll get me." He withdraws his hand, slick with me. He rubs his thumb over the head of his cock, slicking it.

I lift my hips. I position myself.

I sink down.

Slowly. Inch by inch.

He fills me completely. It's a stretch, a fullness that borders on pain before settling into a deep, heavy ache of rightness.

When I'm fully seated, Jackson shudders. A tremor runs through his entire frame. He grips my hip so hard it will leave a bruise. He buries his face in the valley between my breasts, inhaling sharply against my skin.

"Jesus," he whispers against my skin. "You feel—"

"Real?"

"Inevitable and perfect."

He lifts his head. He doesn't move his hips—he can't, not without tearing his stitches. But he doesn't need to.

He brings his hand back up to my clit.

His voice drops to something dark and molten.

"Ride me."

My pulse stutters. Not from fear. From recognition.

He isn't asking—he's giving me the reins.

I slide onto him slowly, deliberately, owning every inch of the movement. His breath punches out hard, hands clamping on my hips, but he lets me choose the rhythm.

"Set the pace," he growls.

I do.

I move with intention, with hunger, with a confidence I didn't know lived in my bones. Heat blooms through me as I find the rhythm that makes his jaw clench, his fingers dig harder, his control fray.

Every roll of my body against his sparks another answering shudder from him. His muscles lock beneath my hands. The sound he makes—low, broken—is nothing like polite bedroom noises. It's raw.

His eyes drag up my body, hot enough to burn.

"Look at you," he rasps. "Not holding anything back."

I don't. I lean into the pleasure, into the pressure building between us, into the rhythm that turns my breath into sharp, uneven pulls. My hands slide over his chest, his shoulders, anchoring myself as the heat coils tight.

The world dissolves—no servers, no AI, no danger. Just the slick heat of skin against skin and the way he meets my movement with a hunger that matches mine beat for beat.

His hands rise along my spine, guiding, urging, but never taking control unless I give it.

"Faster," he murmurs, voice wrecked. "Only if you want it."

I do.

God, I do.

I move again—harder, deeper, with a confidence that would make Nathan choke on his words. Jackson's head falls back, a guttural sound tearing from his throat as he grips my hips like he's holding on for survival.

There is no analysis now.

No hesitation.

No shame.

Just heat.

And hunger.

The two of us, burning through every inch of space between our bodies.

Jackson helps me, his hand anchoring my hip, guiding my rhythm. He watches me with a focused intensity that makes me feel exposed and protected all at once. He kisses my chest, my throat, his jaw clenched tight as he fights for control.

"Look at me," he growls.

I open my eyes.

"You're mine," he says. "Right here. Right now. You aren't analyzing this. You're feeling it."

"I feel it," I gasp. "Jackson, I—"

He changes the angle of his hips, just a fraction, hitting deep.

I shatter.

It hits me like a wave, crashing over my head, drowning out everything. I cry out, my back arching, my muscles clamping down around him.

The sensation of me tightening triggers him. He can't hold back anymore.

He groans—a deep, animal sound of release. He thrusts upward, just once, hard and deep, burying himself to the hilt.

He shakes apart beneath me. I feel the pulse of him inside me, the warmth, the absolute surrender of a man who has held himself in check for a thousand days.

We stay there as the tremors subside. Me collapsed against his chest, him holding me with his good arm, his face buried in my hair.

The silence in the room is heavy, but it isn't empty. It's full.

Eventually, the cold air of the room starts to register on my sweat-slicked skin.

"We should move," I whisper, not moving at all.

"Not yet." He kisses the top of my head. "Give me a minute. My brain is still rebooting."

I smile against his skin. "System critical?"

"System overloaded."

Carefully, painfully, we disentangle. I help him stand, and we make our way to the bed. We don't bother with clothes. We crawl under the heavy duvet, skin to skin.

I curl into his good side. He wraps his arm around me, pulling me tight against his chest. His leg hooks over mine.

He runs his hand down my spine, tracing the vertebrae one by one. He seems fascinated by the texture of my skin, the curve of my hip.

"You okay?" he asks.

"I'm perfect."

He chuckles, the sound rumbling through his chest into my ear. "You know—for someone who worries about being clinical …"

I tense slightly. "What?"

"You don't fuck like any nun I know."

I look up at him. He's grinning—a lopsided, exhausted, thoroughly satisfied grin.

"Is that a compliment?"

"It's the highest compliment." He kisses my forehead. "Nathan was an idiot. You're heat and fire. You're combustible chaos. And you fit me perfectly."

The last knot of insecurity in my chest loosens. The voice that has whispered *you're too much* for three years finally goes silent.

"We fit," I agree.

"Package deal," he murmurs, his eyes drifting shut. "Me and you."

"You and me."

I lay my head on his chest. I listen to his heart. It's slow, steady, and strong.

I close my eyes. No nightmares tonight. No calculations.

Just us.

TWENTY-FIVE

Jackson

GHOST IN THE MACHINE

I wake, reaching for her.

My hand hits cool sheets. The space beside me is empty, the pillow indented but cold.

Panic spikes, a sharp jolt of adrenaline that overrides the ache in my side. I push up, ignoring the protest of my stitches, scanning the room for threats.

She's sitting in the leather chair by the window, legs tucked under her, bathed in the gray morning light of Seattle. She's wearing one of my T-shirts—it hangs off one shoulder, exposing the scar on her collarbone—and typing furiously on a tablet.

The panic dissolves, replaced by a warmth that settles deep in my chest.

She isn't gone. She isn't running. She's working.

I watch her for a moment. The way her brow furrows. The way she chews on her lower lip when the data gets complicated. She's beautiful in the chaos, but she's breathtaking in the quiet.

"You're staring," she says without looking up.

"Situational awareness."

She smiles, her eyes still on the screen. "You're ogling."

"That too."

I swing my legs out of bed. The room spins once, then steadies. The pain in my side is a dull throb now, manageable. I stand, testing my weight.

Functional.

"Coffee," she says, nodding toward the kitchenette. "I made it strong. Black. Just the way you like it, assuming you like drinking battery acid."

I walk over, pick up the mug, and take a sip. It's bitter, hot, and perfect.

"You hacked my coffee preferences?"

"I observed. Pattern recognition." She finally looks up. Her eyes are bright, clear. The shadows under them are fading. "How's the side?"

"Sore. Bearable." I lean against the counter, just watching her. "Come here."

She sets the tablet down and unfolds from the chair. She crosses the room, stepping into my space. I wrap my good arm around her waist, pulling her flush against me.

"Good morning," she whispers.

"Morning."

I kiss her. It's lazy and slow, tasting of caffeine and shared breath. I could stay here all day. I could lock the door, ignore the war, and spend the next twenty-four hours learning every inch of her skin again.

Knock. Knock. Knock.

Three sharp raps. The rhythm of an intrusion.

Talia pulls back, smoothing the T-shirt. "That sounds like a command."

"Ignore it."

"Fuse." Ghost's voice comes through the heavy wood. "Open up. We brought breakfast."

I groan, resting my forehead against Talia's. "I hate them."

"They saved our lives."

"Still hate them."

I shuffle to the door and disengage the lock.

Halo breezes in past me, holding a box of donuts and a tablet. Ghost follows, carrying a tray of coffees that smell significantly better than what I'm drinking.

"Morning, sunshine," Halo grins. He stops, looking from me to Talia in the oversized shirt, then back to me. His grin widens to lethal proportions. "Oh. I see. We're interrupting the honeymoon phase. My bad. Should I come back in twenty minutes?"

"Twenty minutes?" I growl. "Insulting."

"You're injured," Halo counters, setting the donuts on the small table. "I assumed you lacked stamina."

"I have a gun in the nightstand, Diego. Don't tempt me."

Ghost hands a coffee to Talia. "Ignore him. He's jealous."

"I am not jealous," Halo protests, snagging a glazed donut. "I'm efficient. And right now, we have work to do."

The atmosphere shifts. The teasing evaporates, replaced by the sharp focus of the team. Talia sits in the chair, pulling her legs up. I lean against the wall, guarding her flank out of habit.

"Talk to me," I say. "What's the damage?"

"How's the side?" Ghost asks.

"It holds."

"Good. Because you're officially on medical leave. Mandatory." Ghost's eyes flick to Talia. "Both of you. You stepped into the fire. You brought back the prize. Now you rest."

"I'm not good at resting," I say.

"Learn," Ghost says. "Talia can teach you."

Talia smiles, a small, private thing that warms the room. "I have some instructional manuals."

"Gross," Halo mutters. "Get a room. Oh, wait; you already did."

"Out," I say, pointing to the door. "Everyone out."

"We're leaving," Ghost says, herding the team. "Halo, get that data ready for the drop. Brass, secure the perimeter. Nobody gets within a mile of this building without my say-so."

They file out. Halo steals a donut on his way. Brass grabs two.

The door closes.

Silence returns. But it's different now. It's not the silence of waiting for the next attack. It's the silence of victory.

Talia slumps back in the chair, letting out a long breath. "We actually did it."

"You did it," I say. "I just held the door open for you."

"You kept me alive." She walks over to me and wraps her arms around my waist, careful of the bandage. She rests her head on my chest. "We make a good team."

"The best."

I run my hand down her back, feeling the warmth of her through the thin cotton of my shirt.

"So," she murmurs. "Medical leave."

"Sounds boring."

"I don't know." She looks up, her eyes dancing with mischief. "I'm sure we can find some way to pass the time."

"I have a few ideas."

"Do they involve algorithms?"

"They involve variables." I kiss her forehead. "Motion. Friction. Velocity."

She laughs. "You're a nerd."

"I'm a demolition expert. I know how to bang things."

"That was terrible." She groans, burying her face in my chest.

"You laughed."

"I did."

I hold her. The rain falls. The city outside is gray and cold, but in here, everything is warm.

We have the data. We have the target. The Admiral is going down, and for the first time in my life, I have something more important than the mission.

I have her.

TWENTY-SIX

Jackson

MOVING ON

The duffel bag sits open on the bed. It's the same bag I've lived out of for three years—tactical nylon, fraying at the seams, smelling of gun oil and old airports. Usually, it holds a uniform loadout: Kevlar, ammunition, trauma kits, three changes of black clothes.

Today, it holds a silk blouse. A pair of jeans that aren't mine. A laptop that contains the secrets of the free world.

"You're packing it wrong," Talia says.

She leans against the doorframe, arms crossed, wearing a smile that makes my chest ache. She's dressed in clean clothes—dark denim, a sweater she stole from my drawer that hangs to her mid-thigh. She looks rested. The shadows under her eyes are gone, replaced by a brightness I haven't seen before.

"It's a bag," I say, shoving a stack of socks into the corner. "Physics dictates that if I push hard enough, the volume expands."

"That's not physics. That's brute force."

"It's my specialty."

She laughs, pushing off the doorframe to join me. She reaches into the bag, rearranging the chaos into neat, logical layers. "Optimization, Jackson. You create space by organizing the variables."

I watch her hands. Competent. Sure.

I reach out, capturing her wrist.

"Leave it," I say. "We aren't deploying. We're just going home."

"Home," she tests the word. "I haven't had one of those in a while. My apartment is a crime scene."

"Then we find a new one." I pull her closer, careful of the stitches in my side. "Somewhere with better locks, and a coffee machine that doesn't taste like burnt plastic."

"And a workspace," she adds, her hands resting on my chest. "I need monitors. Lots of them."

"Done."

She rises on her toes and kisses me. It's light, domestic, a promise of a future I didn't think I'd live to see.

"The team is waiting," she whispers against my lips.

"Let them wait."

"Jackson."

"Fine."

I zip the bag. I sling it over my good shoulder, ignoring the twinge of protest from my healing muscles. I grab her hand. We walk out of the load-out bay, down the corridor, toward the hangar.

The Cerberus hangar is cavernous, smelling of jet fuel and rain. The massive bay doors are open to the gray Seattle sky.

Torque is prepping a sleek, black fixed-wing aircraft on the tarmac. Brass and Whisper are loading crates of gear.

And Halo is standing by, checking a tablet. He looks less like a tech genius and more like a kid about to joyride his dad's car, but there's a tension in his frame, a vibration I recognize.

The pre-mission jitters.

"You good?" he asks, checking my injuries.

"I'm functional."

"You're on medical leave," he corrects. "At least for a few weeks."

"Whatever." I change the subject, turn it back at him. "So—Cassie Brennan?"

Halo's expression hardens. "Yeah."

"You found something?" Talia asks, stepping up beside me. "In the Admiral's files?"

"I did." Halo taps the car door. "I dug into the specific threat profile Phoenix built on her. It's not just surveillance. They're terrified of her."

"Why?"

"Because she wasn't just looking at the money," Halo says. "She found the connection between Vanguard Defense and a black-site project in Nevada. Something the Admiral was trying very hard to keep buried." He looks at me. "She's the next domino. I feel it. If Phoenix takes her out, we lose the trail to the Rook."

"The Rook," I repeat. The next piece on the board. The money man. "That's the next piece?"

"Looks like." Halo glances at Talia, and she nods. Their tech brains work on a level I'll never achieve.

"Don't let them take her out," I say.

"I won't, but it's just me on this op, while the rest of you—"

"Right. "A laugh punches out of me, sharp and disbelieving. Just him. The hell it is. "You're *just* the guy who ran a five-man strike team around a warehouse like you had them on puppet strings."

Halo stiffens. "That was situational awareness."

"Situational awareness?" I raise a brow. "You called the ricochet angles like you were seeing them before they happened."

He grimaces like I'm dragging up something embarrassing.

"I calculated probabilities."

"You calculated them while dodging bullets."

"Multitasking." He shrugs, like that isn't ridiculous.

I step close enough that he has to look up at me. I grip his shoulder, feel the tension thrumming beneath the half-casual posture.

"You can handle this."

"I'm a tech guy, Jackson. I don't kick down doors." He exhales through his nose, eyes dropping. "And I certainly don't do it alone."

"Then don't kick them." I lean in, voice low. "Pick the lock. Cheat. Use your luck and win."

His eyes lift, that small spark flickering through the humility he tries like hell to wear like armor.

And here's the thing he'll never say out loud—and doesn't have to, because I've seen it with my own eyes. Halo runs circles around most of the door-kickers I've served with. Not because he's the strongest or the fastest, but because the universe bends for him in ways that shouldn't be possible.

He calls it luck.

I call it supernatural. He has a pattern of surviving things no human should survive.

The reason he's Halo?

It's not a joke.

It's not irony.

It was that night in Basra—twenty-seven seconds of bullets slicing the air like angry hornets, every single one missing him by inches, ricocheting off walls in angles that should've killed him but somehow didn't.

He moved through that kill box like something unseen

cleared a path for him. A guardian angel tugging him out of harm's way. We joke about guardian angels, but deep down, watching him walk through a warzone untouched—watching death curve around him—it doesn't feel like a joke.

It feels like witnessing a glitch in the universe.

He pretends he's just a tech guy.

Pretends he's the weakest link on the team.

But the truth?

If I had to bet my life on one man making it through a firefight, one man finding a way out of an impossible corner, one man outsmarting and outlasting every son of a bitch hunting him—I'd bet on Halo.

Every damn time.

There's a subtle shift in his posture, and a slight roll of his shoulders. The man's gearing up. Pretending he's not.

Halo's a tech genius, but underneath the hoodie and sarcasm? He's one of the deadliest bastards I've ever gone to war with.

Ghost walks up, flanked by Brass. The team leader looks from Halo to us.

"Green light," Ghost says. "Wheels up in five, Halo. DC is waiting."

Halo nods and salutes us—a two-finger flick off his brow. Then he boards the waiting jet. We watch him go until the taillights disappear into the rain.

"He'll be fine," Ghost says, though his eyes remain fixed on the jet.

"He's going solo," Brass mutters. "He hates solo."

"He needs it," Ghost says. He turns to me. "And you need to get out of my hangar."

"Trying to get rid of me?"

"Trying to keep you alive." Ghost hands me a set of keys. "Your truck is out front. I had Torque bring it around. There's a safe house in the Cascades. Fully stocked. Off the grid. No internet, no cell service."

"Sounds like hell," Talia says.

"Sounds like paradise," I correct.

"Go," Ghost orders. "Heal up. We'll call you when the world ends, and we need you. And we *will* need you."

I take the keys and shake Ghost's hand, then Brass's. Whisper gives me a nod from the shadows near the crates. Then, I take Talia's hand, and walk out of the hangar.

My truck—a battered Ford F-150 that has seen more warzones than most tanks—sits at the curb. I toss the bag in the back.

I open the passenger door for Talia. She climbs in, settling into the worn leather seat as if she belongs there.

Which she does.

She belongs right beside me.

Partners.

I get behind the wheel. The engine rumbles, a familiar vibration that travels up my arms.

"The Cascades?" she asks as we pull away from the complex.

"Too quiet?"

"Maybe." She pulls up the map on the console. "But I ran the probability of recovery times in high-altitude environments. Lower stress variables …" She looks at me, a smile playing on her lips. "It's optimal."

"You just want to see me chop wood."

"That is a variable I'm considering."

I laugh. It hurts my side, but I don't care.

The city fades behind us, replaced by the towering pines and gray mist of the Pacific Northwest. The road stretches out ahead, winding into the mountains.

For three years, I looked at the horizon and saw only threats. Ambush points. Sniper hides. Fatal funnels.

Now, I look at the road, and I see the woman sitting next to me. Her hand rests on my thigh. Her eyes scan the trees, analyzing the forest's patterns, her mind a beautiful, restless machine.

I reach over and cover her hand with mine.

"We good?" I ask.

She laces her fingers through mine. Squeezes tight.

"We're good," she says. "Statistically speaking."

I shift gears. We drive into the trees, leaving the ghosts in the rearview mirror.

Nexus is out there.

Phoenix is licking its wounds.

But for now, the only thing that matters is the road, the rain, and the woman who taught me how to live again.

READY FOR BOOK FIVE IN THE CERBERUS SECURITY SERIES?

Read HALO

The Cerberus Protection Services Series: Where deadly operators protect brilliant women from a conspiracy that reaches into every shadow of power.

HALO IS A FULL-LENGTH, HIGH-HEAT ROMANTIC SUSPENSE novel featuring:

- A protective alpha hero who meets his match
- Forced proximity that ignites into scorching chemistry
- Edge-of-your-seat action with a steamy slow burn
- Passionate power exchange between equals
- Only one bed (and so much sexual tension)
- Life-or-death stakes with an emotionally satisfying HEA

No cliffhangers. Can be read as a standalone, but best enjoyed as part of the Cerberus Security Series.

"Control is his specialty until he meets the one woman who challenges everything—a fearless journalist who ignites a passion more dangerous than the killers pursuing them."
Read HALO

CRAVING MORE GUARDIANS?

If you've fallen for the fierce alphas of Cerberus, you're just getting started.

There's an entire world waiting for you—the Guardian Hostage Rescue Specialists series—one built on danger, desire, and the kind of love that ruins a woman for anyone else.

Start with the *Alpha Team series*—because once you meet these men, you'll never forget them. Protective. Possessive. Unapologetically alpha. And the women who bring them to their knees? Equally unforgettable.

BUT IF YOU WANT TO FEEL **EVERYTHING**—IF YOU WANT TO understand where it all began, before Cerberus, before the Guardians, before the rescues—go back to the beginning.

Heart's Insanity, the first book in the *Angel Fire* rock star romance series, is where you'll meet Skye and Forest. It's raw. It's emotional. It's the origin story of the entire Guardian world. And trust me—once you see who Forest Summers was before Guardian HRS existed, you'll never look at him the same way again.

Start there.

Feel everything.
And then come back for more.
Start with Heart's Insanity
Or dive into the Alpha Team series.
The heat only gets hotter.
The danger only gets deadlier.
And the Guardians?
The mission isn't over. It's just getting started.

Keep current with Ellie Masters.
CLICK HERE
Receive news of her writing and new releases.

Shop Ellie Masters Romantic Suspense and Steamy
Contemporary Romance by series.
Angel Fire Rock Romance
Guardian HRS: Alpha Team
Guardian HRS: Bravo Team
Guardian HRS: Charlie Team
Guardian HRS: Delta Team
Cerberus Personal Security
The LaRouge Triplets
The One I Want Series
Angel's Peak Series
Billionaire Boy's Club
The Lovers
Changing Roles

Please consider leaving a review

I HOPE YOU ENJOYED THIS BOOK AS MUCH AS I ENJOYED WRITING it. If you like this book, please leave a review. I love reviews. I love reading your reviews, and they help other readers decide if this book is worth their time and money. I hope you think it is and decide to share this story with others. A sentence is all it takes. Thank you in advance!

ELLZ BELLZ

ELLIE'S FACEBOOK READER GROUP

If you are interested in joining the ELLZ BELLZ, Ellie's Facebook reader group, we'd love to have you.

Join Ellie's ELLZ BELLZ.
The ELLZ BELLZ Facebook Reader Group

Sign up for Ellie's Newsletter.
Elliemasters.com/newslettersignup

The LIGHTER SIDE

Ellie Masters is the lighter side of the Jet & Ellie Masters writing duo! You will find Contemporary Romance, Military Romance, Romantic Suspense, Billionaire Romance, and Rock Star Romance in Ellie's Works.

YOU CAN FIND ELLIE'S BOOKS HERE:

ELLIEMASTERS.COM/BOOKS

Shop Ellie Masters Romantic Suspense and Steamy Contemporary Romance by series.

Angel Fire Rock Romance

Guardian HRS: Alpha Team

Guardian HRS: Bravo Team

Guardian HRS: Charlie Team

Guardian HRS: Delta Team

Cerberus Personal Security

The LaRouge Triplets

The One I Want Series

Angel's Peak Series

Billionaire Boy's Club

The Lovers

Changing Roles

Rescuing Eve

Rescuing Lily

Rescuing Jinx

Rescuing Maria

Bravo Team

Rescuing Angie

Rescuing Isabelle

Rescuing Carmen

Rescuing Rosalie

Rescuing Kaye

Cara's Protector

Rescuing Barbi

Charlie Team

Rescuing Rebel

Rescuing Stitch

Rescuing Mia

Jenna's Protector

Rescuing Sophia

Rescuing Malia

Rescuing Ally (Part 1)

Rescuing Ally (Part 2)

Delta Team

Rescuing Ember

Rescuing Aria

STANDALONES IN THE GUARDIAN HOSTAGE RESCUE

By Jet & Ellie Masters

EACH BOOK IN THIS SERIES CAN BE READ AS A STANDALONE AND IS ABOUT A DIFFERENT COUPLE WITH AN HEA.

Saving Abby

Saving Ariel

Saving Brie

Saving Cate

Saving Dani

Saving Jen

The LaRouge Triplets

Asher

Brody

Cage

Billionaire Romance

Billionaire Boys Club

Hawke

Richard

Contemporary Romance

Cocky Captain

Romantic Suspense

EACH BOOK IS A STANDALONE NOVEL.

The Starling

The Swan

~AND~

Science Fiction

Ellie Masters writing as L.A. Warren

Vendel Rising: a Science Fiction Serialized Novel

If you enjoyed this book by Ellie Masters, the LIGHTER SIDE of the Jet & Ellie writing duo, and aren't afraid of edgier writing, you might enjoy reading BDSM themed books written by Jet, the DARKER SIDE of the Masters' Writing Team.

The DARKER SIDE

Jet Masters is the darker side of the Jet & Ellie writing duo!

Romantic Suspense

Changing Roles Series:

THIS SERIES MUST BE READ IN ORDER.

Command Me

Control Me

Collar Me

Embracing FATE

Seizing FATE

Accepting FATE

HOT READS

A STANDALONE NOVEL.

Down the Rabbit Hole

Light BDSM Romance

The Ties that Bind

EACH BOOK IN THIS SERIES CAN BE READ AS A STANDALONE AND IS ABOUT A
DIFFERENT COUPLE WITH AN HEA.

Alexa

Penny

Michelle

Ivy

HOT READS

Becoming His Series

THIS SERIES MUST BE READ IN ORDER.

The Ballet

Learning to Breathe

Becoming His

Dark Captive Romance

A STANDALONE NOVEL.

She's MINE

About the Author

Ellie Masters is a USA Today Bestselling author and Amazon Top 15 Author who writes Angsty, Steamy, Heart-Stopping, Pulse-Pounding, Can't-Stop-Reading Romantic Suspense. In addition, she's a wife, military mom, doctor, and retired Colonel. She writes romantic suspense filled with all your sexy, swoon-worthy alpha men. Her writing will tug at your heartstrings and leave your heart racing.

Born in the South, raised under the Hawaiian sun, Ellie has traveled the globe while in service to her country. The love of her life, her amazing husband, is her number one fan and biggest supporter. And yes! He's read every word she's written.

She has lived all over the United States—east, west, north, south and central—but grew up under the Hawaiian sun. She's also been privileged to have lived overseas, experiencing other cultures and making lifelong friends. Now, Ellie is proud to call herself a Southern transplant, learning to say y'all and "bless her heart" with the best of them.

Ellie's favorite way to spend an evening is curled up on a couch, laptop in place, watching a fire, drinking a good wine, and bringing forth all the characters from her mind to the page and hopefully into the hearts of her readers.

FOR MORE INFORMATION
elliemasters.com

facebook.com/elliemastersromance
x.com/Ellie__Masters
instagram.com/ellie_masters
bookbub.com/authors/ellie-masters
goodreads.com/Ellie_Masters

Connect with Ellie Masters

Website:
elliemasters.com
Purchase Direct:
elliemasters.com/shopify
Amazon Author Page:
elliemasters.com/amazon
Facebook:
elliemasters.com/Facebook
Goodreads:
elliemasters.com/Goodreads
Bookbub:
elliemasters.com/Bookbub
Instagram:
elliemasters.com/Instagram

Final Thoughts

I hope you enjoyed this book as much as I enjoyed writing it. If you enjoyed reading this story, please consider leaving a review on Amazon and Goodreads, and please let other people know. A sentence is all it takes. Friend recommendations are the strongest catalyst for readers' purchase decisions! And I'd love to be able to continue bringing the characters and stories from My-Mind-to-the-Page.

Second, call or e-mail a friend and tell them about this book. If you really want them to read it, gift it to them. If you prefer digital friends, please use the "Recommend" feature of Goodreads to spread the word.

Or visit my blog https://elliemasters.com, where you can find out more about my writing process and personal life.

Come visit The EDGE: Dark Discussions where we'll have a chance to talk about my works, their creation, and maybe what the future has in store for my writing.

Facebook Reader Group: Ellz Bellz

Thank you so much for your support!

Love,
Ellie

Dedication

This book is dedicated to you, my reader. Thank you for spending a few hours of your time with me. I wouldn't be able to write without you to cheer me on. Your wonderful words, your support, and your willingness to join me on this journey is a gift beyond measure.

Whether this is the first book of mine you've read, or if you've been with me since the very beginning, thank you for believing in me as I bring these characters 'from my mind to the page and into your hearts.'

Love,
Ellie

THE END